IF
WE
SHADOWS

D.E. Atwood

Harmony Ink

Published by
Harmony Ink Press
5032 Capital Circle SW
Suite 2, PMB# 279
Tallahassee, FL 32305-7886
USA
publisher@harmonyinkpress.com
http://harmonyinkpress.com

This is a work of fiction. Names, characters, places, and incidents either are the product of author imagination or are used fictitiously, and any resemblance to actual persons, living or dead, business establishments, events, or locales is entirely coincidental.

If We Shadows
© 2014 D.E. Atwood.

Cover Art
© 2014 Anne Cain.
annecain.art@gmail.com.
Cover content is for illustrative purposes only and any person depicted on the cover is a model.

ISBN: 978-1-62798-820-9
Library ISBN: 978-1-62798-822-3
Digital ISBN: 978-1-62798-821-6

Printed in the United States of America
First Edition
March 2014

Library Edition
June 2014

For my family.
Mom, Dad, Kevin, Danielle, Ryan…
I couldn't do it without you.

Acknowledgments

They say it takes a village to raise a child, and I'd say it's the same for a book. I have so many people to thank.

My family, again. You have believed in me, and just as importantly, you have done dishes, cleaned the house, taken out the trash, cooked, and done all these wonderful things around the house so that I could write. I love you!

To kori, without whom I would have been floundering. I am incredibly thankful for everything you helped me find, learn, and understand along the way.

To both of my writing groups—Just Prose and Anticiworkshop—this book is better because of you, just as I am a better writer because of your critical efforts. You all rock.

To Jackie, who believed in me and my words even when I wasn't certain, and to everyone at the dojang who helped me understand that strength and perseverance aren't just words for when I am on the mats, but also words I need to remember in my daily life.

To all of my friends, who have been there with me for the long ride, and to everyone I may have forgotten (because as we all know, I have a brain like a sieve). Thank you.

PART ONE
Auditions

JOURNAL: Monday, October 5

I DREAMED last night about Puck. It was a crazy, mixed-up dream, about auditions and everything I've got going on today: the play, my birthday, and my appointment with you. I don't think I need to talk much about that last. You know why I'm anxious, and I really hope you finally give me the go-ahead. I'm seventeen. It's time.

But the dream.

I jerked awake in the middle of the night because something was rustling around in my room. I thought maybe it was the cat, but he always sleeps in with the girls. Or maybe it was James doing some stunt for my birthday. I sat up and blinked, trying to get my eyes to see in the moonlight.

That's when I saw the boy, and I knew it had to be a dream. He was standing past the end of my bed, small and slim, staring at something in his hand. I cleared my throat and he looked at me. The sudden grin was like a bright white light in the darkness, and he leaped up, landing on the wrought-iron footboard, his long, bare toes hooked around the top rail, one hand down to balance himself.

Yeah, it was that vivid. And totally weird. He just *looked* at me, his head cocked like *I* was the alien thing in the room. And my whole body was frozen. I heard my heartbeat in my ears, thundering along. "Who are you?" I finally managed to ask.

He didn't answer, but I figured it out without him needing to say it. There were streaks of brown and green on his face, and his ears were gently tilted, his chin coming to a sharp point as well. And there was a mischievous light in his eyes. He was Puck, just like in *A Midsummer Night's Dream*.

I guess it made a kind of sense that I'd dream about him, since that's who I'm trying out for today. I was reading the play just before bed last night.

He leaned forward, still precariously balanced, and held out one hand. There were three tiny glass bottles resting on his palm, each filled with several droplets of liquid that shimmered in the moonlight. "I give thee three potions: true sight, true seeming, and true love." He paused, the musical lilt of his voice fading into the silence of the night. Head cocked, he regarded me solemnly and added, "Don't mix them up."

"Shouldn't those be flowers?" I asked because I felt like I needed to ask the question. I mean, I've read the play several times, and that isn't how it goes. The only potion is true love, and he drops the nectar from the flowers on Lysander's eyes. Then havoc ensues.

Yeah, like I'd ever even think about using some kind of potion like that.

He laughed then, the ringing of bells tolling deep. A toss of his head pushed bangs back from his forehead, letting me see his eyes, narrowed and green like the slits of a cat's eyes. "Dost thou imagine that life never changes? Modernization, Jordan, even amongst the Faerie." Another pause, and he thrust his hand forward even more, the long blue nails on his splayed fingertips brushing against my T-shirt. I shivered. "Take them," he told me.

Fine. It was just a dream, so I held out both my hands, cupped together, and watched as he spilled the little glass bottles into my grasp. One liquid was pale blue, one purple, one green. I frowned at them. "Which one is which?" Because suddenly it seemed incredibly important to know, like maybe I *would* actually use them. Like maybe giving someone true sight or true love would really work. Then there's "true seeming"—I had to look that one up online this morning. That means looking like myself. Like I really should look.

I think you know just how much I'd like that.

Anyway, he didn't answer. I looked up and he was gone, like he'd poofed out of existence. Again, dreaming, so I wasn't entirely surprised.

I don't remember anything else until I woke up in the morning with James pounding on my door to tell me that my alarm had been going off for fifteen minutes already and was I ever planning on getting out of bed? He had some other things to say, but you get pissy when I swear, so I won't repeat them.

I yelled out that I was awake, and he barged in. I really hate that there's no such thing as privacy when I've got four siblings. Even though Karen's gone off to college, it's bad enough with just James and the two younger girls around.

James plunked down on my bed, all dressed and ready to go, his hair standing up spiky and wet from the shower. He shoved a box at me, the corner of it poking me in the chest, and that's when I remembered the dream. I opened up both hands and looked, but nope, no little thingamajiggers full of potions. I was still half-asleep enough that it almost seemed like I ought to've had them, I guess. I shook off the last of the haziness and focused on the gift from James instead (a vest, which isn't magic, but looking in the mirror might as well be, the way it changes my shape).

Today's going to be a good day, I can tell. There's chocolate cake for breakfast, and I'll tell you how the auditions go when I get to my appointment. I'm nervous. I've always stayed with a role in the chorus before, and I'm not sure I'm ready to be front and center. But if I want to go into music someday, I'd better get used to it. Singers don't belong in the background. Being on stage is easy; it's being in the spotlight that scares me. But I love *Midsummer*, and even if it's some weird musical version, I know I can sing, and I know I can rock the part. It's mine.

Anyway, I'd better get going. Just remember, when I come in, you're going to give me the letter for my GP so that I can start T as soon as he lets me.

I'm seventeen today. And I'm ready for everything to go my way.

CHAPTER 1: Breaking Up Fights

IT'S HARD to keep still on the drive to school. I cross my legs, pushing my toe up against the dashboard, watching the small dent in the vinyl and the dusty mark left from the bottom of my shoe. James leans over and slaps my leg, and I elbow him back. He's supposed to be driving, not paying attention to what I'm doing. "It's my car, too," I remind him. "I mess it up, I clean it up."

"And I promised to give Britney Jenkins a ride home after auditions." He shrugs like that doesn't mean anything, but I know it does. She's one of the hottest girls in the senior class, and I should probably congratulate him for getting even a second look from her. On the other hand....

"I've got my appointment at four thirty," I remind him. "I need the car to get there."

"I didn't forget. I'll drop you off at that, then I'll take Britney home and hang out there for a bit, then I'll swing back and pick you up, okay?" He reaches across to ruffle my hair, like I'm six or something, and I roll my eyes. "Today's the big day, right, bro?"

"God, I hope so." I pull down the visor and pop the little mirror open, peering into it while I push my bangs back into my face where they belong. "Dr. Hewitt said we'd 'revisit the issue' when I turned seventeen. If she gives the go-ahead today, I've already got my physical set for next week, and if my doctor says the blood work's okay, I could have my first dose by Halloween."

Yeah, *this* is a big deal. Testosterone. T. The thing that will change my whole life.

James's breath lets out in a soft rush, his expression tight, and I know there's a lecture coming. What I don't get is *why*. He already knows how important this is to me, and that I've been researching it for years, and there isn't anything about hormone therapy that I haven't read, or already experienced, since I've been doing hormone suppression therapy since I was eleven. I'm not going into it blind. And even more important, it's something I *need*.

He doesn't say anything yet, just parks the car in the student lot. I cross my arms, my jaw tight and stubborn. "What?" I ask.

"Are you sure?" His lips pressed together. "Absolutely, positively, completely sure? It's a big step and you can't really go backwards after you start."

"I don't want to go backwards, James." Like he really needs me to remind him about the details of my life; he's been there all along. I glare at him, as if that's going to help. "You know that. I can't go backwards from where I am anyway. I stopped being female when I was *eleven*. I've been waiting for T for years, now, so I'm not going to suddenly start wanting it any less. This is what I am. *Who* I am. I'm your *brother*. I deserve to finally go through puberty as much as any other teenage boy."

Okay, so maybe no one really *deserves* puberty. But I actually want mine, as long as it's the right one.

"It's dangerous," James said flatly. "And there are side effects. Like the guys who end up with heart problems, or roid rage." It wasn't as if taking steroids was a complete unknown in the high school experience. There were guys who tried it, to bulk up. But they weren't me, and they weren't doing it the right way.

My jaw sets and I end up staring at the roof of our car. There's a rip in the fabric, and I fix my gaze on that, thinking about anything else but yelling at James. I don't want to start the day fighting with my brother. I don't want to ruin my birthday. So I think about the car, and how we bought it two years ago when James turned sixteen, a whole year before I was ever going to be able to drive it. We did it together like we've done just about everything together since I was born less than a year after him. And my throat feels tight and painful, like I'm going to cry.

"Why are you arguing with me about this?" I force the words out without looking at him.

"Because you're my brother, and you're the only brother I've got."

Did he seriously just say that? "And that's exactly why you should stop worrying," I snap. "Because I'm your freakin' *brother*." I push the door open and step out, slamming it behind me. Sometimes it's like my family gets so *stupid*. They understand, and they love me, I know that, but they still keep trying to second-guess me. Can't they just shut up and support me like they say they will? I know what I'm doing, and I'm not being rash or reckless or stupid. I'm making me *right*.

If they're like this now, I can't even think what they'll be like when I save up for surgery someday.

James touches my shoulder, and I glance at him. "Hey," he says. "You're still on for auditions, right?"

It's like we weren't even fighting. I guess if he's letting it go, I should too. But I can't. Not quite yet. "You sure you really want me to do that? Someone might notice something funny about me when we're getting changed into costumes backstage." James is protective of me, and I'm digging at his insecurities. It's petty and mean, but it feels good.

Thing is, they're my insecurities too. I love acting, and I love singing even more. I've been a theater kid ever since we moved to this school district, but I've always managed to hover under the radar. I've just stayed in the chorus, never trying out for a lead role that would make me stand out. My voice is good, so I get a solo during a big group number sometimes, which is enough for me. But this play has a small cast, and no matter what part I get, I can't hide in the crowd. And I really want to play Puck, which would be putting myself front and center.

But what I said is true; who knows what they'll see in the dressing room? I could play it safe and not try out, giving myself a better chance of getting through senior year without anyone ever having the chance to guess about me. Or I could try out, get the part, and show everyone just how good I am. I guess I'm willing to take that risk. I nod slowly. "Yeah, I'll be there."

James already knew I would. He claps me on the shoulder. "You'll be a perfect Puck." He starts walking, and I follow along in his wake.

I hate this part, when we're walking into school. It's like running the gauntlet. There's a group of tough guys that hang out on the stone wall next to the stairs. It's a suburban school, with about four hundred kids in each grade, and in a town about as white as white gets. But these guys try to pretend they're gangsta, and they don't even know what it means. To them, it's wearing wife-beater shirts with their jeans hanging off their butts, and a lot of chains, and saying "yo" while they talk about the weed they're getting together to smoke during third period.

Usually they bug the hot girls with their wolf whistles and *give me some of that, mama* calls. Sometimes they pick on the freshmen, especially the small geeky ones. I guess you can't look tough unless you're giving someone a hard time. I know there's absolutely no reason for them to pick on me, just a guy walking into the building with his brother, but I'm still wary around them. And I worry that they can smell fear, like dogs, that they'll somehow know that I've got something to hide. Stupid, I know, since these people don't even suspect that there's anything different about me.

I tell myself James doesn't know how I feel, but he keeps me talking and focused on him, so yeah, I'm sure he actually does. We've just made it to the top of the stairs where I can see safety in the form of the door into the school when we hear the shriek.

It's a girly sort of shriek, high-pitched and short, cutting off sharply. I can't help it; I look back over my shoulder to see who's so upset.

They—and by "they," I mean the tough-guy-wannabes—are tossing a phone back and forth between them. And there's a kid standing there with a deer-in-the-headlights look. He makes a face and leaps onto Brandon Josephson (the self-proclaimed leader of the toughs), clawing at his shoulder.

The kid's got guts, but maybe no brains, because that's when things get nasty. Toby Miller throws a punch, and the kid lashes back. And while everyone else takes a step back, James starts down the steps toward them.

It's the right thing to do, stopping the fight. I know that. But I'm scared, and rooted to the steps, and can't make myself do it.

I hear the grunt as one of them gets James with a solid blow in the side.

Then Toby calls the kid a girly-boy who can't throw a punch to save his own life. Which is starting to look like it might be true.

Then the insults get rude, and they threaten to strip the kid and show his girly body to the school. One of them grabs the collar of his shirt and the first few buttons come undone.

I see red.

I don't remember wading in, just that I'm in the middle of things, and I *do* have a really good right hook and I'm strong from lifting weights. I get a few good shots in and take a few in return before I manage to get the kid behind my back and safe while James rescues the phone Brandon stole. Three of the thugs stand, fists clenched, and James and I face them down best we can. We've reached a standoff, and everyone's bruised.

"Stop fighting right now!"

The thugs look at the top of the stairs and immediately try to scatter. Principal Jackson may be small, but she's tough, and even Brandon's a bit afraid of her. She comes down the stairs, grabs him by the collar, and pushes him toward the door to go inside. She glances at me and James, lips pursed before she turns back to Brandon. "I saw who started it." Her voice is firm and carries that note of *you're not getting off this time.* "Into my office, Mr. Josephson. All of you."

She doesn't look at James or me again, so we hesitate. When she walks the thugs away and leaves us behind, I can finally relax and look back at the kid.

He's smaller than me, maybe coming up to my chin; he probably hasn't had that growth spurt most guys get around freshman year. And he's skinny, his chest hairless and flat. Definitely not a girl. Crap. My face heats up as I try to pretend I didn't look.

His back stiffens and he buttons his shirt up with careful dignity. "It's the voice," he says with a soft lilt. "They'll stop saying it once it changes."

"Not every guy's voice is deep," I assure him, even though I hope mine will get deeper eventually. Someday. That is why I need to start T.

He considers me and James, then nods politely. "I'm Paul," he says. "And thank you." He smiles when James hands him back the phone, checking to make sure it hasn't been damaged. "My dad keeps telling me that if I turn the other cheek, they'll ignore me."

"Your dad's an idiot," James and I both say, and we laugh. James taught me to fight a long time ago, just in case. I rub my knuckles against my side, trying to pretend they don't hurt as much as they do. It was my first actual fight, and I'm still in shock that it happened, and that I didn't get into trouble for it. Although there's still plenty of time for Principal Jackson to change her mind and call us down to the office. At least she saw that Brandon and his group were bullying Paul and that was how it started.

As people go into the school, Britney Jenkins and another girl slip out around the edges, coming to join us on the stairs. And oh. Wow.

Just.

Wow.

So this is what speechless feels like.

The other girl is pretty. Not model-gorgeous, like Britney, but there's something about her, even while she's fussing over Paul, that just pulls me in. She has red hair—dark, not carroty orange—pulled back with a thick headband, and her eyes are a sort of jade green. Her brow is furrowed with worry. She's short and a little curvy, and she's dressed like someone who wants to be herself and doesn't care what everyone else thinks. I like that in a girl.

"I can't believe you jumped him," she chides Paul. Not just scolding, *chiding*. I can hear it in every word. "Are you nuts?"

"Dad would've killed me if I lost my new phone," Paul protested. Looking at them together, I figure they've got to be brother and sister. Same face shape, same nose, just different eyes, and his hair is more brown than red.

The girl turns to look at me, smiling.

Um.

"Thanks for helping Paul out." She holds out her hand, and after a moment, I realize she's expecting me to take it. So I do, and it's warm and oh right, shake, that's what she's doing. When she lets go, I'm still standing there, hand out, and she giggles just a bit. "I'm Pepper. I don't think I know you."

"Jordan." And that's about all I can manage coherently.

"Well, Jordan, you're sweet, and there aren't many guys that'd do that for someone they don't know. So thank you. Both of you."

Both of—oh right, me and James. "That's James," I tell her. "My brother." I've mastered cave man speak. Go me.

"Hey." James greets her. He has moved next to me, pressed close in like he can somehow move me bodily up the stairs without quite touching me. Britney is on his other side, just watching.

I take a step up the stairs, then another step, and Pepper paces right along next to me. We inch toward the door, this odd amoeba of people, slightly bruised and apparently lacking in English skills.

"Look, it was nice to meet you, but we've got to go." Pepper takes a step away from me, Paul with her. "Maybe we'll see you around."

"Maybe," I manage to respond.

Then she's gone. Air rushes back into my lungs, and coherent thoughts enter my brain. Holy freakin' *God* is she ever gorgeous. Amazing. Beautiful. Wow. Okay, less than coherent thoughts, but still, there are words, and I might even be able to express them.

I blink when Britney giggles, and try to glare at her, but glaring isn't really my mood right now. She only giggles more.

"If you could see your *face*," she says. "Oh, that *look*. I could use your picture for my vocabulary homework. Flummoxed."

James snorts. "Jordan was *flummoxed* when he met the girl of his dreams."

What? Wait. Oh hell. "I can't," I protest. I can't like her. I can't even *think* about her like that.

"Why not?" Britney asks. "She's pretty. Just ask her out."

She makes it sounds so simple. Britney knows the things about us that everyone knows. That James is ten months older than me so we're in the same grade at school. That we act like twins, and some people treat us like twins, but we're not. But she doesn't know I wasn't born a boy.

James looks at me, and I know what he's thinking, because I'm thinking the same thing: I can't have a crush on Pepper. At least not one that can ever have a hope in hell of going anywhere. My parents would absolutely kill me before they'd let me go on a date. My life is just too complicated, and they think it's too risky for me to get involved in a relationship.

His expression softens and he claps my shoulder. "We'll get it figured out, Jordan. You probably don't want to be a monk forever."

I don't want to be a monk. But if I want to survive high school, it might be easier if I just avoid relationships. It's too much of a risk.

James and I may be in the same grade, but we've got totally different tracks of classes. He punches my shoulder as the bell rings. "Happy birthday, Jordan. Make it a good one, and I'll see you at tryouts."

CHAPTER 2: Role-play

YOU'D THINK that in a school the size of ours, there'd be more than twenty or thirty people at the auditions for the fall play. There's a gaggle of maybe four or five freshman girls (perfect for the fairies, if Titania's fairies need to giggle) right up front. I see a few of the guys who are in chorus, and are probably here under protest. I lift my hand slightly as Ryan—we played soccer together back in eighth grade— nods at me. James is sitting in the second row of seats, and he waves me over. I vaguely recognize most of the others in the auditorium, and might be able to put a name to them, but I don't really know them all that well.

I sink down into the seat next to James, slumping and putting my feet up on the chair in front of me. "Hey." Of course, now that I'm there, James ignores me, so I wave one hand at him, repeating, "Hey. It's your brother, here and talking to you."

"Have you seen Britney?" He's looking around like he's trying to be casual about it, but he has his car key in his hand, and that's a sure sign that he's nervous. James doesn't need a worry stone; he's worn the sides of the key smooth.

"Nope." And if James weren't so antsy, I wouldn't really care. Britney's hot, but she's not really my type. I like intelligence more than I like boobs, and Britney's bust size way outweighs her IQ. Okay, so maybe that's not entirely fair; she's in all the advanced classes, so I know she's far from an idiot. But she *acts* like a bimbo and I get exhausted trying to have a conversation with her. Why do girls even do that, try to act like they don't have brains?

My phone whistles, and I thumb it open to see the text.

'sup

It's Maria, a girl I met during some not-quite-group-therapy sessions with Dr. Hewitt. Maria's a year younger than me, and she's… volatile. Her text is weirdly low-key, so I'm pretty sure that means she's actually bouncing off the walls over something.

James is still ignoring me, and I don't see any sign of the drama coach, so I settle in for some texting.

Me: *Nmuch. At auditions 4 Msummer Nights Drm*

Maria: *wut about T???*

Me: *LATER*

Maria: *srlsy? when??*

Me: *Seeing Hewitt after this. Done 5:30?*

Maria: *Pick you up there. No argumnt*

There isn't any point in me arguing with her, not really. Whether I say yes or not, she's going to be there, waiting for me to come out so she can pounce and see how it went, so I text back *kk* and let it go. She sends one more thing—*hppy birdy*—and I have to laugh. Besides, the change of plans will make James happy. "You can stay at Britney's as long as you want after you drop me off," I say without looking at him. "Maria's going to pick me up."

He hesitates, and I'm not sure if he's thinking of asking whether Maria will end up at our house for dinner afterward or if he just hasn't heard me. He and Maria don't always get along, which is frustrating since they're my two best friends. Maria kind of wigs him out ever since she had a mad crush on him last year. She's over that now, but I can't fix how James feels, and I'm not going to bail on one of my best friends just because my brother is being weird about things.

James finally nods, pats me on the head, and heads off, leaving me on my own so that he can catch Britney just as she walks in the door. It's a brilliant interception, with a kiss that looks like it might involve tongue. I start picking at a frayed thread on my jeans. It's not fair. He gets the girl, I get the fear that if I try to get the girl, I'll be outed as a fraud, and that could be deadly. I can't even think about getting the girl.

Wait a minute.

Holy crap.

It's the girl.

Mr. Dower introduces her—Pepper Sullivan—then introduces himself for the few people who don't already know that he's the drama coach. Dower goes on to tell us about this scriptwriting class that happened over the summer where people had to create a new work by doing a mashup of two existing classic scripts and modernizing the final play. He thinks Pepper's play should be produced, so here we are. A senior from jazz band helped her with the music to go with her lyrics—he's not here today, but he'll be helping with rehearsals.

So Pepper's a playwright who wrote something good enough that Dower's willing to take a chance on it. And she also wrote lyrics, even if someone else wrote music to accompany them. Plus she's going to be working with Dower as his assistant during the show, although he assures us he's got the final say on everything.

Which all means that I have to get up there and do my thing right in front of her.

Um. Right.

It's times like now that I'm kind of glad I'm not physically a boy. Because with my luck, this would be one of those absolutely mortifying moments. Just looking at her is distracting, and makes me warm all over. If I had the right parts, I'm pretty sure they'd be waking up to stand at attention.

"That's the girl from this morning." James comes back, Britney tailing along after him. He sinks into the seat next to me, leaning over to talk calmly like I'm not gaping at the stage. "I put your name down on the sign-up sheet for you, and your e-mail and phone."

I indulge in a brief daydream about Pepper going through the sign-up sheet, trying to figure out which one is me so she can have my contact information. Then I realize how incredibly stupid that sounds and I groan.

James snorts. "Still *flummoxed*, huh? Go on and daydream. It can't hurt anything."

Just don't do anything about it. It's as clear as if he said the words aloud. "Our parents would kill me just for thinking about a girl," I mutter.

Besides, what's the point? I don't like dealing with things I can never have. So I take a deep breath and let it out and try to get my focus back. Puck. Mischievous and silly and fun. I run lines in my head, waiting for my turn on the stage. Next to me, James leans in to comment quietly on how good that one guy is, or how off-pitch the next one happens to be. He'd be a good casting director; except for when it comes to me and Britney, he's fair-minded and has a good ear for a voice.

When I'm called, I walk up toward the stage, remembering to take my hands from my pockets. I find the center, under the lights, and look out at the auditorium. It's hard to find the right angle so that I'm facing both the audience and Dower and Pepper at the same time.

"Face them. Forget we're here," Dower instructs in his gruff voice.

Okay, then, I'll pretend nobody's watching me. I turn so that I'm set right for the audience, which doesn't actually help because now I can feel her eyes on my back.

"What role are you auditioning for, and what are you planning to sing?" She asks me the same question she's asked everyone else, and I have to resist turning as soon as I hear her voice.

I answer, projecting my voice out into the auditorium. "I'm auditioning for Puck today. I'll be reciting from the beginning of *Midsummer Night's Dream*, when Puck places the drops." As I say it, I remember my dream from last night, and the three vials. *True sight, true seeming, and true love: don't mix them up.* I shake my head, clearing away the cobwebs of the dream. "Then I'll be singing a song by Queen, 'The Show Must Go On.'" I know a lot of people are going with show tunes, or something upbeat that's modern pop. I've decided to go with a classic band, but one of the lesser-known pieces; it highlights my voice pretty decently, and not everyone can pull off Freddie. Plus it shows off my range.

"Go on."

At Dower's words, I close my eyes for a moment and push away the real world. Shake my arms and upper body, slipping into Puck's skin, or what I think it should feel like. Light on my feet, and again, I remember the way he crouched on my headboard, and I unconsciously mimic that body language, uncomfortable with shoes still on. "Through the forest have I gone, but Athenian found I none on whose eyes I might approve this flower's force in stirring love." Disappointment rings out in my voice, my body radiating frustration and mischief.

I turn, looking around me, hunting high and low. "Night and silence!" I run on light feet to one side, crouching down as if to look in the brush. "Who is here? Weeds of Athens he doth wear: This is he, my master said, despised the Athenian maid." My voice is light, airy, with a hint of laughter and cheer. "And here the maiden, sleeping sound, on the dank and dirty ground." I stand, looking back out at the audience.

"Pretty soul! She durst no lie near this lack-love, this kill-courtesy. Churl, upon thy eyes I throw all the power this charm doth owe." Bending, I sweep my hands over where Lysander's eyes might be as he sleeps on the ground. "When thou wak'st, let love forbid sleep his seat on thy eyelid: so awake when I am gone; for I must now to Oberon."

With a smirk, I bounce to stand, not quite skipping off to the side. Once there, I stop, and take my own guise back, and glance over at Dower and Pepper, who are both watching me. Nothing. No reaction other than the scratching of pens on paper.

Dower finally glances up and gestures at me. "Sing."

So I do.

The song is off of one of Queen's later albums, *Innuendo*. It has an eerie, almost dirge-like quality, but it's more haunting than sad. I let my voice echo, bouncing words off the sweet spot of the ceiling so I can almost whisper and still be heard in all corners of the auditorium.

I have Pepper's attention. I glance over and see her staring at me, her pen placed between her lips, and I stumble over the next few words. I have absolutely no idea how long I'm supposed to sing for, but I figure I'll just keep going until one of them says stop. I make it into the third verse before Dower cuts me off.

Then I stand there, watching as they confer in whispers. They haven't told me to stay, but they haven't told me to go, either, and Dower's usually pretty definite about things like getting people off his stage. After a moment, Pepper walks over, a script in her hand as she pages through it. "We'd like you to read for a couple of other roles as well," she says as she places the script into my hands. "The purple marker is Sebastian, the blue is Viola, and the green is Helena."

Wait. What? "Those are girl's roles," I say. Everyone's staring at me, I know it. My heart's thundering so loudly she has to be able to hear it. Did someone tell them? Does someone know? Did someone in the administrative offices let my records leak out?

Pepper nods. "I know, and we're having boys read for some of them. By combining the two plays, the storyline has changed, and not only does Puck cast love spells, but he makes it so Viola actually becomes Cesario for a time, and Helena might be changed to a male part." She smiles slightly. "This isn't your traditional Shakespeare."

No, it's definitely not.

I don't want to play a female role, even if it is changed to male or partially changed to male. I can't even think about it. But I do want to play Puck and I don't want to get a reputation for being some kind of drama queen. So I suck it up and start reading. I don't know *Twelfth Night*, but it's easy to tell the language has been changed. "How can I be standing there?" I declare. "I never had a brother. And I'm not a God, splitting myself in two. I had a sister." I put soft emphasis on *sister*; the phrasing bites a deep chill into my bones. "She was drowned, stolen by the water. Who are you?" I look at the person who isn't actually there—the one Sebastian speaks to. It's hard not to imagine myself in Viola's place. "Where are you from? What's your name? Who are your parents?"

I wait a moment, but neither Dower nor Pepper speaks, so I go on to Sebastian's next lines. "I'm a ghost, sure, but perhaps from the same womb as you when we were born. If you were a girl, I'd be crying with delight to find my sister Viola alive and well."

Silence. I glance at the table, and Dower simply says, "Viola now."

It's awkward reading for Viola, then Helena, declaring my love and affection for some guy. Viola's part at least has her dressed like a guy, which, well, that's familiar enough. Still, it all feels wrong, like I'm wearing a mask inside the character. When I finish, I walk over and set the script on the table. I don't want to even look at them, don't want to give them a hint of just how bad that was for me.

"Thank you." Pepper's voice is quiet, and I finally glance at her. She smiles at me. "You have a beautiful voice. Don't plan anything for Friday. We'll be having callbacks then."

I'm pretty sure she's not supposed to say that to me, not yet, and her smile widens as I nod, then walk away.

James is up next, reading for Oberon. They have him read for Sebastian as well, and he has a swagger that looks dead-on perfect for the part. I've never perfected that kind of swagger. I'll definitely make a better Puck than Sebastian.

He comes over to sit with me when he's done, and we watch Britney audition (bland, but pretty, and James can't take his eyes off of her), then I get caught up in watching a girl, Cece (strong and gorgeous, we're something like occasional study-buddies).

The last name they call is Paul Sullivan, and it's the kid from the morning. He looks tiny on the stage, standing there, his hand curled by his side. Maybe one of the fairies, I'm thinking, if they don't want them all to be girls. I wince at that, because it'd give the thugs even more ammunition.

"If we shadows have offended, think but this, and all is mended." His voice rings out with merry authority, cajoling us, teasing us to see his point of view. And in that moment, he becomes Puck. I slide to the edge of my seat, arms resting on the back of the seat in front of me, and I remember.

I see the shadows of bark and leaves across his face. I see the sharp point of his chin and bright snap of his eyes. I hear his laugh, and see the flower he holds in his hand, showing it on his palm as he begs us to give him our hands. I open my own hand then, staring at it, half expecting to see three small vials of colored liquid there.

It was only a dream.

Right?

James nudges me. "You're white as a ghost," he whispers.

But I can't explain. How ridiculous would it sound, saying that I dreamed about Puck last night, and he was *that exact kid* who was on stage, who I hadn't ever met until today? "It's nothing," I say.

"Nothing?" he looks dubious.

"He's good."

"You're better."

He's lying and we both know it. I've lost the part I wanted, and I'm afraid I'm losing my mind.

CHAPTER 3: Moments of Truth

DR. HEWITT says she'll be with me in a minute and directs me to step into her office while she steps out to talk to her nanny. It's convenient for Dr. Hewitt, having her office at the back of the house, but if the nanny needs something important for BethAnn, she'll interrupt us. It's not the first time it's happened. They head down the hallway while I close the door to the office so I can be by myself for a little while and pace around the room. I'm so far from relaxed that I can't seem to stop moving.

I look at her diplomas, hanging on the wall. I started seeing her about six years ago. She was the fourth psychiatrist I saw; the first three tried to tell me it was all in my head and that the panic attacks were just teenage hormones. She was the first person who ever took me seriously. She'd also only been out of school a year when we started meeting, and I was the first person she'd ever met with Gender Identity Disorder. She was the first person who ever listened to me and took what I was trying to express for what it was. She helped me find information, and learn that I'm not alone. She's the one who convinced my parents that putting me on hormone suppression therapy was the right thing to do.

Things were really rough for me for a while. If it weren't for Dr. Hewitt, I'm not sure I'd be alive. So I'm pretty fond of her. We've been through a lot of ups and downs. I've been dealing with the suppression therapy and trying to grow up to be a boy; she's gotten married and had a baby. We're not friends, but we aren't strangers who just talk about thoughts and feelings, either. She gives her personal number to those whom she considers risks, like me and Maria, and some others.

I'm comfortable with her. I *trust* her.

Which reminds me…. I take my journal out of my bag and open it up to the entry I wrote this morning and put it on her desk. Out of everything from the last couple of weeks, that seems like the most important. Today is the most important.

My fingers tap against my leg as I step away, walking from desk to window, window to chair, chair to door, then back to the desk again. Turning in place, I reverse the path around the room again. I've managed to do four laps by the time she comes in.

"I'm very sorry, Jordan. BethAnn has been running a fever since last night." Dr. Hewitt motions to the chair, but I wait until she sits before I flop into it.

She looks tired, with circles under her eyes. "I hope she feels better soon," I offer. "Or at least that you can get some better sleep tonight."

It's small talk, and I tap my fingers again as she goes silent and starts to read. She flips a few pages back, skimming the entries since the last time we met two weeks ago, then closes the book.

"Did you write the letter?" I ask, not waiting for her to bring up the subject. I want to leap forward and look over her desk, trying to find it. I want to shake her, I want to beg. But I can't do that. I sit as quietly as I can, trying to look like some lazy guy where none of this matters, tangling my fingers together and holding on so tight that my skin turns pale in places.

She smiles then, and I know this is it. This is the beginning of the rest of my life.

"Yes, Jordan, I have your letter."

She holds out an envelope, reaching to bridge the gap between us as I lean forward to grasp it. It's real. She wrote it, I have it, I get to go to my physical in a week, and I'll get the prescription. And everything is going to change.

"That's your copy," Dr. Hewitt tells me. "I've sent the original to your physician, and pending the results of your physical, you should be able to move forward as planned. I'll be seeing you regularly to evaluate your psychological progress, and he'll take care of your physical reaction."

"It's going to be awesome," I say, voice rough. "Amazing. I can't wait. This is just—" I'm embarrassed by the dampness in the corners of my eyes. It should be easy; I've been thinking about it all day. But it's overwhelming at the same time.

It's not like I've been obsessing over this forever; just for about the last year. I've been on the suppression therapy for years, which helped, but we didn't start quite soon enough. No one knew we could even do it, or that it was what I needed. But the sooner I start T, the more my body will change in reaction to it. I feel like I need to do it before I stop being a teenager. I don't want to start puberty all over again when I'm twenty.

God, I'm going to have a beard. And my voice... it's going to change. I hope I can still sing. My hands are shaking, my heart racing, and I bounce up out of my chair and walk away, fingers tapping against my jeans again.

"How did auditions go, Jordan?"

Scene change: pan away from the nervously excited boy and over to the sulky actor. I sigh. "There's a guy there who's better at being Puck than me, by far. I'm sure he'll get the part. He's like what people think when they think Puck, y'know? I never thought I'd say it, but right now I'd be better off if I were short and skinny, and hadn't worked out."

"Are you still working out?"

We'd talked about it when I started, because I was trying to bulk up, prepare my body for when I could take the testosterone. I nod, and we go off on a little sidebar about what I'm benching now, and how I'm balancing cardio and weights, and even a little bit about diet. I can't resist rolling up the sleeve of my shirt and showing off the muscle (I'm not Popeye, but I'm no slouch). Which takes off on another tangent about the vest I'm wearing and that brings us back around to body image when I comment how it's almost as good as binding, the fabric's so stiff.

Which reminds me. "I need you to talk to my parents." A flush starts to rise to my cheeks.

"Oh?" She sits forward, hands clasped together on the desk. "Is something wrong at home?"

"God no." Well, nothing that's worth talking about. Yeah, my folks are still sometimes weirded out by me. But it's not like Maria's, where they actively refuse to call her by her name, and where they try to keep her from going out dressed as a girl. My folks try to accept me, but some things just aren't easy for them. Or for me to say, either to them or Dr. Hewitt. "I want to buy something. Online. And my mom's going to think it's some kind of perverted toy, even though I think it's pretty obvious it's not. I need you to explain it to her."

I see understanding dawn, and Dr. Hewitt smiles gently. "I'll make an appointment to talk to both your parents about it. But you will need to talk to them yourself, as well. I can tell them it's not sexual, but you need to explain some of the rest. It'll mean more when it comes from you."

I so don't want to try to explain to my *mother* that a real boy needs something to be his boy bits since nature wasn't good enough to supply them. I can't even imagine that conversation without choking. But Dr. Hewitt is giving me the look that says that it's for my own good, and if I'm hoping to get something better than the homemade solutions I can use now, I'd better nod and say yes.

"So, if you don't get the part you were hoping for, will you still be in the play?" She sits back again, hands folded.

"I don't know." I flop back down into the chair, looking up, shoving my bangs out of my face. "I mean, I wasn't sure I wanted to do the show to begin with, but James wanted me to. It's just that there aren't any chorus parts, no place to be a part of the crowd. And well, I studied Puck so much, and I already knew his lines and how he acts. I don't know if I'd be as good as someone else. But if I walk away just because I don't get the role I want, then everyone thinks I'm a total prima donna." Especially Pepper. And if she casts me as someone else and I walk away, I'll be letting her down.

But what if she casts me as one of the girls?

I press my lips together, looking down at my jeans. The frayed bit is getting worse, the little threads easy to pick at now.

"Jordan?" Dr. Hewitt's voice is gentle, and she's silent until I look up at her. "Are you going to walk away from it?"

"They might cast me as a girl part." I speak quickly, words tumbling out in a rush. "Not because I'm girly. The kid who'll probably play Puck is more girly than me. We rescued him from a fight this morning. But he's not—a girl, I mean. God, I felt awful that I even looked at his chest to see if he was, y'know what I mean? But I saw red when Toby called him that, it just got to me."

I trail off, and she's still looking at me. Waiting. I sigh. "There's this girl, and she rewrote *Twelfth Night* and *A Midsummer Night's Dream* into a single play. And she's doing some gender-bending twisty stuff with it. They had me read for Viola and Helena. And I don't want to be either of them. I don't want to pretend to be a girl in front of everyone."

Because biology aside, it would be pretending. "I don't do drag," I add.

She's quiet, like she expects me to keep going, but what else is there to say? So I cross my arms stubbornly and prepare to outwait her.

"Is it that you don't do drag, or that you're afraid of what others might see if they look at you in that context?" she finally asks quietly.

My gaze drops, my breath slipping out in a rush like she punched me in the gut. The horrible thing is, I can imagine it. I've seen it, in my nightmares, and she's heard that from my journal before. Me, up on stage, in some ridiculous long dress, my body all sharp angles the way it's supposed to be. But people look at me and stare and they see the girl I was born as. I start to shiver, fists clenching, nails biting into my palms. "Fear," I admit, voice shaking. "I—" The shudder rolls over me, violent and hard, my pulse pounding in my ears.

Panic attack.

The world is gray around the edges, and Dr. Hewitt is crouched in front of me, her hands over mine. "Jordan," she says softly. "You need to think this through now, before you're confronted with the decision in school."

Because if I had one of these panic attacks in school that'd just suck.

I stare at her, trying to unclench my hands, or find a way to breathe, or think, or anything.

"If you're given the part of a female character, Jordan, what will you do?"

I shake my head. "I don't know. I don't know."

We sit there for I don't know how long until the shivering subsides. I suck in a long breath, holding it in my lungs because it just feels so good. It escapes in a shaky whisper of sound, and I drag it back in again. In and out, slow and steady until my heart rate lowers. "I'm okay," I whisper, and we both know I'm lying. But I'm as okay as I'm gonna get right now.

She doesn't push me about the part again, and I'm happy to leave it. Besides, I figure she did exactly what she wanted to do: she's making me think about it. I'm not going to be able to stop thinking about it, and maybe by the time it might matter, I'll know what to do without blacking out.

Dr. Hewitt hands me back my journal, and I carefully put that and the letter (which is getting put into my journey book when I get home) into my backpack. My voice is steady when I say good-bye, and that I'll be back in two weeks. She promises again to talk to my parents and says she'll e-mail me when it's done, and I thank her politely (without blushing).

When I step out into the waiting room, I get an armful of Maria.

"You're pale as a ghost," she tells me once she's done hugging me. She grips my shoulders and leans back, looking me over.

I nudge her arms free and point to the door. "Out." And I smile as she skips to the door, turning to walk backward and motion me along faster.

We make our way downstairs to where she's parked on the street. She has a cute little bright-purple Mazda that her parents bought her for her sixteenth birthday as a bribe for her to dress "properly" at home. I don't know how she does it.

She sits on the hood. "So? Did you get it?"

"Oh yeah, I've got the letter." I can't help but grin, and she throws her arms around me, dragging me in to plant a sloppy wet kiss on my cheek. "My physical's in a week. I'll let you know when I get my first shot."

"And I'll be watching to see when you get your first facial hair." Maria touches my upper lip, then pulls back, grinning brightly. "I'm so envious of you, Jordan. Mama gave me the over her dead body speech again last night. I was thinking about—"

"No," I cut her off. We've had this conversation before and I know where she's going with that thought. "You've got less than two years until you're eighteen, and you can do it legally and safely. Do you really want to travel an hour to a city that has enough drug trade to get it, and then hope you don't die making the deal, and that it's clean enough to use?"

Her jaw sets. It's total role reversal from the moment I had with James earlier, with me sitting where James was. But I'm right this time. Illegal hormones are a stupid idea, and if it weren't for TV telling her she could do it, Maria wouldn't even consider it. But she's so damned desperate to get to be herself, and she thinks that if she had breasts, her parents couldn't try to turn her back into a boy anymore.

But illegal estrogen is going too far, and she knows what I think, so we drop the subject.

"We should celebrate," she suggests. "Ice cream?"

"I have to get home for dinner. But we could pick some up on the way and you could stay. It's pot roast night." I hold out my hand, waiting.

It only takes a moment before she drops her car key into my palm. She's on the phone, chattering in Spanish at her mother, faster than I could ever hope to translate with the three years of language class I took before I bailed. She'll talk, I'll drive, and a half gallon of Rocky Road will make a great celebration.

CHAPTER 4: Impossible Things

DINNER TURNS out to be more and less chaotic than I thought. On the one hand, James is AWOL, apparently out for a burger with Britney, so I don't have to worry about him and Maria butting heads. But on the other hand, my two younger sisters won't shut up. Samantha's going on and on about the intricacies of seventh-grade relationships, and Leigh keeps trying to talk over her about soccer. My head starts to ache and no one even thinks to ask me how my appointment went. We did birthday things in the morning, so it's life back to normal for dinner.

Maria and I both take thick slices of chocolate cake and big globs of ice cream on the side and head upstairs. My parents are normally wiggy about me spending private time with anyone, but Maria's the exception, since she knows everything there is to know about me.

I flop on my bed, leaning back against the wall next to the window, and Maria sits at the other end. The cake is thick and dark, the ice cream super sweet, and together they're a quick burst of flavor in my mouth. I make a small noise and decide that eating is better than talking, at least right now.

Maria eats with dainty forkfuls, completely at odds with the tomboy sprawl of her long limbs. I nudge her leg to remind her that she's wearing a straight skirt, and she switches from sprawling cross-legged to pressing her knees together and tucking her feet back under her, sitting on one hip. It's the little things that she's still learning.

"When do you have to be home?" My cake's half-gone, and I set the plate aside to let the ice cream melt into it more.

"How about like, never?"

She gives me a beseeching look, and I shake my head. No matter how many times she asks about crashing at my place, it just isn't possible. It gives my parents a headache trying to figure out sleepovers ever since it all came out when I was eleven, so they've just banned overnight guests for me altogether. Not to mention that Maria herself adds another layer of complication on top of it all.

She sighs. "I got into a fight with my folks last night. Again."

"You said something about over your mama's dead body?" I prompt.

"Exactly." She sits up, jabbing her fork at me. "She said that the only way she's going to see her firstborn son become a woman is over her dead body. Like boobs are threatening her or something. She doesn't understand that I just want to be on the outside who I am on the inside. I'd probably have less trouble at school."

"You could start stashing stuff in your locker and dressing when you get to school," I suggest. Stupid idea, but I lay it on the table anyway.

She shakes her head. "Wouldn't work. I'm still on the records officially as Felipe, and everyone there's known me since I started school. I'm not like you. My parents won't let me change schools. They won't even let me change my name. I'm lucky they haven't cut my hair while I was sleeping." She winds a hank of that hair around her hand, twisting it. I've seen her when she's in her boy drag during the day, with her hair yanked back into a ponytail. It makes her look weird, like I can't quite find the girl I know inside that face.

I reach out and rub my hand over her knee; it's the only thing I can reach of her. I know I've got it good compared to her. We picked up and moved here the summer before eighth grade so I'd be closer to Dr. Hewitt and I could have a fresh start. My school records, which are private except for teachers and administration, have all my birth information on them, but outwardly, I've been male since the beginning of eighth grade. In that respect, my parents are awesome. And the teachers have been decent, too. I'm really, really lucky, and I know it.

"I'd say I could talk to her, but your mama doesn't like me."

That makes Maria laugh because it's true. The first time her mama met me, she was all about what a nice boy I was, and couldn't Maria try to be more like me. Then Maria told her where we'd met, and her mama realized we already were as alike as opposites could get. She hasn't said one word to me since, other than *thank you* when I used to drop Maria off before she got a car of her own.

There's a flash of light outside, and I lean up, pulling the curtains aside just enough to peek out. Yep, there's James coming home, his hair all a mess and a strut in his step. I don't even want to know what he's been doing, although I can definitely guess and that pricks at me all over again. I let the curtain drop back before he notices the light from my room. "James has a girlfriend," I comment.

"Oh? That blonde bimbo you were telling me about?" Maria looks like she doesn't care, which means she does. It's only when she's pretending that she's ever this calm about things. I'd been wondering if she was totally over that crush, and I guess not so much. "That reminds me." She slants a glance toward me. "There's a guy…."

It takes me a second to figure out what she means. "A guy… does he know?" It's the first question I have to ask, and she looks away without answer, so no, he doesn't. "Maria, we can't date," I tell her. "What if he tries to feel you up?"

"I've got balloons." Maria poked at her makeshift chest, amplified by salt-filled condoms that had been prodded into shape. I know because she showed me, in detail, one day. Tits are a lot less traumatizing when they aren't stuck on me and a lot less interesting on someone else when they're made of rubber.

"And he's not going to, Jordan," she continues. "It'll be some kissing, and I can distract him if he wants to get physical, but I *don't* want to get physical, not yet. I'm not right yet."

"So you think we *should* date." She's talking about this guy, but I'm thinking about Pepper again. And it isn't a question, not at all, because I don't know how to make it one. There are footsteps coming up the stairs, and I hold my breath, waiting to see if James comes in or goes by. The footsteps go down the hallway, and I hear the bathroom door slam shut, then the water start running. Evening shower. Huh.

Maria is silent. I finally look over at her, confused by how quiet she is. "What?"

"Each other?" she squeaks softly.

I'm lost. "What are you talking about?" My cake is nice and gooey now with the melted ice cream, and I pick up the plate so I can polish it off.

"Do you think we should date each other?" She strings both our questions together like maybe I meant it that way. Next thing I know, she's hammering on my back as I'm choking on the cake I inhaled in my surprise.

"No!" I shake my head vehemently. "That wasn't what I meant at all. You were talking about that guy. And I met a girl."

"Oh." She looks down, idly nudging at portions of her anatomy that don't quite seem to look right at the moment. "You going to ask her out?"

"Hell, no. My parents'd kill me. And what would I say to her if I did?" I get the shivers just thinking about telling Pepper about me, not to mention my folks. They're supportive, yeah, but they still have limits. To keep me safe, they say.

Maria snuggles up next to me, her arm around my back, head tipped on my shoulder. I have to put the plate down or she's going to end up with chocolate crumbs all down her front. I put my arms around her as well so we can hold each other. "Don't be ashamed of who you are, Jordan Lewis," she tells me sternly. "She'd have to be amazing to deserve you."

The shivers slow and fade. "She's pretty amazing," I admit. "She wrote the play, and she's helping direct, and she's drop-dead gorgeous. She has freckles on her nose. I didn't even know I liked freckles."

Maria's pocket buzzes, and with a grumble, she fishes her phone out and swears at it. "Mama's pitching a fit and Serena says she says if I'm not home in fifteen minutes, I'm grounded for a week. That's barely time to drive there." She looks at me, and she's considering staying—I can see it—so I shove at her without saying a word. If she's grounded, she'll lose the car. That means no psych appointments, since her parents won't take her, and no visiting me. She knows all that as well as I do, so she just sighs. "Fine, fine, I'll go."

We untangle ourselves and she kisses me on the cheek. She runs down the hall, tapping sharply on the bathroom door to call out, "Bye, James!" His response is muffled, but Maria just laughs and blows the door a kiss. Then she hurries down the stairs and is gone. It's a twelve-minute drive from her door to mine, if she doesn't get stuck at lights. It's gonna be close.

I should probably clean up so Mom doesn't get pissy about me having dirty plates in my room. I grab Maria's from the bed, and reach for mine on top of the dresser. And I stop, Maria's plate tilted in my hand, ice cream dripping onto the floor, because my plate isn't the only thing on my dresser.

There are three small glass vials, tiny enough that they could fit all together on the palm of my hand. One is filled with blue liquid, one with purple, and one with green.

I give thee three potions: true sight, true seeming, and true love. Don't mix them up.

No way. No fucking way.

I set the one plate down on the other with a thunk. Then I pick up the vials. Purple was first, I think, so that'd be true sight. Then green, no wait, blue was the second in my dream, making that true seeming. Which leaves green for true love.

Crap, I'm hallucinating. This can't be real. I put the vials back down and rub at my eyes. When I open them… they're still there.

"You okay?"

I spin around, putting my back to the bureau, blocking the vials from view, and smile tightly at my brother. He's got a towel in his hand, rubbing it against his wet hair while he talks.

"I heard Maria leaving," he says, "and you look kind of weird. Everything go okay at your appointment today?"

Oh. Right. That. I nod quickly. "I've got the letter, and she sent a copy to Dr. Patil's office already. As long as I pass my physical, I can start the new therapy as soon as everything comes together for it."

James frowns, stepping into my room. He comes up close, and he's taller than me by a few inches. I keep hoping that when I start T, maybe I'll grow again and make it to six foot like him. He's looking at my face, and he seems worried. "Shouldn't you be happier, then?"

"I am," I insist. "Best thing to happen to me since I started seeing Dr. Hewitt and she put me on the hormone suppression drugs. It's just…." My voice trails off, because I am not going to explain to him that things from my dreams last night are somehow sitting on my bureau.

"The play?" he prompts.

I seize on that. "Yeah. I don't think I'm going to get Puck. That kid we rescued from the thugs was kind of amazing at the tryouts. And it's his sister doing the casting, I guess."

"And you're a senior and he's a freshman," James pointed out. "They always give the best roles to the seniors because it's our last chance."

"Great, just what I want, a pity casting," I grumble. "I'd rather not play the part if that's why they give it to me." I shake my head because if we keep going, we're going to end up talking about the other parts I read for and honestly, one panic attack a day is more than enough. "You did a good Oberon. We'll probably find out about callbacks on Thursday. Don't they have another round of auditions tomorrow?"

"For the guys who couldn't make it today, yeah." James puffs up when I compliment his Oberon, thoroughly pleased with himself. "In a perfect world, I'll be Oberon, Britney'll be Titania, and you'll be Puck. Can't wait to get the script for a read-through."

"It's modernized. I don't like modernized Shakespeare." It feels weird on my tongue, the way the words have gone from fluid to awkward.

"There's probably room for interpretation." James shrugs. He takes one last look at me. "You're all right, then?"

I nod and shove him toward the door. "There's one slice of cake left downstairs. You should go get it before one of the girls tries to sneak it before bed."

When he's gone, I nudge the door shut behind him. With five kids in the family, we're all privacy nuts, and right now, I need that privacy because I have to see if I'm losing my mind.

I turn to look at the bureau.

The three vials look back at me.

I'd say it can't be happening, but it is. True sight, true seeming, and true love.

The question is, what do I do with them?

CHAPTER 5: Callbacks

THE LIST for callbacks doesn't go up until Friday morning. It's pinned to the wall outside the music room, and there's a hand-scrawled note saying that all people listed will be cast in the play, but they need a few more readings before they nail down exactly who will be playing who. I'm on the list. So's James and so is Britney. So far so good. Ryan's on the list as well, and Paul Sullivan and my study buddy Cece Anderson. There are a few names I recognize vaguely, like Tyler Edison (soccer again) and Zach Bennett (he's been dating Ryan for the last year; it's kind of hard to miss the only out gay couple in school). I don't know the rest of them, but I figure I'll get to know them soon enough, right?

It's hard to concentrate today. All I can think about is Puck. Speaking for Puck. *Being* Puck. Then I think of those three vials that I shoved into my underwear drawer at home, and my breath shudders in my chest. But hah, I have the vials, so that means I *am* Puck, right? I get to use them.

By the time we all gather in the auditorium after school, I feel like I can't quite breathe. It's not a panic attack yet, but it's close. I need to be able to read for my part, and I need to be sure of it. I find a corner and settle in, letting my body go loose and limp. Eyes closed: breathe in, breathe out. I watch the movie in my mind of me as Puck. I can do this. And I can do it better than Paul Sullivan.

Once everyone's there's, we're called up on stage to sit in a circle. They want us to read for a few parts, then Dower and Pepper will go off and figure out the final slate. Sounds lovely, except not.

They pull up Ryan, James, and a guy Damien first, and have them read for Oberon opposite Cece and a girl named Caitlyn as Titania. Once that's done, they tell everyone to sit but Ryan, and pull up Tyler and Zach, having them go through Demetrius and Lysander in various combinations. I have to laugh as Zach and Ryan play the parts, adding a whole new level as they take it from bromance into campy romance. Pepper giggles, but Dower puts Tyler back in with Zach and has them do it again the same way only less campy, with Lysander pining for Demetrius. It works surprisingly well.

Next up are me and Paul. He's so tiny that he makes me feel tall. He'd make a good Viola, wouldn't he? Small and thin, he could be a believable girl. We read for Puck, taking turns working with the three possible Oberons, and it feels so good to be in this role. I let everything else go as the words pour out, and Puck takes me over.

It's done too soon, and Dower calls for James and I to stand. We look at each other, confused, as Dower nudges us closer to each other, looking us over carefully. I know what he sees. We're almost the same age—Irish twins born ten months apart, spaced just right that we ended up the same year in school. We're both blond, like everyone else in the family, and our faces have similar shapes, although his is more angular than mine. His hair is shorter and spiked, while my bangs fall in my face. And James is three inches (yes, exactly, I've checked) taller than me. We don't dress a thing alike, but we stand in a similar way, fingers hooked in our pockets as we watch Dower walk around us in a large circle.

I feel like a piece of meat on display. I don't like it, but I try not to fidget; I don't want to fall short when they compare me to James.

Pepper hands us the scripts and tells me to read for Sebastian while James reads for Viola. We end up playing it for laughs, because James can't take it seriously. His voice slips up, high-pitched and vaguely squeaky, as he tries to mimic what he thinks her voice ought to be. I think about trying to make myself butch, but I can't even go there. I'm not as big or bulky as James, and all I can think is what everyone else must see with Viola towering over Sebastian.

A moment later Dower has us switch roles.

The world narrows down to the tiny spots I can see of the script. I can't look up, can't even think. I'm sure as hell not acting, just reading the words in an awkward voice that falters and skips as I force the words out. It feels like an impossible task, but we make it through. I feel hazy and gray as James sits and Ryan stands, and we find a new page in the script and read a scene with him as Orsino and me as Viola being Cesario. This scene is somehow easier, with him looking at Viola as if she was male in truth, and I know that in this version of the play she is, thanks to Puck's magic. My breath slowly eases, and I gain confidence, voice ringing out.

Pepper nudges Ryan away and brings out Caitlyn, pointing us to new pages again and a scene for Olivia and Cesario. And I flirt without trying, finding Cesario inside me in ways that I cannot find Viola. He is easy, so easy for me, because I get him in ways that no one else really can. Here he is, hiding inside the body that has become his. And he finds some comfort in it. I wonder if anyone else realizes how much Viola's life would be changed by her time as Cesario. I wonder if they truly think Viola could possibly go back to the person she began as, once she reaches the end of the story.

Then I'm done, and they have me sit. There are more who read different scenes, but I don't care. And when Pepper and Dower go off to talk among themselves, I settle in to sit cross-legged on the stage, pull out my homework, and try not to think about it.

"What d'you think?" James folds his legs, sitting next to me, hands on the stage behind him as he leans back and looks around.

"I think I have math homework." I don't want to talk about it. Talking about it means thinking about it, and until they come back and announce who's got what part, I can pretend it's all still okay. Right?

But James doesn't take the hint. "They didn't even have me read for Lysander or Demetrius, and it looks like Britney's going to be one of those girls." His gaze drifted to watching the pretty blonde.

"Well, Cece's gorgeous," I point out. "And regal. She'd make a good Titania."

"What about Puck?" He nudges me. "Think you'll get it? They had you read a lot for Viola."

My lips press thin, pencil scratching hard against the paper. I don't answer.

"They're probably thinking about the sibling connection. Sebastian's not as good a role as Oberon, but I'll take it if I get it."

"Pepper and Paul look like siblings." My throat feels tight, and I don't look at James, not wanting to give away how close I feel to a panic attack. "Maybe she should be in the play and they can play Viola and Sebastian. I bet she'd make a great Cesario. I'd be happy to show her how to bind properly." My voice is pitched low enough to be just for James and me, but still, I glance around before I say that, just in case someone's listening.

Thinking about binding makes me think about the reverse. If I play Viola, would I have to wear—God. No. I don't even want to think about the costumes Viola would have to wear on stage, what *I'd* have to wear on stage where everyone could see. "Let me do my math already, James." There's a faint creak in my voice, the panic making it hard to breathe. Pull air in, hold it, see if I can let it out slow and easy. In, out. I need to relax.

"You have all weekend, Jordan," James points out. "Why are you in such a rush to get it done right this second? Nervous?"

I look at the notebook on my lap. "Yeah. Can we drop the topic now?"

A shadow falls over my page, and I glance up to see Paul crouched in front of me. The position seems so natural for him, light on the balls of his feet, elbows resting on his knees as he balances there. He grins at me. "We didn't get introduced properly." His voice is naturally high, lilting slightly. "I'm Paul. And you're Jordan. And I wanted to say I think your singing voice is amazing. Better than mine by far."

"You'll get there by the time you're a senior," I tell him, which is honest. He's not bad. In fact, he's got a nice high tenor, and I'm betting he can hit the high notes even better than me. But he doesn't have the depth that he needs, and training'll give him that. "Just keep working on it. And you're a better actor."

He shrugs. "Not really. I'm just a better Puck. I can't play a role straight to save my life."

I blink, trying to figure out if that's some kind of code and he's coming on to me. Luckily he just keeps talking.

"I don't know what Pepper's got in mind, not completely. She's kept the show totally under wraps and I saw the script for the first time at the same time you guys all did, during auditions." Another light shrug, and he tilts backward slowly to land on his bottom, sitting cross-legged like we are.

"For what it's worth, I think you'd be an amazing Viola." Paul gestures at me, so I can't possibly think he means James.

I shudder at those words, another shiver rolling through me when James speaks up. "He's right. Your Cesario is more believable than anyone else's. And I'd be ridiculous as Viola."

"If you ever want to run lines or anything, you should come over. Both of you," Paul includes James in the invitation. "The schedule for the play is pretty aggressive, and we're going to have a lot to memorize in a short amount of time. And I don't know about you, but the modernization of it pretty much freaks me out."

It's such an echo of what I was saying last night about the changes that it sets me off-balance and I just stare at the kid. James answers for both of us that sure, it sounds like a good idea, and we ought to get groups together based on the scenes we're in. He elbows me and says something, but I don't hear the words. I just stand up.

"I need to take a piss." Crude, maybe, but it shushes them both up long enough for me to get away. I'm at the door when Dower's voice calls out to us to gather up so he can announce the cast list.

I look at the door, then back at Dower. I wasn't completely lying; I do need to go. But I can't really miss the announcement, either. So I make my way back to the edge of the stage and stand there, arms crossed, avoiding everyone else as I lean one hip against the edge.

"This show has a smaller cast than if we'd simply merged *Dream* and *Twelfth Night* together," Pepper explains. "What I've done is pull out two storylines from each play—the characters and relationships—and kept the fairy element to affect both storylines. So we have the fairy court, then a quartet from *Dream*, and a quartet from *Twelfth Night*." She cedes the floor to Dower then, for the actual announcement.

The fairies first: Damien as Oberon, Cece as Titania, and Paul as Puck. I swallow past the lump in my throat, and try not to look at anyone else. I don't want sympathy, not now. I don't want to break. The three giggling girls from auditions are Titania's attendants, and I stuff their names—Libby, Sylvie, and Demi—into my memory and hope I won't forget them right away. It's hard to tell them apart, since they're all kind of short and perky, and I suspect they're all cheerleaders.

It's the *Dream* quartet next, and I hold out hope here, that I could be Lysander or Demetrius. They didn't have me read for Helena again, so I hope to God that Pepper changed her mind about *that* at least. I guess she did, since she's cast a tall girl named Lianne as Helena, and Britney's going to be Hermia (which yeah, makes complete sense, since she's pretty and vapid and all). Zach's Demetrius and Tyler is Lysander.

That only leaves four roles for me, Ryan, James, and Caitlyn.

My throat tightens; the light in the room seems to fade as things start to swirl around me. I grip the edge of the stage with my fingers, trying to force myself to stay upright. I could swear I hear James's voice calling my name, and I push away, shoving at whoever is near me as I race for the door.

It closes with a thunk behind me, leaving me in a hallway that seems too dark, almost like a horror movie. I pause, struggling to breathe, then move with echoing quick steps down the hall to the bathroom. I go into the farthest stall and lock the door behind me. I climb up and perch on the toilet, toes on the edge, head bowed down by my knees as I crouch there, fighting for consciousness.

Because how fucking embarrassing would it be to pass out locked in a toilet stall, right?

Hours pass in a haze of warm breath and chills. I hear the door open and the water run, and I wait to hear the door again, for whoever it is to leave.

"Jordan?"

A girl's voice. Am I in the wrong bathroom?

I open my eyes, blinking into the light that seems so much brighter than it was before, and look to my left and right for a telltale wastebasket on the wall of the stall. No, not the girls' room. Thank God.

There's a soft knock on the door to the stall. "Are you okay, Jordan? You didn't look very well when you ran out. People are worried."

I slowly unfold my body and stand. My hand shakes when I twist the lock and let the door swing open to find Pepper there, her brow furrowed and hand still raised to knock again.

She's several inches shorter than me, built as tiny as her brother. The spray of freckles across her nose is scrunched together, slowly spreading out as her expression eases when she sees me. Her red hair is in her face, and I have an absurd idea to nudge it back. My hand half raises, then I remember: she cast me as a *girl*. She has somehow seen through the mask. "I can't do this," I say quietly, my voice hoarse and rough.

Disappointment shows in her jade eyes, but also resignation. "I was afraid you were going to say that," she admits. She backs up, giving me room to come out, then hands me a paper towel soaked with cold water.

I press it to my eyes, feeling the cool on my forehead. The panic is fading, leaving me cold and empty. "I'm sorry." I hate disappointing her. What a great second impression, huh? At least her first impression was of me helping save her brother. Maybe I earned enough points with that to counteract this mess.

She turns away from me, ratcheting out another long string of paper towels, and soaking those as well. She offers it to me silently. I give her the towel that was warmed by my skin, and put the new, fresh one over my closed eyes, not wanting to look at her right now.

"You brother's really worried about you." Her voice is slow and cautious. "I told him I'd check up on you, because I wanted to talk to you. Maybe tell you why I cast you."

Why *she* cast me. Not Dower. Did he tell her the truth about me? He wouldn't do that. Would he? I shiver, and breathe in through my nose and out through my mouth, struggling against the darkness again. This is ridiculous. I can't let it take me over. "Go on," I say.

"It's your voice," she says. "You have this amazing, rough, smoky voice that's so perfect and haunting. You've got the low notes perfectly, and you nail the higher ones when you sing, but it's not like you go into falsetto. I can believe you're both female and male, and you don't seem like you're trying to be fake as Viola. And that's hard for a guy, really hard. Your brother's a good actor, but what he did—it's what most guys do. They turn it into a farce, but you didn't. You were uncomfortable, yeah, but you treated her like she was just anyone else."

I drop my hands away from my face, blinking in the light. "She *is* just anyone else."

Pepper smiles then. "Exactly. We're not aliens, but most guys seem to think we are. Or like the only way to be a girl is to put on tight clothes and prance around in high heels. Viola's just another human being, and she needs to be played straight like that. And I knew you could do it. And you and James are so perfect standing next to each other. Dower really wanted to give him Oberon, but I wanted him for Sebastian because of you."

My laugh sounds a little strangled. "Don't tell James that; he'll be blaming me forever for his losing Oberon."

Pepper touches my shoulder, squeezing lightly. "Come back in and do the read-through, please? And think about it over the weekend. You can tell me Monday if you really can't do it. But I promise you, no one's going to be laughing when they see you on stage. They're just going to be thinking about how awesome an actor you are to pull it off."

I swear, my brain short-circuits as soon as she touches me, and I'm nodding before I really think about what I'm saying yes to.

Her smile is worth it.

I can't resist this time and reach out, one finger hooking in a dark-red curl, nudging it back behind her ear. She flushes, warm rose under the freckles, but she doesn't pull away. I'm playing with fire even thinking anything about her, and my heart's rushing so hard I'm starting to shake again. It's the good kind of nervous, anxious and waiting for something to happen, like that moment before going downstairs on Christmas morning to see the packages under the tree.

The moment breaks as she lets go of my shoulder and takes a step back. "C'mon. Let's go get that read-through done. There's a script in there with your name on it."

I stand there, looking at her. "Is there going to be a roster handed out? Your brother suggested that a bunch of us could get together and run lines. I know we all gave you our info when we signed up." It seems like one way of subtly getting her number and e-mail.

Her smile sparks impish, and my heart trips over itself in a syncopated beat. She steps forward and picks my phone from where it peeks out of my pocket. She carefully taps for several moments, then holds it out at arm's length to take a picture of herself. She hands it back to me, showing her name, phone, and e-mail woven in with her smiling image. She curls my hands around it. "There." She blinks innocently, adding, "You can use the home number to reach Paul, too, of course. You should text me soon, so I've got your number, too."

"Of course."

She steps to the door, and looks back at me as she opens it. I can see James standing down the hall. He walks toward us, and that jars me into motion. I shove the phone back in my pocket and walk through the door that Pepper's opened for me.

INTERLUDE: Pepper

PEPPER SAT on the edge of the stage once everyone was gone, waiting for Paul to come back from his trip to the boys' room. It had been a long rehearsal; getting through all the callbacks, then the thing with Jordan, and finally doing the first read-through of the entire script. They paused often during the read-through to discuss the changes from the original manuscripts for both plays, and talk about the musical numbers. Pepper had introduced TJ Reid, who wrote the music for the show, and they'd handed out CDs of the accompaniment for each of the songs. Pepper had also handed out a schedule for rehearsals. For Monday she had placed the fairies on the stage with Dower for large blocking, sent the *Dream* quartet off to music, and she'd take the *Twelfth Night* quartet for smaller blocking off-stage. They'd rotate in groups throughout the weeks.

It was a long road ahead, but she was sure it was going to be worth it. Some of what she wanted from the play had peeked through as the cast members had simply read the lines cold, and she knew there was so much more that would emerge as they rehearsed. She couldn't wait to see how the production would shine when it was polished.

"Ms. Sullivan."

The voice came from the darkness in the middle of the auditorium, around the aisle that split the lower and upper levels. Pepper recognized the principal's tone and immediately pushed herself off the stage and started walking up the aisle. "Yes, Ms. Jackson? What did you think of the read-through?"

"I think you have the potential for a very interesting production." The words sounded as if they were carefully chosen by the principal.

Pepper's stomach sank at the quiet, almost flat tone. "You haven't changed your mind, have you?"

"I haven't." Ms. Jackson gestured to one of the chairs, waiting until Pepper sat before she took a seat, leaving an empty space between them. The principal turned slightly to face her, ankles crossed neatly and tucked back, hands folded against her skirted lap. "I have already agreed to support the production, and to sponsor your script for the Miller award. You are still interested in submitting your work, yes?"

"Definitely." Pepper nodded quickly. "I need to do some cleanup on it first, but it's mostly minor revisions and I'm hoping to go through it this weekend. No matter how many times I read it out loud, hearing it in other people's voices still showed me some places that they'll trip over the lines." Not to mention that there were a few points where she'd heard the actors insert the lines they already knew, in the old language, and she thought they actually worked better. So she'd do some quick revisions, print out new scripts, and hand them out Monday. She didn't think anyone was likely to start memorizing until they started blocking the scenes anyway. At least she hoped they wouldn't.

"Good. I'd like to take a look at the final revision before I write my letter to the committee on your behalf. And I believe you need a full recording of your cast performing the music, am I correct?"

"Either a recording of the final performance or a video of selected scenes in rehearsal and the recording of the musical numbers," Pepper confirmed. "I'm going to e-mail out release forms for everyone to sign. I'd been going to wait for everyone to become comfortable with the material, but I don't want to end up surprising them with the recording."

Ms. Jackson tilted her head, regarding Pepper quietly. "Do you believe that your entire cast will become comfortable?"

"I hope they will."

Pepper felt like Ms. Jackson had something else that she wasn't saying as the silence stretched on. She knew Ms. Jackson had observed Jordan's rapid exit and his return, but Pepper didn't really want to talk about Jordan's possible issues in the play. "Is there something else?" she ventured quietly.

"Do you remember an Emily Graves? I believe she auditioned for the part of Viola."

It took Pepper a moment, but yes, she remembered her. The girl had a voice like polished glass in that very uncomfortable soprano sort of way. "I do. She's not a bad actress, but her voice didn't suit Viola at all. She didn't really fit in any of the other roles, either, although I might've considered her for Hermia if we didn't have Britney. Why?"

"I spoke with her mother this afternoon. Apparently her daughter remembered what you said about the potential of having Mr. Lewis play the role of Viola and complained when she didn't receive an invitation to callbacks. She is quite upset about being passed over in favor of a male playing a female role." The look Ms. Jackson leveled at her made Pepper's back stiffen with quiet resolve.

"I'm willing to defend my choices, and I know Mr. Dower supports me," she said firmly. "Her mother's welcome to come to rehearsals and see the work we're doing, and why I made the decision I did. Emily's voice never would've suited Cesario. Jordan's got a great midrange voice that'll work well for both sides of the equation."

Pepper met Ms. Jackson's eyes, wondering why the principal wasn't saying anything. Again. It was like there was something Pepper wasn't getting that Ms. Jackson thought she should, and it just didn't make sense. She gave her a look. "Is there anything else, Ms. Jackson?"

"Just know that I'm willing to back you to the school board," the principal said. She stood, and smoothed down her gray skirt. "Given how Mrs. Graves was speaking, I'm expecting it may well come to that. I don't think she approves of anything less than the usual roles. I'll give you a letter to go with your release form, inviting parents to read the script. We're going to need them to be as comfortable as our players are."

Pepper wrinkled her nose, then relaxed, sighing as she stood as well. "Thank you, Ms. Jackson. I appreciate the support. And I promise that the play will kick butt and be something this school will never forget."

Ms. Jackson smiled, and it looked so odd that Pepper smiled back, caught up in that sudden enthusiasm. "Of that," Ms. Jackson said, "I have no doubt. Good luck, Ms. Sullivan."

Pepper let out a slow breath, walking back to the stage where Paul was now waiting for her.

"Sounds like life's going to be interesting." He quirked a smile at her.

"Only if we let it be." Pepper shouldered her backpack, then offered Paul a hand down from the stage. "I think the best thing we can do is just go forward and create the best damn show that this school's ever seen."

Her brother rolled his eyes, hands in his pockets as he walked with light steps. "And you think we can do that?"

"I think it's going to be a really good show," she said slowly. "If our Viola doesn't walk out on the role."

"How'd that go? The conversation with Jordan, I mean. You guys were locked in the bathroom for a while there. Is he really totally opposed to it? He came back out and read and didn't look like he was going to puke anymore."

"Yeah, well…." Pepper sighed, shrugging loosely. "I told him to take the weekend to think about it." She glanced back at Paul. "He really did look like he was gonna be sick, didn't he?"

"Completely. Funny thing is, he didn't seem like the kind of guy to be easily scared when he was fighting, did he?" Paul bounced ahead, turning to walk back, hands spread wide. "More like the kind of guy who charges in when he sees injustice. Him and James were my avenging angels."

"Are you crushing?" Pepper knew better, but she couldn't resist teasing.

Paul snorted. "Not my type, although if he had a sister just like him, I might be interested. It's more like… hero worship." He shook his head, rolling his eyes again. "The only thing the bullies ever manage to get right is that I am a complete and total geek."

"Pfft, so am I. I mean, I took a scriptwriting class for fun and mashed up Shakespeare." Pepper giggled. "We're a geek sort of family. Or are we dorks? Something like that. I'm proud of my dorkitude." But when she thought of Jordan, she sighed slightly. She *was* a dork. And he was cute in a way that meant she wouldn't mind if he could see past her dorkiness. Not that she could date someone in her play. She hated people who did that—it never looked good for a director to date one of the players, and she didn't want to be accused of favoritism.

"I think it's going to pull together," she finally said quietly. She leaned on the door to the school, holding it open for Paul to walk through. "And I think it's going to be pretty much amazing when it does. The school's never going to forget the show."

"What are you going to do when people start talking?" Paul asked, voice just as quiet. "Some people aren't going to like the way the show asks questions about gender, or pokes at sexuality in ways that the originals didn't."

"The originals did," Pepper countered. That was a part of what she loved about Shakespeare, after all. He was right, though; rumors were going around quickly, if they already had someone upset about Jordan getting the role he did. "Look at Viola playing Cesario. Shakespeare liked to push at the gender barriers, and work with what he was given, with the young boys playing the female roles. I'm just drawing that out to a logical place and making it more noticeable."

"And the changes to the targets of the potions?"

"Dramatic license. If we're going to play with gender, we might as well play with sexuality as well."

"What if someone bails because they don't want to deal with all the talk?"

"They've all read it now. If someone comes to me on Monday and they step out, then they step out." It was a valid fear, but Pepper couldn't dwell on it. "I tried to cast people who were serious about the show, who I thought would stick through it."

"Panic attacks aside?"

Okay, that part was still worrisome, Pepper had to admit. She'd never seen someone go absolutely white over something like this before. But she wanted to trust him. "Like you said, we talked for a long time, and I think he'll be okay with it. And I think he was trying to ask for my number, so I gave it to him," she admitted.

"You are *not* going to date a guy to keep him in the play."

"No!" Pepper shook her head quickly. She stopped at the bottom of the stairs, so she could lean in, speaking quickly to her brother. "He's cute. And he was so nervous. So I gave him my number, and said he could call us to set up times to run lines, which *you* had told him he could do already. So I don't know, maybe he's going after you and you'll have to be gentle when you let him down."

Paul smiled, that tiny fey look that he got sometimes, and reached up to tap her nose. "Nope. He went speechless when he looked at you, Pepper. He's into you, and you're going to have to figure out what to do about it."

Complications like that were something Pepper did not need. Life was going to be interesting enough getting to Christmas with a completed production and no outside drama, either from the cast or from the school at large. And she had a feeling it was still the calm before the storm, and maybe she ought to enjoy the quiet.

Then again, she also hoped Jordan would text her like he promised, so she'd have his number in her phone. Just in case.

PART TWO
Blocking

JOURNAL: Monday, October 12

I'M TRYING not to think too much today. It's Monday, and we have our rehearsal after school, of course.

Yes, that means I'm doing it. And I'm sure you'll have something to say about that at my next appointment when you read this. I don't know if I can explain it in coherent words without the panic attack, but I've been thinking about the play since callbacks last Friday. And what it comes down to is that I auditioned. I was given a part and if I ditch, I break the plan they have set for me and James as Viola and Sebastian. Pepper has to go back to square one and recast. And I don't want to do that to her.

I also spent all weekend thinking about asking her out. She's assistant directing. Is that like some kind of sexual harassment if I ask her out? Not that I can actually do it. We all know my parents don't want me dating. But I keep wondering: what could one date hurt? Just like… a movie. And dinner. Or maybe ice cream at the place downtown.

What's funny is that I've been seeing you so long I can hear you in my head asking me about Pepper. You'd ask, "What if it hurt her?"

And I guess you're right. It wouldn't be fair to lead her on like that. But is it fair to me to not even try at all? And God, what if she actually likes me? Could I trust her? Hell no… I can't tell anyone. Especially not now. Not with the Viola thing going on.

The next few months are going to be messy.

But! I see Dr. Patil today, and I already stopped in Thursday morning before school to let them steal my blood for the physical, so hopefully he'll say yes. It's so close I can taste it. I wonder how long it'll be before I have to shave? God. Shaving. Doesn't it sound amazing?

Okay, maybe it doesn't to you, but it does to me.

The only thing that scares me is that my voice will change. Do you know what Pepper said to me? She told me that a part of the reason she wanted me for the role is because my voice is gender neutral. Well, she put it differently, but she liked that it isn't exactly alto and isn't exactly tenor, but sort of fluidly runs the lines between the two. She has no idea why that is, but I'm sitting here thinking right now about how it might change. And I wonder if I'll still be able to hit that alto range without having to go into a falsetto.

It's the only thing I'd miss of what my body is now: my voice. I'm hoping that since it's so low to start with, it won't change much. And I won't mind if it doesn't change before the production's done.

The rest of puberty? Bring it on! I'm ready to get hair on my chest and on my face. I'm ready to bulk up more. I wish I could make my hips narrower, but I'll just have to try for broader shoulders to counteract it.

Someday I'm getting top surgery so I can go shirtless (as long as no one notices the scarring). It'd make life so much simpler in the summer.

Oh yeah, Mom said you made an appointment to talk with them today, which is a godsend. I almost got caught in the bathroom at school the other day. I couldn't wait until I got home to pee, and there were three guys in the bathroom and I had exactly two minutes between classes. I sat there for a count of ninety, I swear, before they finally left and I could pee in peace. I can't do that again. I'll take shit for using a stall, and they'll be all on about how I'm too shy to piss in front of them. I already change in the privacy stall in the locker room for gym. It's nothing I haven't heard before. But standing up to pee? Critical. Absolutely critical. I've been doing my research, and I've picked out an STP packer that I think should work, but I have to order it online. Which is why you need to talk to Mom and Dad.

By the time you read this, you'll already have talked to them, and they'll have talked to me, and I'll either have ordered the thing, or it'll have all gone to hell.

No matter what, socks aren't going to do it anymore. While I was looking online for the STP packer, I started looking into homemade packers, too. They aren't going to help with the bathroom problem, but they'll at least make my jeans look more realistic.

Not that I think anyone's looking.

But just in case.

I'm going to end up layered in fake body parts, you know. Because they're going to expect me to strip down for Viola's female garb (um, no!) and I'll probably have to wear a bra. Which I am not filling with natural parts, thanks. So there I'm going to be with my bindings and a bra on over it, and I'll use Maria's fake tits, and geez… I'm going to be a comedy of errors waiting to happen.

Why did I decide I'd do it?

Oh right. Pepper.

I've never met anyone who made me want to be myself so much. And at the same time, she makes me want to be what she wants me to be. I look at her and every thought in my brain goes right out the window. *Fwoosh.* I turn into a gibbering idiot, and I get the urge to go home and write stupid songs.

And I texted her over the weekend so she'd have my number. Just *hi.* She texted me this morning.

She wants to know what I've decided.

I'm going to say yes.

CHAPTER 6: Packing

THE PHONE lying on my bed doesn't make a sound, but the screen flashes three times, pauses, then does it all over again to let me know a text is coming in. It might be Maria, who can wait, or it might be Pepper responding to me… who has to wait, because I have my hands full. Who knew that hair gel wasn't going to pour easily into a condom? I honestly didn't think I was going to make this much of a mess, but there's green goo all over my palm and I'm trying to figure out how to tie off the condom without making more of a mess.

Apparently I should've started in the bathroom to begin with. But with three siblings in the house, two of them girls and one being fussy about his hair, I didn't want to have people trying to get me to hurry up. What I really should've done was practice over the weekend. It just sounded so *simple* that I thought I wouldn't need to.

I manage to get the thing knotted, and there it is: a makeshift packer to replace the bits in my pants that God didn't see fit to give me. I leave it on my bed, next to the phone (which is flashing for another text now), and go down the hall to wash up.

James is standing in my doorway, looking at my bed, when I get back. Crap.

I shove him into my room and close the door behind us.

"Jordan—" His voice trails off and he gives me the sort of helpless look he gets when he doesn't quite know how to deal with me.

I sigh. "Socks aren't cutting it anymore. They look almost right but not quite, they feel weird, and it's not like I'm going to magically grow my own right now."

He blinks twice. "So you filled a condom with—" He glances at my desk before he can finish the sentence. "—hair gel?"

"I found a tutorial on YouTube." I shrug and leave the packer on the bed because really, he needs to leave before I can finish up here. Instead I pick up my phone, thumbing it awake and smiling when I see that both new texts are from Pepper. The first one is just one word:

awesome!! and the second one asks *see you at school*? I ignore James for the five seconds it takes to type back *at the doors, before we go in? yeah.* When I look back up, he's nodding to himself, like it all makes sense. "What?"

"Pepper," he says. "That's why you need that, right?" He gestures at the bed.

I can't help the flush. "Maybe. I mean, if anyone's looking, I just want to look normal. And feel normal." And I am so not going into the other stuff that I need to get to be *normal* because this conversation is already getting seriously embarrassing. "Did you see the e-mail Pepper sent out over the weekend? There's something we need to get Mom or Dad to sign, about us being in the show."

"So you're gonna do it?" He leans against the wall, half blocking the door. Obviously I'm not getting out of the conversation until he's ready to let me go.

I nod. "Yeah. Pepper texted me a few minutes ago to ask, and I told her yeah. I mean, it's just a part in a play." I try to sound like it doesn't mean anything. "I didn't want to let her down. All we have to do is get the slips signed." I hand him the form and letter I already printed out for myself.

"I don't remember them having us do this before?" James reads the letter, then looks over the form.

He has a point. We've both been in every show since we started high school, and this is new. It talks about the rehearsal policy and the weekend schedule for dress and tech in December. The letter makes it very clear that no absences are allowed. But there's also a release to film the rehearsal and performances for some competition, and an offer to the parents to let them read the script if they are interested.

"It's probably because of the filming." James shrugs. "I'll go print mine before I go downstairs."

My phone flashes again, and I take a look. Pepper will be waiting for me. With Paul, she says, and I'll be walking in with James like usual, and we'll all be passing by Brandon's crowd again, so it isn't exactly like a private rendezvous, but still. Pepper's going out of her way to wait for me before school, which is totally awesome.

"You're grinning like an idiot," James points out, nudging me as he reads the phone over my shoulder to see who it's from. "Jordan...."

"I'm not going to do anything." I pull my thoughts back under control, because he's right. Everyone's right, even if I don't like it. "But there's nothing saying we can't be friends. And someday if I trust her, I can tell her, and who knows what could happen then, right?"

He laughs, and I glare at him, which only makes him laugh again and pull me into a rough, one-armed hug. "You're a romantic," he teases, and I glare more and pull away.

I plant my hands on his shoulders and shove. "Go on out, and take my form down to Mom for me. Cover this part up." I hand him my release form and point to where it says Viola/Cesario at the top. Okay, so I'm avoiding explaining the part I got to my parents. James doesn't question it, just takes the paper and walks out, still laughing.

I close the door behind him, leaning against it. Maybe I am a romantic, I don't know. I just know I can't stop thinking about her. I'll sound her out. Maybe she's not interested in anything physical. I mean, I think I heard that she's a junior. Not everyone's ready to jump in the sack immediately, right? It could be years before she's ready to do more than kissing.

She could also be an alien from Mars. Who am I kidding?

I look back at the lonely-looking thing on my bed, filled with green gel and air bubbles. I lift it slowly, feeling the weight of it against my palm, how it moves and wiggles as I poke at it. Then I unzip my jeans and put it where it belongs, curling it so I dress to one side (the left), and feeling it settle in securely. I wear tighty-whiteys for a reason. They aren't the most attractive or fascinating things, but no one's supposed to see them socially, and they are convenient, considering everything else. And they're pretty good with socks. Or apparently homemade hair gel packers.

Zipping up, I look into the mirror on the back of my door. Normally I hate mirrors, and I won't look into one naked. Ever. But now, once I'm dressed and put together, I look into the mirror and it's almost the image I expect to see staring back at me. I hook my thumbs in my pockets, standing loose-limbed and easy, and grin. It's gonna be a good day.

CHAPTER 7: Drag Race

MONDAY SEEMS longer than usual, but maybe that's anticipation of our first rehearsal. When I get to the auditorium not all that long after the last bell, there are already people there. Dower and Pepper have their heads together discussing something while she makes notes on a clipboard. Ryan's waiting on the edge of the stage, talking to Caitlyn. James is in the midst of the *Dream* quartet, one arm around Britney's waist, his fingers drifting up her side. I can't decide if he's being possessive or if he just can't resist touching her. Zach's gaze keeps drifting over to Ryan instead of paying attention to whatever Tyler and Lianne are saying. I don't see the fairy court anywhere.

The thing is, the cast members aren't the *only* people in the auditorium. Sitting in row five, right where they're close enough to hear us from the stage even if we're speaking normally, thanks to the acoustics, are a group of three girls and five boys. I think I recognize the girls from auditions last week. They whisper to each other, looking over all of us, as I join Ryan and Caitlyn.

"What's going on?" I ask quietly. I don't like the idea of people watching us stumble through the awkward phase of rehearsals. I want to know my mask is fully in place before I have an audience.

Ryan shrugs. "Not a clue. They showed up just after I did, and settled right in like they're planning on staying."

"I remember that one," Caitlyn shrugs toward the girl in the middle of the group. "She was at auditions. I think she tried out for Viola and Helena."

Auditions are a blur in my memory, but I remember her vaguely. If she went up after I had that hellish reading of my own, I probably wouldn't even have noticed her. Lianne must know her, because she waves, and the girl waves back with a small, tight smile. Lianne looks far happier about being there than her friend, who has a sour twist to her expression.

"Dower'll take care of it." Ryan nods. And yeah, Dower's walking up to the little group as Pepper comes over to join us.

Dower pitches his voice low enough to speak to them that we don't hear specifics, just a soft rumble of sound. But the girl sits up straight, her polite smile a plastic mask stretched across her features, and her voice carries well when she speaks. "I'm sorry, but this *is* a school-funded production, right?" She waits for a moment, then her smile widens. "Then it's open to anyone. You don't have to put me on that stage, but you can't refuse to let me watch rehearsal, either. You can't be exclusive, according to the rules of the school. Besides, I'm here to watch my friend." She gives another finger wave to Lianne.

"Shit," Pepper whispers, and it sounds weird coming from her. She doesn't seem like the kind of girl who curses casually.

"What's going on?" I lean toward her, and she echoes the motion, bringing us close enough that our shoulders brush.

"Emily's pissed off that she didn't get into the play," Pepper murmurs. She glances at me, and then the memory fully clicks in, between what Caitlyn said and that look Pepper's giving me.

"She auditioned for Viola," I say slowly. Which means, she *wants* the part I have and *don't* want. "She's pissed that I'm playing the role."

"And on Friday, her mom requested a copy of the script to read over the weekend, since we made a point about how we gave the role to you because Viola is actually changed to Cesario," Pepper says soberly, voice still soft and low. "I'm nervous."

It's totally instinctive what comes next. I mean, what's a guy to do? I slip my arm across her shoulders, squeezing a little, wanting to protect her against a world that can't handle something as stupidly simple as a play. "Nothing's going to happen. You've already got approval for the play, right?"

Here I am defending a part I don't even want. This is… weird.

But she's smiling at me, and leaning into me a little, which makes everything worth it. "Yeah, I've got approval. Dower says he'll back me, and I've already spoken to Ms. Jackson as well. But it doesn't mean it's going to be an easy ride."

We watch as the girl—Emily—sits down and Dower calls the *Dream* group over, pointing James toward us. Emily looks pleased with herself, arms crossed, chin lifted as she smirks. Great. We're stuck with an audience.

"I've been through tough spots before," Ryan offers. "I mean, when I started dating Zach two years ago, there were some people who didn't approve. I just said—" He holds up his middle finger in a familiar gesture. "And we went on with life. We'll do that now, and kick butt up on that stage."

Well, good for him. Ryan's *out*. Zach's *out*. I'm about as far in the closet as a straight guy can get, and I have no desire to have the door ripped off the hinges. And yet, here I go, script in hand, to play Viola. Lovely.

Dower's taking the others up onto the stage, so Pepper gathers us down front, stage left. We start with an early scene where Viola is alone, after almost drowning. She's shivering, cold, and struggling to walk into the woods.

"There's a manor house this way," I say softly, trying to use my vibrato to make my voice shake. I wrap one arm around myself, the other hand too busy holding my script. "They've told me so, and it must be, but I find nothing down this path but woods and more woods."

"Look, what goes there?" Pepper asks, reading Puck's lines in Paul's absence.

I freeze, looking around. When Pepper gestures, I change my stance, and how I pitch my body toward where the audience might be, even though I can't pay any attention to them. "Did I hear something?" My voice lilts up, soft and husky.

"We're supposed to believe that's a girl?"

I freeze at the voice, my fingers tight on the script. I hear my pulse in my ears.

"Ignore them," Pepper murmurs. "They're trying to get under your skin."

"I know." It takes several deep breaths before I'm able to continue, and I nod to Pepper. She holds up one finger, and steps back so that Paul can step in, appearing from God knows where to join us.

He smiles at me, a quick bright grin. "Why look," he says cheerily, "it is a woman lost, and wet here among the leaves. Dost thou come for pleasure, bright one, or dost thou come to lose thyself? Or perhaps thou looks to find thyself here amongst the trees; if thou art lost, it only stands to reason that thou could also be found. What is it that thou seeks?"

I open my mouth to speak, and I realize that the room's gone silent. I cast a glance back over my shoulder, and there are five people in the audience paying oh so close attention to us. The action has paused on stage, Dower's attention on our visitors. My hand shakes, and I reach out to grab the script with both hands to steady it so I can read from it. "The house of Count Orsino," I say, voice soft and flat, tight from my throat. "I need a place to stay the night."

There's a loud snicker, and my cheeks flush red.

Paul's attention never wavers from my face as he reaches out to touch my hair. In the background, I hear Pepper muttering something about needing a wig, and the scratch of her pen against paper. I'm rooted to the ground, staring at Paul, not wanting to be touched but knowing I can't jerk away right now either. "A woman alone to the rogue of a Count? What would the good women say to hear it? What shreds your reputation will become."

"Just tell the count the truth." It's her speaking, voice high and thin, pitched to rise over the distance between us. "Tell him that she's really a man, and no one will be worried. He won't want a guy in drag."

"That's enough!" Dower snaps out, and the voices go silent. I turn to look at him, and at them. Emily sits back with an angelic expression. "You may watch, but if you continue to speak, I have every reason to put you out of this room for disturbing our rehearsal," he reminds her.

She's silent then, but the damage is done. I step away, breath shuddering in my throat. I can't manage to get enough air. Paul looks at me, waiting for my line, but I can't do it. I look down at the script in my hand, trying to focus on that and pull myself out of the downward spiral. *Why is it that my breast marks me different than a man? Why is it that simply because I lack what a man has, I cannot travel as I wish? If not for anatomy, I could be independent of means and safe of virtue.* The words are simple. I open my mouth, then close it again, lips flapping like a fish out of water. I can't do it. Not here, not now, not in front of *them*.

"Go get a drink." Pepper's voice is low, and she doesn't look at me, consulting her clipboard instead. "Ryan, Caitlyn, let's do the first scene with Orsino and Olivia while Jordan's taking a break. We'll get back to this when he returns."

I close my eyes, feeling the shivers course through my body. When I open them, I force myself to walk, not run, to the door at the side of the stage. I retrace the same steps I took last week, when I raced out in a haze of graying light. It's not that bad this time. I'm not going to pass out. I think.

I stop at the water fountain, taking a long drink, then lean against the wall with my head resting on my arm. That prima-donna reputation I didn't want to get? It's starting, I can feel it. Pepper wouldn't even *look* at me.

The door creaks, open, then closed. I hear a voice as soon as it clicks shut. "Oh, I'm sorry, I didn't know you were out here."

I turn to look at Emily, taking in just how much smaller than me she is. I could bench press her, plus another thirty pounds I bet, easy. Her voice lilts with a soft lisp, a good octave higher than mine. She smiles as I look at her.

"You would've been a terrible Viola," I say. I shouldn't provoke her, I really shouldn't, but the words slip out anyway. "No one would ever believe you were a boy. Orsino would've stripped you in minutes and had his way, if you showed up in drag on his doorstep."

"And people are going to believe you're a woman?" She laughed softly, the sound quiet and clear. "Really. Your shoulders are too broad, and you walk like a hulking lug, even if you are skinny. You're going to look like a fool in drag, in front of the entire school and town. You should just get a coconut bra now and play it for laughs, *Viola*. It's going to be that ridiculously bad."

"And you think instead that Cesario should sound like Minnie Mouse?" I counter sharply. "If you sing like you talk, there's no guy on Earth who wouldn't be mortified by that voice."

She scowls at me, and it's possible she might be pretty, but I just can't take her seriously right now. She looks like a little ferret, all pissed off and ready to bite my nose.

And what's weirder yet is that I'm somehow both pleased and offended. She's just told me I look more like a guy than Viola. Which is good, right? And yet, I'm pissed off that she's telling me there's no way I'll be any good as a girl. I have half an impulse to pull my shirt open and show her just how good I'd be.

Then the shaking starts again because *God* no, I am *not* doing that. I take three steps back, struggling to breathe all over again.

She sniffs at me. "If you run away every time you start talking about this, no one could possibly take you seriously on stage. An actor who can't even make it through a rehearsal." She glances at the ceiling, shaking her head. "Oh yes, you're such a better choice for the role. I've already let Mr. Dower know that if he needs an understudy, I'd be happy to learn your part." She smiles sharply. "Just in case you bolt on opening night."

I don't need to listen to her anymore, but I can't leave her with the last word, either, so I struggle against the oncoming attack and stand my ground. "I won't bolt," I say quietly, and take just one step back. "And I don't need you as an understudy. So go home. I don't want you at rehearsals anymore."

"And that is exactly why we'll be here again tomorrow."

Her giggle follows me as I escape into the boys' room and lock myself in a stall. I know, I know, but what else can I do? I just need five minutes alone to put myself back together; then I'll go back in. I can do this. Pepper needs me, so I have to do it.

CHAPTER 8: Seeing True

"JORDAN?"

I have a distinct moment of déjà vu, panic seeping into me, but I know this time I'm in the right bathroom. Boys' room, same stall as I sat in before, waiting out the panic attack. This time I measure the time in minutes, and know it hasn't been all that long since I walked out. And this time it isn't Pepper who's come to find me, but Paul.

I nudge open the door and stand there, and he looks at me. "You're pale," he says. "Here." He holds out a bottle of soda and I take it.

"I'm not going to pass out from hunger or something," I tell him. I crack open the soda anyway, and take a long gulp. It's sweet and cold, and it gives me something to focus on. Plus, it feels nice to get my throat wet, so I don't feel like I've been swallowing sawdust.

"Didn't think you were." He steps back and considers me. He has his hands on his hips, fingers curled against his pants. "C'mon. Pepper's busy with the others right now, so we can get out of here and talk."

I take another swallow to give myself time to think. "And go where?" Is he hitting on me? No, he can't be. Can he? "You're not hitting on me, are you?"

He flashes a sudden, sad smile. "No, I'm not hitting on you, Jordan. In fact, the girl I've been crushing on since starting here in the fall just managed to completely kill any inkling of attraction I had for her. Which is disheartening, because she's gorgeous until she opens her mouth and the hate spews out."

"You had a thing for Emily?" It distracts me, and I'm able to move. Together we walk out the door and down the hall. He doesn't go to the door to the auditorium, but instead to one that leads directly backstage. We go into the wings, then up the metal stairs at the back corner. They lead up to the catwalk, high above the stage, but we don't go that far, pausing halfway up instead and sitting on the stairs of metal lattice work. "Our voices will carry here," I whisper.

He shakes his head, perching on the stair above where I sit. "The curtains that block it from view also muffle all the sound," he told me, but his voice was pitched quietly just in case. "It's private. And yeah, I thought I had a thing for her. But that's how it goes sometimes, doesn't it? We fall for the face we see, and it only lasts until the truth of a person comes out." He pauses, then adds, "She left just after you did."

I look down, relieved that there won't be any more insults today. I know he's talking about Emily's ugly interior and pretty exterior, but for a moment it feels like he's talking about me. "Some people just aren't very good at showing who they really are," I say. "It's not their fault."

"And that's not so bad, if they don't turn out to be poison on the inside," Paul muses.

"That depends on what you think is poison, doesn't it?" I'm veering too close to the personal here, so I try to push my side of the conversation back on track. I take a quick gulp of soda. "Some guys might think her sharp tongue and her absolute binary straight view of life is a good thing."

"But not me." He's crouched rather than sitting, and he rises up on his toes, twisting to look out at the stage. "I'm glad I got to see her with true eyes before I ever asked her out."

True sight. My hand shakes, and I look down at the bottle of soda. And it's still a soda. It hasn't changed, even though his voice is echoing in my mind now. "True sight," I murmur, and he grins.

"Exactly." His attention swivels back to me. "And you? If you could have one thing to make your day better, what would it be?"

"True seeming." The words slip out, and he laughs, the sound soft and rolling, lilting like a woodland fairy song; I'm reminded sharply of Puck from the dream. The world swirls and I sway uncertainly. That wasn't even the right answer, although in some ways it was. *Testosterone* is the best thing that could happen to me today, if Dr. Patil says yes, and if they can do my first shot right away. But true seeming would be pretty cool too.

I look back at Paul, and wonder what's in my soda to make my head spin like it does. I thought it was just a cola, and it was still sealed when he handed it to me.

He nods at me, as if what I've said makes perfect sense. I wonder if he sees what I see right now, or if the world looks flat and normal to him. Leaves are sprouting out of the steel stairs and handrail, and vines are twining around him. I grip the steel with unsteady hands, and a tendril grasps my wrist to hold me down. I don't feel bound, though, I feel safe. Protected. Here, halfway to the rooftop on unsteady stairs above the stage, we are perched in a place out of time.

Puck's gaze shifts away from me to look at those below us on the stage floor. "Mischief waits," he murmurs. "Not the bite of an asp, but the sweet bray of an ass, bringing laughter and tears instead of poison. For we all make an ass of ourselves when love awaits around the corner, do we not? But the question comes, what is true of truth? Is true love true to heart or true to mind, or simply true to the moment? Does true seeming speak to heart or body? Does true sight see what is real or what lies in the heart? Complications upon complications, all waiting to be found. Mischief waits, and mischief comes, to pounce and play, the lamb enticing the ass to show his true voice and bray his hopes for all to hear."

It must be a part of the play I haven't read yet. I've focused on my scenes and those little bits with Puck where he changes me from Viola to Cesario. The room wavers and swims; I close my eyes against the motion. "And if we wish to see mischief gone?" I ask quietly, my voice soft and a little high, as if Viola speaks through me.

"Then we must wait and see it gone. It is the fairy night, after all, and you will come out the other side unscathed but changed." He flashes a bright grin, but his expression quickly grows concerned. "Jordan? You don't look so good."

Paul peers out at me through the vines that grow along the railing, as if he doesn't even notice them. He slides a step down and touches my forehead with the back of his hand. "You're white as a sheet," he continues, concerned, "but you're not too hot or too cold. You should've said something if you don't like heights."

No, it's not the height, it's the vines. But I can't say a word because they're gone again, and we're crouched amidst steel cast in a waffle pattern, and Paul nudges me to move down to the stage once more.

"I'm ready to rehearse," I tell him. My throat feels tight, but the words come out strong.

He goes ahead of me through the curtains, winding across the side of the stage, well away from where Britney and Tyler are rehearsing the blocking for a scene, stopping every few words for Dower to reposition them. I pause in the darkness and reach into my pocket. I draw my hand back out empty, surprised. I feel like the vials should be there, even though I know I left them buried in my underwear drawer at home, and haven't looked at them for days. They are an impossible thing, and yet, so is what just happened up on those stairs. I saw Puck, I know I did. At the very least, I had a cola-induced hallucination, and I'm lucky Paul doesn't think I've gone completely nuts aside from my panic attacks.

I look at the empty bottle of soda in my hand, my mind still on the vials. It would be so easy to spike my own drink and just sip at it one night, waiting to see if they saw me as I truly am.

And it would be cheating, too. I don't need magic. I just need to be me.

I make my way to the edge of the stage and wait there as my brother finishes his impassioned speech to Caitlyn's Olivia. James is good, but then he always has been, and he's a charming rogue. Perfect for the part, really. And it hasn't gone unnoticed, with Britney distracted by our little scene, and Dower trying to recapture her attention.

I wait until Pepper sees that I'm there, and when she smiles, I smile back at her, relieved that she's not shouting.

"Better?" she asks.

"Better," I say, and I slip down off the stage and retrieve my copy of the script. "We were just at the point where Puck transforms Viola, right?"

She looks at me closely, and I stand very still. My hands are still shaking, just a little, and I wonder if I'm still pasty pale. However I look, she finally nods, and motions for me to step over by Paul. "Exactly. Now that we don't have any hecklers, though, I'd like to start that scene again from the top. I want to work on the blocking for Viola and Puck, and on Viola's transformation. I don't want any doubt in the audience's mind that they've just seen a woman become a man in front of their very eyes."

Breathe in, breathe out; I center myself and find the role. And this time Viola's words flow out easily, slightly panicked after nearly drowning, and confused by Puck. Paul's confidence is infectious, and I find that same confidence for Viola, talking back to Puck, enjoying the witty banter as they negotiate. Then in that moment, when Viola looks down, I spread my hands and speak, "What truth is this, seen by my own eyes?" I like the new script better, the way it has been changed to make it modern English but with an almost Shakespearian cadence to the words. "I am female cast into male form, my curves fled for muscles, soft skin traded for angles. I am Viola no longer."

"Thou art what thou art," Paul says, circling around me, Puck looking at me from all angles as Pepper shows him exactly where to go and where to stop. "And thou art Cesario."

CHAPTER 9: Awkward Walk

BY THE time the rehearsal's over, I'm torn between feeling completely wrung out and totally jazzed. We all pack up and walk out in a clump, splitting up into smaller groups once we're outside. James goes off with Brittany, saying they're going back to our house to study. Yeah right. I wonder if Mom'll believe it.

I walk more slowly with Pepper and Paul. I've got her backpack over one shoulder while she carries a box of scripts and costume information. "If you want, I could give you a ride home," I offer, not wanting her (well, them) to have to struggle home with all their stuff.

"Mom's waiting right over there." Pepper turns slightly, pointing toward a black SUV pulled up to the curb. "Probably impatiently."

She looks at me, though, almost as if she's disappointed, and I try to figure out how I could make this work. "Well, um, she doesn't have to pick you up every day. James and I share the car, but there's plenty of room to give you guys a ride any time."

Pepper pauses, and we stand there, halfway down the stairs. Paul makes it two more steps, then turns around and comes back up to join us. I hear a car door in the distance, and I'm pretty sure that if I look, I'll see her mom watching us.

"It's not a throwaway invitation," I tell her. "I mean it." I sound so serious, even though it's only a ride home. But maybe it's the bare beginnings of figuring out how to be friends, or more.

"Take the ride today," Paul says. "I'll tell Mom that you'll be home right away. You can put the things in the car, take the long way home if you want."

I feel the flush rising in my cheeks as he so obviously tries to push us together, and I try to run with it. "That'd work. You won't be too late, either. I mean. I've got someplace I need to be in about thirty minutes and all." That might make me a few minutes late, but Dr. Patil never runs on time, especially for the evening appointments.

She smiles then, soft and slow, blooming into a bright grin that almost matches her brother's mischief. "I think that sounds great. C'mon, let's go put the stuff in the back of Martha. Mom won't let me go anywhere with some strange guy she's never met."

"I'm innocent, I swear it!" I spread my hands. "I couldn't hurt a fly."

"And yet, you're carrying two backpacks that'd probably knock me over," Paul pointed out. "I'm betting you're stronger than you look."

Okay, well, yes, maybe just a bit. But I don't look like a thug. Generally parents like me, as long as they don't know the truth. And I don't intend to let anyone know, if I can avoid the topic. I smile politely to Mrs. Sullivan, going around to the hatchback as she pushes a button and it slowly rises by itself. "Martha?" I have to ask.

"We name our cars." Pepper shoves her box in, then takes her backpack to push in as well. "No, I have no idea why Dad named this one Martha, but that's what it's been since we got her five years ago." She pulls the hatch down, slamming it closed as I step back out of the way. She reaches out, catching my hand and linking our fingers together. It's just a casual motion that probably doesn't mean a thing, but I like the way it feels anyway.

Pulling me forward, she introduces me to her mom, and her mom to me. I hold out my hand and we shake. "I won't bring her home late," I promise. "I have to get to an appointment myself." *So I'll save kidnapping her for another time.* Luckily, I bite my tongue before the words escape, not sure whether her mom would think that was such a great joke or not. My mouth feels tight, trying to hold back the smile, although I'm sure some of it leaks out.

The charm works, though, and Mrs. Sullivan agrees. Paul climbs into the SUV, and it pulls out, leaving Pepper and me there by the curb. My fingers are still curled around hers, and she doesn't seem to be pulling away. That small point of contact has short-circuited my brain, narrowing my focus to the flaring nerves in my hand. My thumb slowly glides along the side of her finger, testing that little bit of touch, so unfamiliar and strange. When I look at her, she's smiling at me.

"I thought you said you had to go somewhere?" She takes a step closer to me, raising her free hand slightly as if to reach out toward me.

My mind fills in the next moments in a quick flash of images: Pepper putting her hand against my chest, then swaying close, me bending down to brush my lips against hers. And I want to. I really, truly want to so desperately that my body tightens with a raw ache. As her hand lowers, I step back, and her fingers brush through the air in front of my chest. "I do," I manage to reply, voice hoarse. "Next time we can take the scenic route."

She lets her hand fall, and I hear a soft whoosh of breath. Her answering smile is slightly shaky, uncertain, so I squeeze her hand to reassure her. I feel like we're having a major conversation without a single word, but I can't even begin to find the language for it. Instead, I point toward the only car left in the lot, and we head over and get in. I toss my backpack into the back seat.

"So you've got somewhere you have to get to? I guess I shouldn't invite you in when we get to my house," Pepper said, looking out the window as we pulled out of the parking lot. "Go on up to Main and turn left. You need to drive straight down that until the speed limit picks up, then my street is on the left at the third light."

She lives out on the edges of town, further out than my own house is. We're in the northern part of town, in the thick of the suburbs, where houses look like a Monopoly grid. I have to pay attention because while we're still in the center of town, there's a light every few streets, but we can still talk.

"Next time," I say. "Unless you're just being polite." Because I can't quite believe that she said that, and God, if it weren't my physical, I'd so be there. I wonder if Dr. Hewitt would understand if I bailed on one of her appointments because I had a chance at something almost date-like. I have a feeling she wouldn't *like* it, but she'd understand.

"I'm not just being polite." Pepper's smile flickers into existence then it fades away again. Her hands are folded in her lap, fingers twisting around the seatbelt.

"Then next time I'll come in," I say, answering her smile with one of my own.

The light changes and I move forward, inching our way through the low-speed center of town. I feel like something has changed for the better, like maybe we've actually gotten somewhere in that conversation we weren't quite having. "Friday," I say, while the feeling is still good and I haven't lost my nerve.

"Friday?" she asks, twisting in her seat to face me.

Fair skin flushes warmly, and I push at my bangs. "Um. Yeah. Friday. After rehearsal. Maybe um. We could get dinner. And go catch a movie. Or something. If you're interested. And your parents don't think I'm a complete thug."

I risk a peek at her, but she's looking out the window now, and I can't see her expression. My grip on the steering wheel tightens. I got it all wrong. That was too much. "Or not," I say quickly.

"No," she says with a soft sigh.

Crap.

"I mean, don't take it back." She's still not looking at me as she speaks. "I'd like to go out. But I'm not sure I should. Since I'm helping Dower, and you're in the play and all. I don't want anyone thinking you're getting some kind of special treatment. Especially with Emily…."

Oh right. I hadn't thought about any of that. Hell, I'd barely managed the guts to ask the question in the first place. "Maybe something—maybe something quieter, then. I mean. Not public. Like you and Paul could come hang with James and me for video games and pizza. Just a totally friends thing." My throat's still dry because now I'm pushing when she's already said no, but it sounds like maybe she's actually interested. "Or we could just wait until the play's done. You could promise me a date for New Year's Eve."

"Done."

Seriously? Oh hell, I'm choking on air, coughing while we're stopped at a red light. She pats me on the back, and I try not to think about what she might be feeling through the jacket. My eyes water, but I manage to clear out my lungs and breathe again. "Which one?" I ask, voice cracking slightly.

"Both." She smiles, and her hand falls to cover mine briefly. "Paul and I will come over Friday. And I'll save you a date for New Year's Eve. But you have to let me pick the place for that one. I'm very particular about how I like to ring in my new year. It sets the tone for the next three hundred and sixty five days, you know."

Wow. Just... wow. Whatever words I had in my mind, they're gone now. I have a sort-of-maybe date for Friday night with a girl who must think she likes me if she thinks she'll still want to go out with me in a few months. Holy crap. Wow. I just—wow.

"Jordan?"

"Hm?" I look over, and she's pointing at the light, which is now green. Flushing faintly, I hit the gas and get going again. "Cool. I mean, that's cool. Are you vegetarian or hate mushrooms or anything? James and I like everything pizzas."

"You sound like Paul, eating everything in sight." Pepper laughs. "I'm not picky. Whatever you guys want, I'll eat. Whatever video games you guys play, I'll either play too, or I will cheerfully mock you. And if you have any of those karaoke or band games, I will kick your butt." She pauses a moment, then admits, "Okay, Paul will kick your butt at karaoke, but I'm a mean drummer on the band ones. I can carry a tune, but my voice isn't anywhere near as good as you guys. Is everyone in your family talented?"

"We're not all stage hounds," I admit. "That's mostly me and James. Our older sister Karen's the brainy one: she's in a pre-med program. She says she's going to go to Tufts, and I believe her. Leigh's the jock; she plays soccer in the summer, basketball in the winter, and runs track in the spring. And Sam... well, Sam's our social butterfly. She's bright and outgoing and everyone seems to adore her."

"Kind of like James."

It ought to hurt that she doesn't say anything about me being charming, but it doesn't. I know that James and I are opposites in that. He's outgoing and charming, and I'm the quiet one. But when it comes to music, it all switches around and I'm the one who glows. We're used to it, and we use that. "Kind of like James," I agree. "But she doesn't act, or sing more than chorus. James is the actor. And I'm the musician. Guitar, and songwriting, and someday I want to record. I'm thinking about going to school for music next year, if I can get into a good school." Which means auditioning, and not panicking, and yet another administration being let in on the secret.

"That's right, you're both seniors." Does Pepper look disappointed? She points at the light, then left, and I realize we're already to her street. I pull in to the left-turn lane and wait patiently for the light to cycle. "We're five houses down on the left. You'll probably see Martha in the driveway."

It's funny, a week or two ago, I was really looking forward to doing all my applications and auditions, and getting out of this town. Now I'm thinking I might miss things around school. Just a bit. "Right, we're both seniors," I agree. "College will probably be the first time we've ever really been apart. It'll be weird. We were raised pretty much like twins, even though we're not. I just turned seventeen last week, and he'll be eighteen in December."

"I'll be seventeen next April," she says. "You aren't so much older than I am."

"I'm one of the youngest in my class," I point out, even though that's pretty much obvious. The conversation is inane, and silly, but it's nice to be with her and talking about anything at all. I look for her house and when I spot Martha, I pull in to the driveway next to it and throw the car into park. Pepper doesn't get out just yet.

And I have to ask the one thing that's been bugging me all week. "How come I never noticed you at the school before?"

"Maybe you weren't looking," she says with a smile. "I've been there since I was a freshman. We were probably just doing different things. I'm mostly a geek, and the bullies love me because they made me cry on my first day freshman year." Her smile is soft and rueful. "I wouldn't be doing this play now, but I love writing, so I did a playwriting camp over the summer that Dower recommended. The guy who taught that program sent my script back to Dower, and oh look, here I am."

It's hard to think of her without confidence, since she seems to exude it, from what I've seen. She seems so settled when she talks about the play, so ready to conquer the world. But right now, her walls are down, and I itch to bridge the distance between us. Slowly, so she could move if she wanted, I reach out and lightly touch one red curl where it rests against her cheek. I twist it around my finger lightly, then nudge it back. Her eyes widen, her mouth slightly parted, and my throat goes dry when her tongue darts out to wet her lips.

I pull my hand back. "Is that what you want to do with your life? Write plays?"

She nods quickly, her skin flushed rose under a faint spray of freckles. "I just want to write. Books for kids, plays for kids. Well, teens. I want to write things that'll make a difference."

"The play's pretty incredible," I tell her, because it is. "I had my doubts on the whole Shakespearian musical thing, but you did it well." She blushes, and I have to smile because words slip away again. Seriously, I could just sit here, staring at her. And I do.

"Didn't you say you had an appointment?"

What? Oh hell. The clock reminds me that it's twenty past six, and if I don't get a move on right now, I'm going to be seriously late. "Crap, yes, I do, at six thirty and it's a good fifteen minute drive. I need to bolt, Pepper. But—" I look back at her. "Tomorrow. I'll give you and Paul a ride home?"

She nods once quickly, reminding me, "You and James." Because if it's a group thing, then we're not dating or anything. That doesn't stop her from covering my hand with hers and holding on until I turn my hand in hers to hold on as well. My hands are large, considering, and hers are smaller, so they seem to fit. We both look at them, and I can feel myself smiling. I wonder if it's the same stupid smile James was teasing me about. Probably. I'm not going to look in the mirror to find out.

"And Friday," I remind her.

"And Friday," she agrees. It's not a date, but it's a date, and God, I can't wait. Getting through the week is going to be so much easier with that to look forward to. I feel like I can weather anything, even the crap that Emily wants to sling at us during rehearsal. If my reward is getting to spend time with Pepper, I could even fly.

She leans forward, and I freeze, because no, she isn't—but then she is, her lips soft and warm against mine, pressing for only a second or two. I don't know if I kiss her back, I'm so surprised, but my hand tightens on hers and I don't want to let go. I want to do it again.

"You need to go," she reminds me with a soft smile, and a nod at the clock. Where did the last few minutes go?

"Crap," I groan. I let go of her hand, placing my own shaking fingers back on the wheel, curling around it to hold on tight and try to hold myself down. Did I say I could fly? Make that blast off into the stratosphere right about now. "You go on in, and tell your mom I'm really sorry I didn't walk you to the door. But I really have to run."

She pushes the door open, and steps out.

"Pepper?" I call, and she pauses, turning and ducking to look back in at me, quizzical. "See you tomorrow?"

Warmth floods her expression. "Outside the doors at the top of the stairs. Yes, we'll be waiting."

"Awesome."

And then she's gone, and I watch her walk up to the door, waiting until I've seen her go inside safe and sound. And now I'd better rush; with my luck, this'll be the one day Dr. Patil's running on time while I'm the one who's late.

CHAPTER 10: T

"WHERE HAVE you *been*?" Maria rushes up to me in the waiting room as soon as I walk in, grabbing my hand and pulling me off to one side for a hurried conversation, while I do my best not to drop the folder I'm carrying in the other hand. "I've been trying to text you for ages, but you weren't answering," she grumbles. "I told them anyway that you'd texted me that you were running late because of your rehearsal, so you're not in trouble, but you need to go check in, chico, because they're waiting. Are you getting the T today?"

My head spins with the sheer rush of words coming from her mouth. I start with her last question. "I don't know, I guess I'll find out, but I hope I am. I've got a whole pile of forms here that say my folks are okay with it. And I was in the car, giving Pepper a ride home after rehearsal. Which had some moments of absolute crappiness."

That distracts her. "Driving Pepper home, or the rehearsal?" She cocks her head, curious.

"Rehearsal." I nudge her hands away from me. "I need to go check in and get going. If they're going to give me the T, I'll ask if it's okay if you come back. They should let you. I have a letter from Dr. Hewitt saying that you're learning how to do the shots too so you can help me." Because honestly, out of all the people in the world, Maria's one of the few I don't mind seeing me naked. Okay, I mind, but I can deal with it without panicking.

That's why she's here instead of my folks. My dad would be weirded out by it all and my mom would be anxious. We had a long talk about it, and I got them to sign off on me doing the injections and this appointment on my own. It'd be easier if I were eighteen already, but I don't want to wait another year for this.

Getting checked in means handing over everything in the folder to the nurse at the front desk. There's the form that my parents had to sign, saying that it was all right for me to get the shots, since I'm not of age yet. They'd come in about a month ago to see Dr. Patil and discuss all the risks. They'd come without me because they wanted to have an adult perspective on it, without me muddying the waters with what I wanted. He'd given them a huge packet of information to go through at home, and we'd sat down and done some of it together, and they'd watched some DVD or something about the health risks. There was a point when Mom freaked, but I found her some research that went against the horror stories she was seeing, and she calmed down.

I reminded her about me being in therapy because my head doesn't match my body. And about that day when I was eleven, before anyone understood and I was so overwhelmed by it all that I did the unthinkable. I showed her the scars on my wrists to remind her, and she agreed. This is for the best.

They came back to see Dr. Patil again last week, after Dr. Hewitt wrote my letter, and when they came home we all sat down together and went over everything one more time. And by the time we were done, my head was spinning with cautionary tales, Mom was crying, and Dad was stoic. But every form was signed.

There are risks, I know. But I think it's worse not to do it.

I have a seat next to Maria in the waiting room, but it's not all that long before they usher me into one of the exam rooms. They leave me with one of those ridiculous paper gowns and instruct me to take everything off, underwear included. I hesitate, and the nurse gives me a dark look and repeats: *everything*.

I don't like this nurse. There are four doctors in the practice, and three nurses who are on at different times. I ask if Nurse Rose is on, and the nurse frowns before saying she'll check to see if she has time for me. Nurse Rose at least… well, I don't know if she gets it, but she handles everything nicely. And physicals? Kind of suck for me.

The thing is, no matter how much I don't want my biological body, I still have it, and everything that can go wrong with it is still a risk for me. So last year they started doing—they started checking on things. Breast cancer. Cervical cancer. All those *things* that girls get. Just because I'm over the age of sixteen, and I guess they don't believe I'm not doing anything sexual, they say they have to check me for them. Dr. Patil convinced my mom last year that it was a good thing, and she signed off on it, so yeah. I can't get out of it.

I just hate this part of it all.

I'm sitting on the edge of the ridiculous little bed, my paper gown bunched up under my butt to hold it together as much as possible when Dr. Patil and Nurse Rose come in. I feel even more naked than ever with my underwear and packer bundled up with my jeans, T-shirt, and binder, all neatly piled on the chair in the corner. But I'm so glad to see the nurse; last year she held on to me when I nearly blacked out and just tried to float through the worst of the exam. She'd whispered to me that no girl enjoys it, and I whispered back that I wasn't a girl, I was a guy. I remember she squeezed my hand and didn't let go, and I might've fallen a little in love with her for that.

She takes my blood pressure and pulse while Dr. Patil looks over my blood test results. "So you're planning on starting testosterone." He speaks matter-of-factly, his accent lilting the sentence up at the end like a question.

This part I have under control. I nod once, quickly. "Yes, today if you're ready for it. I'd like to learn to self-inject, and I have a friend with me who is going to be my... well, she's going to be my moral support. For when I start injecting at home. So I'd like to have her with me today, and for future injections, if that's possible. You should have a letter from Dr. Hewitt about that, and my parents signed all the forms."

For a moment I think he's going to object, because Maria isn't family. But, I can see the folder I brought in, peeking out of my charts. He flips through the forms and letters, scanning for signatures, I guess. "You are aware of the risks, yes?" he asks.

That's why I signed all of that, isn't it? But I hold my tongue and nod instead. "Yeah. My folks and I looked through everything and we know all the risks. But I'm ready for it now, and I don't want to wait any longer. I'm seventeen, and I want to go through puberty while I'm still a teenager." It seemed unfair to hold it off until later, and be all awkward when everyone else was already done with it.

He flipped through the papers again, stopping on one where I could see Dr. Hewitt's letterhead. "Your friend is Maria Jimenez?" he asks. The name sounds awkward on his tongue. I nod, and he makes a note in the margins. "Your blood work looks fine, Jordan, and given your overall health, I have no problems with starting your first shot today. However, your first several shots will be given here, in the office, before you are able to do so at home. And if I observe anything unusual after your gynecological tests today, I may have to change my recommendation."

I hate that word. He mentions the tests, and I feel the shivers starting, my skin cold. "I understand," I say quietly. "Can we just get on with this part? I don't like it." And I'd think he could understand why, but last year, when I was in tears, he just kept saying that he had to do the tests because I was at risk as a young woman. I know I won't win the argument, no matter how wrong that statement is.

He pats the bed, and it takes me a moment to lie back and put my feet where they belong. I can feel the darkness coming, feel my mind checking out. A hand slips into mine, holding on, and I am promised that it won't take long.

It doesn't matter how long it takes. It's the fact that it's happening at all that I hate. That I am being reminded that I am not what I feel like I should be. He touches my breasts first, the ones that are barely there thanks to hormone suppression therapy, but apparently still enough there to be at risk. And he talks to me, like he thinks that'll help.

"Have you become sexually active?"

Oh God, like I want to talk about it. "I haven't even had a girlfriend," I say dryly. "It's not easy, considering I'm missing a few important bits and have spares of others."

He pauses, then says quietly, "That does not mean that you could not be active. There are certainly things that you could do, as I am sure you are aware. If you do become active, that adds a new level of risk, and as your physician, you should make me aware of any such activity."

I close my eyes, scrunching them tightly, and grip Nurse Rose's hand tightly. "I'm not active, okay? I was serious about that. I've only ever even been kissed once." Today, but he doesn't need to know about that. "If you have any more questions about things, can you wait until this is done? I'm just going to pass out here now."

Not really, not entirely, but as he replaces the paper gown over my breasts with a cheerful comment about how everything looks fine, I start to let myself check out. By the time he gets down to the other end of the examination table, I'm not there at all. I don't know where I am, just that it's dark and quiet and peaceful, and I don't have to think about anything until I hear the door closing, and Nurse Rose lets go of my hand.

She hands me a wad of tissues, her smile gentle and soft. "Clean up, Jordan, and you can get dressed. Everything but the jeans, and I'll be back shortly to give you your first shot. You mentioned you had a friend waiting?"

"Maria Jimenez." I feel dazed as I clutch the tissues and clamp my knees close together. "She's out in the waiting room. Just... just give me five minutes before she comes back."

Nurse Rose touches my shoulder. "We'll give you all the time you need." As she steps out, she reminds me where the giant trash bin is for the tissues and paper gown, and I'm left shaking.

I clean up best I can, but I'm still hyperaware of all the parts I do have. Putting my binder back on and tugging my shirt over it helps some, putting at least that half back to rights as much as I can. But even after I pull up my underwear and stuff the packer in, I feel weird and wrong. I like the weight the packer gives me, but I feel... violated. This isn't the right body, those aren't the right parts, and I *never* want to use those parts like that, but that's how the exam works. It forces me to see my body as the girl that I'm not and never will be. I sit back down on the edge of the bed, hands fisted tight and head bent as I focus on breathing.

There's a soft knock on the door and I call out for whoever it is to come in. Maria just sits next to me and puts her arm around me. I can't help it; I lean into her and press my face against her shoulder. I won't let them make me cry, but God, this sucks. So I just sit there with her holding me up until the tremors fade.

I'm mostly composed by the time Nurse Rose comes back, although I'm sure my skin is still blotchy and red. She's pushing a tray on wheels, and she moves it right up to the bed so she can show me what she has.

The little vial of testosterone seems so small. There's a cap over it with a rubber center, and the vial itself is smaller than the ones Puck left with me, not even the length of my thumb, and narrower in width. She has alcohol swabs and a needle in a plastic packet. The needle is huge. I don't just mean it looks intimidating, but the thing is big enough to make me feel sick to my stomach. When I pick it up, she doesn't object; the packaging protects it from germs. "This thing is going to go into me?" I ask cautiously.

"Not exactly." She picks up another package that holds just the tip of a needle, which still is daunting but is also a hell of a lot smaller. "We'll use the larger needle to draw the testosterone up into the syringe, then we'll switch tips to a smaller one for the injection. The testosterone is thick, so it's easier and quicker to move through a larger gauge needle, but that would be painful to inject. So we go with the smaller needle, and it just takes a little more time."

Big needle but over with quickly, or small needle and it being slow. I'm half tempted to ask if I could just use the big one and get it done, but I glance at it again and yeah… no way am I putting that thing into my body. Not even for T.

"Testosterone is administered through an intramuscular injection, and you'll want to change the site you use regularly. The easiest place is the thigh." Nurse Rose touches my thigh, marking out a pattern of nine invisible dots, like tic-tac-toe cells. "You can be sitting down. The muscle is easily available, and there's plenty of it. You'll also switch legs regularly."

I nod, and Maria nods. "I should take notes," I say, even though I don't want to tear my eyes away from what she's doing.

"We have a sheet that explains it all," Nurse Rose tells me. "I'll be sending you home with a packet. Today, just pay attention. It's your first time."

And I realize that she really does get it. She smiles that gentle smile, and okay, maybe I'm not exactly in love with her, but I still like her, and I feel like I have an ally here. Finding one of those is always just… nice. "Is it all right if I make all of my appointments with you, while I'm getting the injections here?" I ask.

"You're more than welcome to do that." She rips open the packaging for the needle, and twists off the cap. She pulls the plunger of the syringe out once, then presses it in, then pulls it out again to measure a half milliliter of empty space. "We're going to inject air into the vial first. It's not necessary now, but this vial will last for several injections, and as more liquid is taken out, it'll create a vacuum in there if we don't replace it with air for the volume we take out each time."

High school chemistry in action. Or is that physics? Either way, it's pretty cool. I nod, and watch as she swabs the top of the vial with an alcohol swab, then inserts the needle tip through the rubber bit in the cap, right down into the liquid. She pushes the plunger in, then starts to draw it out again. Liquid with the consistency of olive oil bubbles up into the syringe, and it takes her a few tries before she pulls it without air bubbles. She shows us exactly how the liquid looks at the measurement line—the meniscus—then tugs the needle free and flips it so the point is up into the air.

Man, that is one huge needle. Maria's hand finds mine on the table, and her fingers wrap tightly around it. I sure as hell don't mind having someone to hold on to right now.

"For this part, keep it up like so, because otherwise you might drip some of the fluid out." She quickly caps the needle and twists that one off, setting aside. She twists the new needle on and pops off the cap. The thing still looks larger than I'm really interested in feeling shove itself into my thigh.

But it's T. I try to force myself to relax, knowing it will only hurt more if I'm tense.

"And that's it, except for the shot itself. Would you like to hold it?" Nurse Rose offers me the needle. I hesitate, because no, not really, I just want it to be over with now. I remember going to get shots when I was little, and my mom turning my head toward her, pillowing it against her shoulder so I could pretend it wasn't happening. I can't do that anymore. This is something I need for my life, for always, and I have to face it.

So I reach out and very carefully take the needle from her. Such a small bit of liquid that's going to make such a huge difference in my life. "I can't wait," I murmur, and Maria squeezes my hand.

Nurse Rose swabs a spot on my thigh and takes the needle back. I want to close my eyes and look away, but I force myself to stare at my skin, watching as she positions the needle then jabs it quickly in. It hurts! I squeeze Maria's hand so tightly that she squeaks and I breathe, trying desperately to relax again.

"Almost done," Nurse Rose says quietly. She starts to push on the plunger, and oh God, I can feel it going in, I swear it. It's so thick and slow, and I can see that it isn't simple to just shove the plunger down and be done with it. Seconds feel like hours, the spot on my leg chills as it pushes into me; then it's over and she pulls the needle free.

There isn't even a spot of blood left to show where it was.

"That's it?"

Nurse Rose laughs. "That's it, Jordan. You've had your first testosterone shot. Congratulations."

I'm still staring at my leg, as if it ought to suddenly start sprouting thicker, darker hair than the soft blond fuzz I've always had. James's leg hair is darker than mine, more coarse, and I wonder if mine will change now. And how long it'll take. And when I'll get to shave. I can't wait to shave. A slow grin starts, and everything bad about the day is gone, just like that. Emily? Who cares. Stupid physical exams? Not a worry. I am a boy with boy hormones and life is *good*.

Maria hugs me and kisses my cheek before Nurse Rose ushers her out so I can put on my jeans. I pull them up and button them, then take a moment to look over the things still out on the tray. She'd left them there so I could look, saying she'd put them in the biohazard bin for sharps as soon as I was done. And now that no one is watching me, I take my time and linger over them. I twist the vial of testosterone this way and that, looking at how oily it seems and how it flows. Then I look at the needles—both of them—without touching. I'm going to learn how to do it for myself, and right now I believe that I can.

I hitch up my jeans and adjust myself to make them more comfortable. Then with a grin, I walk out, feeling better than I have in a long, long time.

CHAPTER 11: Games & Things

WHEN REHEARSAL ends on Friday, Pepper and Paul pile into our car to come home with me and James. No Britney, because it's not a date night; it's just friends hanging out. When we walk into the kitchen, all talking at once, it's obvious Mom and Dad are confused by Pepper being there when Britney isn't. Obviously they think she's somehow with James, because she can't possibly be with me. I'm not going to correct them. It's easier to do it this way for now.

James and Pepper go into the kitchen to order pizza and wings, and they'll set up the games downstairs while Paul and I hunt down some music.

We'd gotten to talking in the car, and Paul wanted to see my CD collection, so we head up the stairs. I can hear Mom calling out to both me and James to keep doors open, and I roll my eyes.

"My parents think I'm gay, too, sometimes. Or an equal opportunist or something," Paul shrugs as he steps into my room. He doesn't stop politely at the door, just moves in with fluid footsteps over to the CD rack that runs floor to ceiling against one wall. "They must think I give off that vibe or something. I've tried to tell them that not all theater guys are gay, but after about a hundred lectures about how they'll love me no matter what, I've pretty much given up."

What the hell do you say to that? "My parents don't exactly think I'm gay," I try, then stumble to a stop when Paul gives me a look like I'm supposed to explain that better. So I just shrug right back at him. "I haven't dated, so it's not like they've got empirical evidence either way."

"Are you?"

I shake my head quickly. "No way. It's girls all the way for me." I can't even imagine being with a guy like that; it just sounds weird to me. Not that it's wrong for guys like Ryan and Zach. It's fine—they can do what they want. But the only place I need to see guy bits is attached to my own body, thanks.

"Same here." Paul crouches in front of the CD rack, looking at the ones on the bottom, and I guess our male bonding is done. Which is good, since tonight is my sort of not-date with his sister, and really, that's just an awkward discussion.

He touches the cases, paging through them with a faint click-clack as he moves them. "Not many people buy CDs anymore," he comments.

"I like the way they feel." I sit on the edge of the bed, watching as he goes through them. "I have a lot of music that's only in electronic format, but there's something about having a CD in my hands that I really like. Especially the ones with lyrics. Plus there're some songs only released on certain versions of the CD."

"Is that why you have two of some?" He taps a pair on the next to last shelf, and I nod.

"Yeah. I've got Best Buy special editions, Target editions, Hot Topic editions, and some other lesser-known ones, plus special editions from the online services. I'm kind of a music whore," I admit. "When I like a band, I want everything. You're looking at where most of my allowance goes, if it's not going into an instrument or movies."

He starts picking CDs from the shelves, and I can't fault his taste. It's a mix of rock and punk with some off-the-wall alternative thrown in. "What do you think I should hear that I probably haven't heard?"

I nudge him aside, and he steps back, staying close enough that I'm aware of him behind me, his skinny body radiating warmth. It's uncomfortable, not because I'm afraid of him or anything, but the world's starting to spin again, fuzzing around the edges. Are my shelves turning green? I reach out and touch them to steady myself, surprised by the unexpected feel of moss under my fingertips, cool and spongy.

I close my eyes for a moment, wrestling the world back under control; when I open them again, the shelves are back to normal and Paul's standing over by my bureau. I quickly grab a half dozen or so CDs off the shelf, all small bands I found either opening at live shows or pushing their music at Warped.

"What's this?"

When I look, Paul's leaning against my bureau, smiling slightly with one of *those* vials in his fingertips, the glass reflecting purple light against the wall from the liquid inside. Instinct says to push it out of his hand, but I don't want to break it. I haven't decided if I'm going to use them yet, but that doesn't mean I want to lose them either, right? The other two vials are there as well, sitting on top of the bureau in a neat little line as Paul sets the one down again. Didn't I leave them in my underwear drawer? *Under* my underwear?

I walk over and pull open the drawer, peering inside. Did Mom put things away for me and pull them out? But no, everything's just like I left it, except that those vials were in the drawer, and now they're not, and this is going to drive me insane, I swear. "Magic potions," I deadpan, sweeping them into my hand and shoving them back where they belong. At his look, I manage to laugh. "Nothing illegal. Just these stupid things that are all like herbal supplements. Supposed to make you see things, but I'm figuring it's totally in your head, right?"

He watches as I close the drawer, head cocked, expression interested. His fingers graze the top seam of the drawer. "You haven't tried them yet?" His smile slips wider then, and the world whips around, leaving me wobbling on my feet. There's a gentle point to the tip of his ears, and his fingers seem longer than I remember, almost pointed as he taps the wood. "Use thy gift," Puck says quietly. "It does thee no good in a drawer." He withdraws and turns, doing a little skip and spin I've seen him do during rehearsal this week, almost a trademark Puck move. But when he looks back at me, it's Paul once again looking out from his eyes.

Hanging out with Paul gives me whiplash. One moment he's just a guy like anyone else at school, and the next moment I swear I'm seeing Puck. I'd blame it on the hormones messing with my mind except it started before those ever did. Maybe I'm going insane, I don't know, but I think if we get downstairs (and leave the vials upstairs), everything'll be fine.

"Why haven't you tried them? Afraid of whatever you put in when you made them?" Paul laughs at my expression. "You could always foist them off on someone else, see what happens?"

I'm so relieved that we seem to be back in reality that I answer honestly. "Do you really think I'd do that, give something I'm not even sure isn't poisonous to a friend?" I protest with a shake of the head. "I don't think so."

"It doesn't have to be a friend."

Okay, so maybe he has a point there, but I don't want to waste these on someone I don't like. If they're real, they're useful. If they're not real… well, who knows what the products of my hallucination could do to someone. "They'll keep," I say, pushing the drawer again even though it's already closed. "It's not like something's going to spoil."

I need to get out of here before Puck shows up again. I'm not comfortable with either Puck or Paul questioning me about the vials.

I hold out the CDs I picked toward Paul. "There's a ten-shot CD player down there. It was my dad's when he was in college." I'm not sure they even make things like that anymore; they just figure we'll all rip our music onto our MP3 players and listen that way, I think. "Why don't you go set things up. Oh, and tell James I'll be down with the pizza money in a minute. I've gotta make a pit stop."

Lying, yes, but it gets Paul out and down the stairs and I can then hear my folks pointing him toward the finished basement.

I pull the drawer open again and move things around so I can see the vials. "You need to stop haunting me," I tell them, like they're somehow going to listen. "I'll use you when I use you, but not before. So just cut it out." I touch the green one with the tip of my finger, because it's actually kind of tempting. It's a first date. What would it be like if Pepper really saw me the way I'm supposed to be? No confusion, no explanations needed. Just a guy and a girl and a couch and some kissing maybe. Well, only a little, since our brothers'll be in the room. But still. She couldn't doubt me, after that, could she?

The vial is cold against the palm of my hand as I lift it out of the drawer and close my fingers around it.

No. This is a really bad idea.

I shove the vial back into the drawer and bury it under my clothes, then push the drawer shut. Then I grab my wallet and run downstairs, slamming the door to my bedroom behind me. "Sorry!" I call out when Mom gets cranky over the whole door thing, and again when the basement door slams as well (not my fault this time, it just swings shut too quickly). I jump from the last few steps, landing almost lightly at the bottom.

"Hey." James looks over at me, holding up the plastic pretend guitar he's wearing. "Pepper's claimed the drums; Paul said you could take what you wanted, he's good with either bass or vocals."

Paul's over by the stereo, poking it with the delight of someone who loves retro electronics, and that makes me grin. And I know he's a guest, and I should give him the better thing, and I know he's got at least as good a voice as I do. But I want to show off, and this is my game, and my basement, and I know how to rock these acoustics. Much to my parents' frustration—they keep saying they're going to soundproof, but haven't yet. "Vocals," I choose.

I pick up the microphone, and Paul joins us, and for the next twenty minutes, it's all about notes speeding across the screen, singing at the top of my lungs, and a hell of a lot of laughter. We don't stop until Mom yells down the stairs and we have to pause right in the middle of one of my favorite songs because the pizza dude is waiting at the door.

I gesture at my wallet and James and Paul take off up the stairs with it to go pay the guy, leaving me alone with Pepper.

The door slams closed at the top of the stairs. Mom'll be thrilled, I'm sure.

Pepper stands as they go, stretching her arms up toward the ceiling, then spreading her fingers to stretch those. She makes a funny little sound as she does so, and that noise hits me right in the stomach, a sucker punch of *oh hey I like that*. I take a step toward her, she moves as well, and we meet in the middle, almost like we planned it that way. Her hands slip up to my shoulders as she looks up at me. I only have a moment to think *I should kiss her* and then I am, or she's kissing me; it doesn't actually matter much who started it.

What matters is that I've been thinking about kissing her since Monday night, and now it's happening again and it's just as good the second time around. Better, even. Thinking is almost impossible, but instinct is right there, so I wrap my arms around her and pull her in closer. She tucks herself in close easily enough, and we don't stop the kiss.

I'm liking this. A lot.

Her hands slide up, playing with my hair, and I try to deepen the kiss. I don't want to give away that it's my second kiss ever, but I'm hesitant. There are supposed to be open mouths involved, and tongues, which all seems kind of desperately awkward. Except once I try it out, it isn't awkward at all; it's amazing, and when we finally stop, I'm not sure how long it's been. It seems like hours, or not long enough, and I want to start over. I'm breathing hard, my heart is hammering, and I don't think I've ever wanted anything or anyone this much in my life.

Some faint corner of my brain comments *increased libido* and I shove it away. Whatever. I'm also a *teenager*, so aren't hyperactive hormones supposed to be a part of the package? I'm just lucky enough to actually have some hormones to be hyper now.

Pepper's flushed, and her lips are as red as if she's put on fresh lipstick, only more appealing. I run one thumb across her lower lip, and she smiles, tongue darting out to touch my skin.

God. Um. Whoa. Who knew that my thumb was connected to my lower bits like that? Not me, that's for sure.

If the thing in my jeans were real, I'd need to shift, and as it is, I'm suddenly uncomfortable with my body's alien reaction. Pepper lets her hands slide down over my chest, then slips her arms around me and holds on, pillowing her head against my shoulder. I'm so glad I wore a vest today, because it gives a reason for why my chest feels odd; she just feels the vest instead of just a shirt over binding, and I'm safe.

That thought is all it takes for me to feel guilty, and to worry at the same time. What if she knew? Would she think I'm not enough for her? Is this even fair to her? Or to me? God, I have never been so wound up and here I am, my skin tingling all over and wanting to be *touched*, and I can't do anything about it.

I just hold on to her and try to wrestle my breathing under control.

"Jordan?" she says quietly.

"Yeah?" My voice is hoarse, deeper than usual, which is kind of a nice side effect, I guess.

"I really think I like you." She's whispering with her face still pressed against my shoulder, her words like warm puffs of air over the skin of my throat. It feels good. "Kissing you is somewhere past amazing, and you kiss pretty decently. The last guy I dated kissed me like he wanted to swallow me. It was a little like drowning. Pretty gross. But you don't do that."

Awesome, considering I didn't have any practice, either. I just did what felt good for me, and I don't think I'd want to be swallowed alive, either. Um. Okay, not going there. "I like kissing you too, can't deny it," I tell her. "Why am I worried there's a 'but' coming?"

She's quiet. Too quiet, and I nudge her back a little, wondering if maybe that hand resting against my vest *did* feel something it shouldn't. "What?" I ask worriedly.

Pepper shakes her head quickly. "No, no, nothing bad. Just... it's kind of overwhelming. Every time I kiss you, it's like my brain just switches completely off."

"I know the feeling," I admit with a rueful smile. "Only change that to every time I *see* you. You're lucky to get coherent sentences out of me."

"You're doing just fine." Both hands against my chest, she uses them for leverage to go up slightly on her toes and brush her lips against mine. "Just... I keep thinking what if you—" She flushes brightly with that. "Maybe we should keep it to just kissing. Until we get to be better friends."

God help me, I want her. Just standing here, I want her more than I'd ever thought possible. As she steps back, I shove my hands into my pockets and take my own step away, using the motion to try to quietly shift the packer someplace a little more comfortable than where it is pressing against right at that exact second.

Her flush intensifies at my motion, and I feel my own face warm. "Sure," I say quickly. "I don't want you doing anything you don't want to. I'm okay waiting. I'm not going to force anything." In fact, it's a little bit of a relief. Only not. It means I don't have to worry about making an idiot of myself, except, I *want* to. Crap. Hormones are confusing. Very confusing.

The door at the top of the stairs opens, crashing into the wall as James yells, "Napkins are on the table. Grab a big handful, okay?" We both jump a little farther apart just as James comes down the stairs, thumping onto every step. I meet him at the bottom and he gives me a curious look, one eyebrow arching up. I don't know how to answer him with just an expression, but my cheeks warm again and he starts to grin. "Everything cool?" he asks.

"Totally chill," I reply, and I take the wings off the stack of boxes he's carrying. "Did you order enough for an army?"

"I figure you'll eat a half a pizza, and I'll eat half, and Paul'll eat half... that leaves some for Pepper, if she's quick enough to catch it before we go back for seconds." He gives her a lazy smile, ducking when she lightly thwaps at his shoulder.

Paul comes downstairs then, the door slamming closed behind him (again). He's got napkins, plates, a couple of bottles of soda, and some cups. And just like that, the mood dissipates and I can think again. I don't ache quite so badly, although I'm still warm every time I look at Pepper, but we can laugh easily. We curl up on the sofa, all four of us squeezing in close together while we eat, and her body is right up against me. I like it.

She leans into me like she belongs there, and who knows? Maybe she does.

INTERLUDE: Maria

MARIA SHOVED things into her backpack carefully, hoping to finish before anyone else came into her room. Her little sister had already been in twice, until Maria had threatened to tell Mama about seeing Serena kissing Juan out behind the school. That shut Serena up good, and for the moment, Maria had a bit of privacy.

She rolled the skirt up, knowing it would wrinkle less that way, then carefully tucked in a knit top as well. A small zipper bag held her makeup, which she buried under the clothes, and then she started putting books in on top. She didn't worry about the shoes, knowing the boots she was wearing under her jeans would work well enough with the long skirt, and the less she had to change, the better.

She took the stairs down two at a time, hoping to get out of the house before anyone noticed and tried to drag her in to dinner.

"Felipe!"

Mama's voice was sharp, audible throughout the house, and Maria stopped on the last step with a sigh. "Sí, Mama?"

She came out of the kitchen, a spoon in her hand, gesturing. "Where are you going, Felipe?" she asked, a frown twisting her expression into disapproval. "It's dinner, and we're doing dinner as a family here, tonight."

Friday was the one night they were all home. Serena didn't have vocal lessons or dance, Dom didn't have soccer, and Maria—as Felipe—was supposed to stay in. She hated these family dinners, where Mama and Papa refused to acknowledge her by her proper name. She shifted from foot to foot, shrugging one skinny shoulder. "I'm meeting up with a guy at the library," she said, pulling her phone out of her pocket to show off the text from Marco. "We're working on a project."

The text actually said, *C U library 7pm* and nothing about a project. But that's because Marco wasn't from school; he was from a club two towns over where Maria had gone to the under-21 night and flirted outrageously. But Maria knew that if she pushed it as hanging with the guys and schoolwork, her Mama would waffle and hopefully cave.

"It's due Monday," she clarified, which was semi-almost-true. She *did* have a project due on Monday. It happened to be a book review, on a book she'd already read and done a half-assed write-up on, good enough to get her the usual C that kept her going at school. "I'll be back by eleven."

Mama's lips pursed, but she didn't say no, which Maria took as a good sign. "Library closes at nine, mi hijo."

"Well, yeah." Maria spread her hands in another shrug. "Me and Marco, we're gonna hang a bit after we're done with our work, yeah?" She pitched her voice a little lower, tried to be butch like the guys at her school. Which was exactly what she never had been, and the sparkling pink case on the phone in her hand didn't help the image at all.

Mama was wavering, almost there, so Maria didn't give her a chance to say no. She just bounced up and hugged her, giving her a quick kiss on the cheek. "Thanks, Mama. I'll text you when I get to the library, and I'll let you know where we go after."

"Calm down, Felipe," Mama pulled her in for another hug. "The guys won't like it when you bounce. Can't you act a little more... like them?"

No, she really couldn't. She just forced a smile rather than answering. "I'll see you at eleven, Mama. Not one second later, I promise."

Then she slipped out the door.

She finally breathed when the door was closed and it didn't open again right away. She'd half expected Mama to come after her, or worse, for Papa to start bellowing *that name*. But no one came, and she was free to go. On a date that Mama had no idea she had.

It was going to be amazing.

She drove to Waltham first, then stopped at a McD's and slipped into the ladies' room when no one was watching. Using the handicap stall, she wriggled out of Felipe's clothes and into her own, yanking up nylons to smooth her legs where they were bare above the boots, and carefully placing her falsies into her bra. She tried to nudge her flat chest together, but she was too skinny; this was one time that carrying a little baby fat might not be so bad. She'd read techniques about taping just the bottoms of her boobs to pull them together and give herself cleavage, but she needed boobs to start with for that trick. So instead, she stuck with shirts that had a high neckline, but also showed her flat belly, and the tiny belly button ring she'd forged her Mama's signature to get two months ago. The shirt clung to her makeshift curves, showing them off in a way Maria thought looked good, and as long as no one was groping her, they ought to pass.

Thank God she never had to shave, or else passing would be an absolute nightmare. Still, before she applied makeup she did a final check in the mirror, tweezing away any stray hairs that had magically appeared. Once her transformation was complete, she felt right in her skin again, and she sashayed from the bathroom, grinning at the boys who stared when she walked by.

She always felt like she was faking things every day at school, then again at home. The only times she could really be herself were when she was all alone in the house, at Dr. Hewitt's, or with Jordan, or out on her own. Not that she was supposed to go out on her own, but she'd been doing it since she got the car, and she knew Jordan and Dr. Hewitt were just being fussy. Nothing dangerous had ever happened, and nothing was going to. Maria was in control of her own life, and she knew how to manage the men around her to keep them under her control as well.

Marco was waiting on the steps of the library when she got there. He stood and pushed away from the stone, coming to meet her as if he couldn't wait to get away from the library, which was just fine with Maria. There were definitely better places to go.

When he reached her where she waited by her car, he wrapped his arms around her, hands at her back and just below her waist, rubbing his thumbs against her bare skin. When she shivered, he grinned, and oh God, she couldn't help but grin back. He was so cute! Absolutely perfect, really, with dark-chocolate eyes and the little dimple in his chin and a scar over his right eyebrow (from when he'd fallen when he was two, he'd said). "You didn't really mean studying tonight, did you?" he asked.

He was a senior, and he was large, which made Maria feel tiny. She was pretty sure his hands could swallow hers. When he cupped her face with those hands, she felt delicate and petite, and it made her shiver right down to her toes. Because *this* was right. *This* was exactly who she was and who she was supposed to be. And yeah, maybe she was a little jealous of Jordan who was so far ahead of her right now, with his hormones and his not-date with Pepper tonight, and the perfectly charmed life where he passed because no one knew the truth. But Maria could pass, too, and soon enough it'd be her turn to rewire her body (well, parts of it anyway) with hormones. But for now… there was nothing wrong with having a little fun.

Marco bent closer, and her breath caught, and she leaned up to meet him for that first soft kiss. She felt that small touch all the way down to her toes and back up her spine, turning her body to jelly. She wanted to lean in against him, press close, but she knew there were dangers in that. Better to stay in control. So she nudged him back and smiled, fingertip trailing down his chest.

"There's a place I know where people like to go and just hang out." Because no one called it parking anymore. "If you're willing to go for a few ground rules."

When his finger started to echo that same motion down her chest, she nudged his hand away. "No groping," she said with a little pout. "I'm not a quick lay. I'm the kind of girl you date and bring home to Mama before you're going to get in her pants." And hopefully, by the time they got that far, Marco'd be so head over heels, he wouldn't be upset to find a little something extra in those pants. It'd take time, Maria knew, but it happened. There were guys out there that just didn't care. And she was sure that Marco had the potential to be one of them. "But you can have all of this," she went up on tiptoes and kissed him again, just the way she knew she was supposed to, with tongue and everything, letting it go for a while before she pulled back. "All that you want," she finished her sentence, a bit breathless.

So maybe his hands strayed, just a little, over her back. Maybe he was tempted, Maria couldn't be sure since he didn't say anything. But he didn't disagree with her terms, either. And when she opened the passenger door, he climbed in, and she went around to the other side so she could drive.

They kissed at every stoplight, and by the time they reached the shore of Lake Cochituate, Maria was wishing more than ever that they could do more. She pulled the blanket out of the back seat, and hand in hand they walked out of view of the road. Just before they sat down together, Maria set her phone off to one side, open so she could see the clock, and so she'd hear the alarm that she had set for ten thirty. Marco was adorable, but he wasn't worth getting grounded for. Maria definitely wanted to be able to do this again.

PART THREE
Off the Book

JOURNAL: Wednesday, October 21

MOM ORDERED me the STP packer yesterday. Thank God because Tyler almost caught me when I was desperate to pee during rehearsal yesterday. I was in too much of a rush to be careful and he walked in while I was there. I covered but when I got home, I made sure to talk to Mom and Dad (again) because of it. She even put it in for priority delivery, so it ought to come in early next week. Can't wait. I just hope it's comfortable.

It's been an amazingly busy couple of weeks. The rehearsals are seriously intense. The bell rings at 2:30 and we have to be in the auditorium or music room by 2:45. We go straight through until 6pm, except for Wednesdays where we go an extra hour. I'm glad you're able to do evening appointments for me until the play is done; I'd go nuts if I didn't have you to talk to until after December. Although I could just drop this off, and we could talk on the phone, I guess. I talk enough here for about three sessions, I'm sure.

There's just so much going on. Like the shit everyone's saying about the play. Emily Graves is still causing trouble. She doesn't watch rehearsal every day, but she's there enough that we can't just forget about her. She's quiet now, so Dower can't throw her out. But she watches everything I do. And she watches the *Dream* quartet too. Then she starts spreading things around the school.

It's only been a couple of weeks, and already you can hear two camps forming. First, there are the people who don't care what's going on. They're the ones who maybe signed the petition for the GLTBQ alliance when it started up. Or maybe they're the ones with gay brothers or sisters or someone in their family. Or maybe they just honestly don't care and are willing to let people be.

Then there are the other ones. They're the ones who hate fags. The ones who make sure everyone is aware what "trouble" is walking their hallways. They're the ones who are offended because in our version of the play, when Puck misplaces the drops, Demetrius wakes up and spots Lysander first thing. Or who are horrified that a guy would wear a dress to play Viola.

It's funny. I never wanted the part, but I'm so absolutely *pissed off* at these idiots that I wouldn't let go of it if you paid me. Even if it wouldn't hurt Pepper for me to back out now, I couldn't do that. I want to show these guys how it's done. Besides, don't they know their history? Guys always played all the roles in the original productions for Shakespeare. This just makes it normal. Well, according to the outside view.

But it's not making my life easy, at all. Guys follow me down the hallway, asking if I'm a girl.

Yeah, really.

I mean, if only they knew.

I think about it, sometimes: what would happen if someone got it into their head to check. If they did to me what they did to Paul, I'd be a dead man. I'm worried sometimes that it could get dangerous, but I don't know. Maria says I should live and let live, because if I just ignore it and don't let it get to me, they won't think there's ever a *reason* to check. She probably has a point.

Speaking of Maria.

This is the part where I break confidence, just a little. She might've told you about it, but she also might not have said a word. Did you know she's seeing a guy?

Yeah, that's what I was thinking, too.

But she says he's really cool, and he doesn't want anything from her. Unless he's really unique, I think he's lying. And I think she's lying, too, because I think they've done more than she's told me about (she said just kissing). Not that I think Maria lies a lot or anything, but it's the way she doesn't look at me when she says it. And the part where she's so completely gone on him. She can't stop thinking about him, and she's sneaking around to meet up with him. I think I've finally convinced her to at least let me know when she's going out, even if she's lying to her parents.

I know it puts you in a weird spot, me writing about it in my journal, since you probably now need to tell her parents. And maybe I'll rip this page out before I hand it to you, I don't know. I've got some time to think about it. I'll keep an eye on her until then, I promise.

Everyone's really getting into sex lately, I think. James is… never home, I swear. He goes over to Britney's after rehearsal a lot, to do "homework." Or sometimes they come here, and "homework" is done downstairs in the basement. Mom sends me down to check up on them, but I stomp on the stairs enough that they know I'm coming.

Honestly? I think I'm jealous. He has it so easy, and he doesn't even know it. Britney's hot, even if I don't like her. And he just can do whatever he wants because he was born that way. Sometimes I feel like it isn't fair.

And the worst part is? I'm horny all the time. TMI, I *know* but seriously, it's true. They say guys think about sex like what, every five seconds? I don't remember the exact amount of time, but that's what it seems like lately. If I had the parts, I'd be a walking hard-on. I keep daydreaming about my almost-sort-of-maybe girlfriend, and wishing we had something more. It's awesome, but at the same time, it's distracting. I want things I can't have. I'm taking out my frustration on the punching bag and the weights downstairs. That's helping, some.

Okay, so maybe I'm exaggerating a little. And maybe it's because I have someone to think about, and I've never had any kind of a reason to think about sex before. But yeah. It's on my mind, a lot.

Now that I've embarrassed the hell out of both of us, I need to go get ready for school. I'm seriously thinking of ripping this page out before my next appointment. It'll save us both a lot of misery.

CHAPTER 12: Decisions

So, IF I were a true love potion, would I be purple, green, or blue? I consider the three vials on the palm of my hand and decide that purple is obviously love because it's closest to the color of a heart (purple's close enough to red, right?) and set that one back in the drawer. Blue for sight, and green for seeming, then. Not because I'm sure, but because it just feels right.

I'd think that after telling me not to mix them up, Puck might've come back and told me which one was which. Or maybe he did tell me, but I forgot, because I don't usually remember my dreams.

Don't usually find things on my bureau that I was given in a dream, either.

Nothing about this is usual, I have to admit. Still. I tuck the blue potion back in the drawer as well, and tug the underwear over it all.

I don't know what I want to do with the vial still in my hand. I'm pretty sure it's true seeming. Remembering back to the dream, I think green was the second potion he gave me. *True sight, true seeming, true love.* Yes, that was it. But do I really want to drink this thing when I don't even know where it came from?

I close my hand around it, feeling the cold edges press into my fingers and palm.

James nudges my door open. "You coming? I need to get in early and meet up with Britney. I figured you wouldn't mind some extra time with your *girlfriend*." He keeps his voice low and grins at me; I grin back. She's not my girlfriend, not publicly, and not exactly. But then again, she sort of is.

And it's amazing.

Abso-fucking-lutely amazing.

"I'll be down in a minute. Grab me something to eat, huh?"

He goes thundering down the stairs, leaving me with the vial that I still have to decide exactly what I'm going to do with.

I set it back down on top of the bureau for the moment and go to the mirror on the back of my door. I peer into it, looking closely at my face. One hair, just one hair would make my day right now. But no, as hard as I look at my chin and upper lip, I don't see anything. Thing is, we're all so fair, even James only has to shave because if he doesn't he gets a patchy pale beard that dots across his face in wisps and blotches and looks ridiculous. Right now, I wouldn't mind if I looked ridiculous like that. A hint of peach fuzz would go a long way toward making me feel better.

People at school have started calling me Jordana because of Viola. That was never my name. It's Jordan, and it has always *been* Jordan; yes, I know, I got lucky in the naming lottery. Guys ask me about my skirts and threaten to snap my bra. It's like… there's nothing anyone can do anything about. We're a zero-tolerance school, but they are all careful not to get caught. And I can't go tell on anyone, because if I make a big deal out of it, it'd be like waving a flag of surrender and saying they're right.

So I just have to ignore it. Let it all roll off my back, because if it didn't mean anything to me, then I wouldn't care. As long as I'm secure in my masculinity, I'm okay.

Thing is, I can't help it. I hear people saying things and I have to check and make sure everything's put together right. I need to make sure I'm still passing, and that something hasn't slipped out of place. They don't know. They can't possibly know unless someone's actually gone into the records that are locked in Principal Jackson's office. And I don't think anyone would ever even think of doing that, because when it comes down to it, they don't actually *believe* that I could be biologically female. They're just giving me shit, and it's all started because people don't get the fact that gender isn't just as simple as being born one way and staying that way forever.

The play is confusing people, which pisses them off. No one likes to feel confused. I get that. But I'm so sick of them taking it out on me.

And there's still no hair on my face, no matter how hard I look.

I straighten up and look over at the vial on the bureau, and it feels like the vial stares back at me.

I palm it and shove it deep into the outer pocket of my backpack. Hopefully I don't knock into anything and break it during the day. I don't even want to think what that'd do.

I shrug into a hoodie, wearing that over the denim shirt I'm already wearing over a faded band T-shirt, and then I shoulder my backpack. Both shoulders, so I don't have to listen to Mom warning me that my back's going to get all bent out of shape and won't I be upset when I hurt too much to walk (like that's going to happen before I graduate high school and don't have to carry a heavy backpack all the time anymore).

When I walk into the kitchen, James hands me a muffin. Mom reminds us that Karen is coming by for dinner with her new boyfriend, and that Sam and Leigh are actually going to be home, and it's Chinese food night, so could we stop off and pick up the order on our way home from rehearsal? She gives James money, and he hands it straight to me because I'm less likely to lose it. I shove it deep into a pocket where I'm sure it won't slip out, and we head out to the car.

On the way, I grab a couple of water bottles, stuffing them in my pack for later. I figure if maybe I want to do it—the vial, I mean—I can dilute it in a bottle of water. That way if it tastes bad, I won't even notice. And I have to bring two because James always steals my water bottle. It's like I'm the only one who ever remembers to bring one. I don't know what he's going to do without me in college next year.

"I was thinking about bringing Britney over for dinner tonight," James muses.

I'm not even sure he knows he said it out loud. He looks like he's concentrating on driving, his gaze resting on the stoplight where we're paused for the moment. "Tonight?" I have to ask. "With Karen. And her boyfriend. And a hundred serious conversations about futures?"

He gives me a look. "Not like that."

"If you bring her over tonight, it'll be like that," I tell him. "Mom's in meet-the-parents mode, and she'll be all over Britney, trying to find the brain cells she rubs together and making sure she's good enough for you. Is it really that serious?"

I've gone too far; I can tell by the sharp set of his jaw. "She's not some stupid blonde, Jordan. She's in the AP chem class, and she might be smarter than you and me put together."

"Can't prove it by her conversation. Or her giggling." I refuse to back down, crossing my arms. It's for James's own good—if he can protect me, I should do the same for him. Why does it matter if she's smart if she tries to act so dumb? "She's never said one intelligent thing to me. In fact, most of what she's said to me has been *where's James*? So I'm not sure she even notices me as anything other than a handy thing to point the way towards you."

He shakes his head and lets it go. "I didn't know Karen was bringing her guy over when I talked to Britney last night."

"So you already invited her over."

"Yeah."

Oh, great, so it's not something he can easily undo without causing girlfriend drama. "I guess I could ask Pepper to come over, too. Maybe that'd dilute things. It'd certainly take any heat off of you and Karen, both." Because if my parents had any inkling that I was doing something like *dating*, they'd freak out in a heartbeat. Pepper hanging around our house hasn't changed anything; they just think we're all friends. I think they've even stopped thinking James is going behind Britney's back with Pepper.

"No way, Jordan. Not worth it."

Good to know he thinks that, since I'm actually there too. But still. "So what're you going to do about it?"

He shakes his head, navigating his way into the student parking lot. "I don't know. I guess I'll talk to her during rehearsal. I don't think she wants to have them looking at her like something serious, either. We're just having fun."

I think Britney's doing more than having fun. Did I mention that she's always looking for James? She's hooked on him, big time, and honestly, I think he's pretty hooked on her, too.

The car comes to a stop, and we just sit there, looking at each other. "Uninvite her," I say as sagely as I can.

"We'll see," he replies.

It'd be for the best. It's a family dinner. Britney's not family, and if she comes to dinner, it's like saying maybe she's *like* family. But James is also a nice guy, and he doesn't want to break his girlfriend's heart. So I guess dinner's going to be crowded tonight. And interesting in the Chinese proverb sort of way. Can't wait.

CHAPTER 13: Good Closets

BEING IN the closet has a loaded meaning. But there are some times when the closet is exactly the right place to be, like when Pepper sends our group to take five, then asks me to help her get a few things from the storeroom off the choir practice room.

We don't have very long at all. The others will be back soon, and the door to the storeroom doesn't have a handle on the inside, so we can't close it all the way. But that doesn't matter. We've been stealing tiny moments all week, just a quick kiss here and there, a taste to whet the appetite, and it's been driving me insane. Pepper still doesn't want to get hot and heavy, and that's not so bad since I haven't told her the truth. And we're still trying to pretend to everyone else like we're not together at all (for whatever definition of together we are).

Truth is, I'm falling for her. And I feel guilty every time I think it, because I wonder if she deserves someone better than me. Someone who won't make her life complicated.

Then her hands slip over my shoulders and she's pressed tight against me, our lips brushing momentarily before I deepen the kiss and she makes that cute noise that she always does.

Right. Thinking. Not happening.

I try to keep myself aware, listening for footsteps, but it's not easy. There's conversation out there somewhere, James's voice in the distance. But it doesn't seem to be coming closer, and I wonder if he's trying to keep everyone out of the room and give us a few more moments.

Sounds awesome. I trust my brother, and I let go my awareness, sinking into the moment with Pepper.

The sound of a throat clearing, half polite and half angry, catches my attention. I feel my face heat up as we break the kiss and both turn to face the door where Ms. Jackson stands, hands on her hips. Dower's behind her, but thankfully, none of the cast is there.

"Care to explain?" Ms. Jackson asks.

I groan inwardly because if they wanted to, these two people could absolutely ruin my life. For one, they could tell my parents, because I'm sure the adults talk about what is appropriate behavior for me while I'm on school premises. And for second, they could tell Pepper the truth, because they both know. I can't read Ms. Jackson's expression, but Dower doesn't look like he approves. I let go of Pepper, my hand falling to my side, and she interlocks her fingers with mine and squeezes gently.

"We were kissing," Pepper says with a smile, as if it's nothing. Of course, to her it isn't. She's a girl, I'm a boy, we're in a closet, and we're making out... totally normal teenage hijinks.

"I saw." Our principal's tone is dry. "And this once, I'll let it go. But I should advise you to remember that the school has a policy against public displays of affection, and that includes anywhere on campus, no matter how unobserved you think you are." Her attention turns to me, and I can hear the layers of meaning in her words. "I thought better of you, Mr. Lewis."

I carefully disengage my fingers from Pepper's, not looking because I don't want to know if she looks hurt or angry with me. I nod once, my smile flickering. "I'll try not to take after my brother again." Because James gets away with these things. James was making out with Britney in the seats of the theater through half the rehearsal on Monday, right up until they needed Britney on stage for a scene. No one said a word.

Pepper's fingers brush mine, and I cross my arms to get them out of the way. I want to apologize, but I have no idea what I'd actually be apologizing for since I can't explain what's going on. It's not like I can blame my parents when she's already seen what James gets away with. Life would be so much simpler if God had gotten it right on the first try.

I think about the vial buried in my backpack. I could fix that. One swallow, that's all it would take to have people see me true.

"If you'd both step out, I have something to discuss with you." Ms. Jackson motions for us to join her, so we do. My stomach lurches, because if she's including me in the conversation, and it's not about finding us in a closet, it still probably isn't good.

"As I was telling Mr. Dower, the school board has received an official complaint about the show." Ms. Jackson perches on the edge of the table at the front of the room. She crosses her arms, tiny but fierce. "The complaint is twofold. First, it complains that a role designed for a female was given to a male actor."

"But, the role *isn't*—"

"Ms. Sullivan." Ms. Jackson cuts her off. "The other is, of course, the subject matter of the play as a whole. It seems that some of the parents are uncomfortable with both the gender issues and sexuality which will be presented."

Now I want to reach out to Pepper and hold her hand, but this time she's the one who stands apart. Her hands are fists by her side, her body vibrating with anger. "That's not fair," she says quietly. "The whole school board read the script after Mr. Dower asked if I'd be interested in having it performed. We had a meeting. They agreed that it was okay to do, and that there was nothing offensive about it." Her smile is tight. "They agreed because in the end, everyone goes back to *normal*." She doesn't approve, and I half wonder if there's another version of the script where Viola gets to stay a boy. I can't even say how good that makes me feel, because if she wrote *that*, maybe she wouldn't freak out if she knew about me... but then, I could be completely imagining things, so who knows.

It's a pile of what-if, which isn't really worth much.

Then I think about what she's just said, about being *normal*, and I can't help but wince. Ms. Jackson is looking at me, and I shrug, not sure what she wants from me. "People have been letting me know they're pissed off about me playing Viola for a while now, Ms. Jackson," I tell her bluntly. "Nothing violent, but it hasn't been fun, either."

"I'm sorry you've been subjected to that, Mr. Lewis," she says, and her expression is kind. I remember the meeting we had with Ms. Jackson before my freshman year, when my parents were so concerned about how the school would accommodate me. She promised then that she'd do her best to keep me safe, and I can see that echoed in her expression now. I can't say it's okay without making Pepper curious, so I just shrug again in response.

"So what does it mean?" I ask, because there's a part of the story that's still missing. She's told us what's going on, but not how we fix it.

"Do you want to play the role of Viola, Mr. Lewis?"

"Yes." I say it without hesitation. I might not have wanted it when Pepper gave it to me, but there's something challenging about it. And I won't give it up just because a bunch of idiots want me to. My answer might be different if they hadn't been hassling me, so in a way, they have themselves to thank for me digging my heels in.

"Well, we promised Ms. Sullivan that we would support this show when Mr. Dower and I selected it."

I dart a glance at Pepper, wondering if she knew that the principal had had a part in picking her play, and I can't tell because she won't look at me.

"So we will do exactly that." Ms. Jackson stands, head cocked and eyebrows raised as she regards us. "But I would recommend that professional behavior be your guide as you go forward. We don't want rumors getting out that Ms. Sullivan selected you to play the part of Viola because she favors your attention."

I flush and don't look at Pepper. "That started after the play. We didn't even know each other before auditions."

Pepper inhales a rough breath. "We'll be professional," she assures the principal. "No more making out in the closet, or anywhere that anyone else might possibly see us."

"That's probably for the best." Ms. Jackson smiles tightly. "Too few young couples take their time, and once the complications begin, it is too difficult to go back and remedy that."

Oh God, she's giving us relationship advice. The *principal* just told us to get to know each other before we get physical. I think I'm going to die of embarrassment on the spot. "Sure. Yeah. We'll do that."

"Good." Ms. Jackson nods, then pauses just as she seems about to leave. "Mr. Lewis. A word, if you please. Walk with me down to the office."

I glance at Pepper and Dower, and they both nod. "Come back to the auditorium," Dower tells me. "We'd like to begin blocking the final scene, as it's one of the more complicated ones and is likely to take a while to get straight. Be prepared to sing."

I nod at that, then look at Pepper. I try to ask her with my eyes if she'll be okay, and she smiles weakly at me. I feel like getting caught didn't just throw cold water over us, it's shoved us way down under an entire frozen pond, and we can't get out past the ice. My own fault, maybe, for pulling away from her first, but I can't repair it with Dower and Ms. Jackson watching us.

Ms. Jackson clears her throat, and I trail after her like an obedient duckling. We cut through the people waiting in the hallway, too polite to be standing with their ears pressed up against the door. Their expressions are frankly curious, and James looks worried as he sees me following the principal. She seems to notice as well, smiling faintly as she assures him, "I require your brother's help for a moment, Mr. Lewis. I promise, I will send him back, unharmed and without notes on his permanent record."

He relaxes, and we pass by. Behind us, I hear Dower and Pepper rounding the cast up, moving them into the auditorium. Then it's all silence except for the click-clack of Ms. Jackson's heels against the tiled floor.

"You wanted to talk?" I ask, trying to keep my voice quiet, but it still echoes off the lockers and into the empty hallway.

"In my office, Mr. Lewis," she says. She holds open the door and motions me in, and when it clicks shut behind me, I feel nervous and trapped. But when she says sit, I sit. What else can I do?

I tap my toes against the floor, looking around. It still looks pretty much the same as it did three years ago when my folks and I met with her then, except for a few more certificates of some kind of commendation or other hanging on the walls. I look back at her where she sits behind her desk.

"Am I in trouble?" I finally ask.

She smiles faintly. "No. And in fact, that is a part of what I want to assure you of. I have not been unaware of the slurs these last few weeks, Jordan."

She's switched from formal to informal, and she doesn't look like someone's shoved a stick up her back to make her sit straight.

She pulls the glasses off her nose and carefully rubs them with a cloth to clean them.

I have to ask, "Then why didn't you do anything about it?"

"If I stepped in, they'd believe you told me," she said. "And the attacks would only become more subtle, and more vicious. I am not blind to the way the mind of a teenager works."

I offer a small rueful smile. "And that'd be why I didn't tell you in the first place. I've been making sure to stay in public places, and honestly, I'm trying to avoid the bathrooms. I don't figure anyone knows the actual truth."

"They don't. Those records are sealed." She breathes steam on the glasses, rubbing them clean once more before putting them back on her nose. "But if you continue forward in the role of Viola, things are likely to get worse before they get better. I don't think pressing your suit before the school board is going to make the bullies back off."

"I know." And I do. "But I can handle it. I know what I'm doing here, and conversations like this are only going to get me in more trouble, Ms. Jackson." I really don't want to look like the principal's pet.

"Which is why you are running an errand for me." She reaches for a folder on her desk and opens it, checking inside. "This is the brief from the school board. Please deliver it to Mr. Dower and inform him that he is expected to be at the school board meeting next Wednesday, the twenty-eighth, at seven o'clock. It is up to him whether he wants any of his cast, or his assistant, to accompany him."

I nod, taking the folder. "I'll give him the message. Can I go back now?" I push myself to stand, not waiting for an answer.

"Jordan."

I pause, standing there by the chair, looking at her. "Yeah?"

"I am aware that you may feel that the message the play gives, in the end, is perhaps not the best." She speaks slowly, as if she chooses each word with care. "But I believe that the message that appearances are only an illusion, and that we should accept those we love, however they are, is an important one. And it is worth putting my weight behind the production."

Her approval is comforting, and knowing that we have her strength behind us makes me feel more resolved.

"We're not going to give up either," I tell her firmly. "The show will go on."

She laughs then, the sound softer than I would have guessed from the steel she shows us all daily. "The board has never met anyone quite like you or Ms. Sullivan. They won't know what hit them." Ms. Jackson steps past me and opens the door. "Go on back now, Jordan."

And I go.

CHAPTER 14: Slipped Drinks

I WALK into the auditorium and give the folder to Dower as he waves me up onto the stage. Pepper is standing in for me, and she quickly goes over the blocking I've missed. The scene is large and complicated, with Viola and Sebastian's reunion, Olivia and Orsino reacting, and the entire *Dream* quartet coming out from under the effects of their potions and rearranging their alliances. The fairy court is all around the edges, their music interspersed with ours. It's big, we're all on stage, and it's the first and only time I sing as Viola instead of Cesario.

While we're working, the side doors open and a small group of people come in, planting themselves right in the best seats in the house. I stumble over my line and look away from Pepper. James shakes his head, and I focus on him and our scene.

We go through the dialogue for a while first, bouncing back and forth as it goes between the groups. Then Pepper starts blocking the song.

I'm so tired of standing here by now. We haven't had a break in an hour, and everyone's looking a little worse for wear. One of the freshmen fairy girls is shifting from foot to foot, like she's desperate to pee. But when Pepper says sing, we do, going through the song from start to finish.

James isn't surprised at all; he's heard my voice plenty of times, and he knows I can hit those notes. Paul and Pepper have heard it, too, outside of rehearsal. But for everyone else, it's the first time that they hear that I can make it well into the alto range just as clear and pure as when I'm singing tenor. I try not to flush, and I can't look at Emily and her crew at all. They make noises, and I falter just from that, but James nudges me and I'm back on track.

Pepper calls to take five when we finish. The dancing fairy disappears through the side door quickly, her friends close behind. Pepper goes into a conference with Dower while the rest of us grab a break. I go to my backpack and fish through it, looking for water. I can feel watchful eyes on me.

"Wouldn't you know it, she's got the voice of an angel." Emily's giggle reaches me easily.

Don't react, don't say a thing. Can't let her know she's getting to me.

"I'm beginning to think we're wrong about how he got the role," her boyfriend muses.

And that's it, something snaps. I remember the thugs, and how they ripped Paul's shirt, and no way am I letting that happen to me. I fish the vial out of my backpack and open it, dripping about half of the bright-green liquid into the water bottle in my hand.

That's it. All I have to do is drink this and no one will question anything. If it's real. I stare at it, trying to trust it past that quick, bright impulse, and just *drink*.

I hear coughing somewhere in the background. A shoulder nudges me roughly, and the water bottle is taken from my hand. James tightens the lid back on, giving me a small grin. "'Scuse me while I rescue the damsel in distress." And he jumps over the seats to get to Pepper's side and hand her the bottle after he takes a long swig of it himself. She drinks gratefully, and the coughing finally stops. She thanks him with a smile, saying something about allergies.

I can't do anything but stare.

James stole my water bottle. The one with the potion in it.

What if it's poison?

They don't fall over. They don't do anything except stand there, heads bent close together, talking about blocking, I guess, since James is pointing at the stage.

Well, that's good. I'd hate it if I'd killed my brother and my not-girlfriend with a single potion.

But they've got my water bottle and I didn't get to drink it, and it's not like a true-seeming spell is going to do a thing for either of them. Wait, I brought a second bottle for James. I pull that bottle out and tilt the vial, spilling out the last of the potion. It shimmers as it falls into the bottle, and I cap it so I can give it a quick shake, as if I'd put one of those drink packets in.

My phone blurts out. I pull it out—a text from Maria: *911 need help 2nite.*

Groaning, I try to get Pepper's attention, or Dower's. James glances over, and when I point to the door, he shoos me out with a *go, go* hand motion. I shove the bottle deep into my backpack and head out, phone in my hand. *911? Like what?* I type back at her.

Date. Need 2 get chnged.

Date? Maria!

Christ, she just pulled me away from rehearsal because she has a date?

I reply: *2nite is bad. Family thing.*

Pleeeeeeeeease.

How am I supposed to say no?

When I don't type anything back because I'm trying to figure out what to say, she texts again: *B there 4 dinner. C u!*

Seriously? Maria invites herself over to my house tonight, while Karen's going to be there with her boyfriend, and James is bringing Britney? Tonight is becoming one of those farcical situations and I figure Shakespeare would be proud of us for creating this much of a mess all on our own. With a groan, I go back inside and toss my phone into my backpack and reach for my drink.

Crap. My water bottle is missing.

This can't be happening.

I look around, not sure where it's gone. It was in my *backpack.* Someone would've had to actually make an effort to get at it. I can only think it'd be James, but he and Pepper are sitting on the edge of the stage, talking intently. I glance around at the rest of the cast. Ryan and Caitlyn look like they're rehearsing off to one side. The fairy girls are gathered together, giggling (do they ever stop?) and the *Dream* quartet is up on stage with Dower, working on blocking.

Someone took it and drank it, I'm sure of it, but no one seems to have changed that I can see. So maybe I'm just making things up, imagining things since it was just a dream to start with. Puck couldn't have been in my bedroom that night. So all that was in the vials was some water colored with food coloring. Nothing more. I'm sure of it now, because shouldn't everyone have a true seeming that's different from what they show the world?

Dower pulls us back onto the stage, arranging us for the final number again. We go through it, stepping slowly through the blocking once, twice, then a third time at something closer to normal speed. By the end of it, my own throat feels hoarse. My attention is inward on Viola and on the sound of my own voice; Emily has been silent this time, which is a blessing.

We wind down slowly, and Paul comes over, something of Puck still in the way he skips across the stage. "You were definitely the right choice for Viola," he says with a quick grin. "I don't think I could've pulled off that song, not the way you do. Your voice is so clear on the high notes."

My smile is shaky, half thinking that he's a singer, he can see right through me. "Practice," I say, coughing when it comes out rough. I rub at my throat, irritated by the sound. "And my voice changed late." And might still change more, but hopefully not until the play is done. "But thanks. I'll make them eat their words."

I walk to the edge of the stage, jumping down when I get there. James and Pepper are over by his and my packs, talking about something. I can see Britney heading in our direction, too, and Paul's still right behind me, talking.

"You didn't want the part," he comments. "What changed your mind?"

"Honestly?" When I ask, he nods, and I smile wryly. "First, your sister. I didn't want to disappoint her. Then her." I jerk my chin toward Emily, who's still sitting there, watching everyone with avid eyes. "There's something about telling me I can't do something that makes me want to do it more than anything, y'know?"

He laughs. "Oh, I know, I know. For what it's worth, I'm glad you changed your mind. I think a lot of the play's success is going to hang on your shoulders."

"Way to layer on the stress. Thanks." My tone is dry, and it only makes him laugh again.

"Tonight?" Pepper's voice is loud and startled, and it attracts my attention. Paul falls silent as well.

James has her hands in his, looking down at her, while she looks back up at him. What's going on? That body language—I don't get it. They shouldn't look like that. He's looking at her—he's looking at her like *I* look at her.

I feel someone on my other side and hear a soft "What the hell?"

Britney looks just as confused as I feel. I look to Paul, then her, then back to my brother and the ridiculous expression on his face as he stares at *my* not-girlfriend.

"Tonight," James says. "We've got a family thing going, so I can't get out. But you can come on over and join us for dinner."

"Huh?" I look at Britney again. "You're coming over tonight, right?" And Pepper can't, because my folks don't know about us not really dating, and then we'd have to ask Paul, and Maria's going to be there. My head spins with all of it.

"I thought so." Britney's voice is high-pitched and wispy soft. "But then James said earlier you have a dinner tonight with your sister and that maybe I shouldn't come because your parents would totally think we're serious. And I like him, but I'm not planning on getting married right out of high school or anything so sure, I agreed. But why's he asking *her*?"

Pepper leans up on her toes, brushing her lips against James's mouth, a soft smile lighting her lips. "Sure. Sounds lovely."

Oh. That answers that.

We're all silent. Me, because I can't even think past what I'm seeing. This can't be happening. My brother's stealing my not-girlfriend.

"With hearts made true, deceit hides among the shadows, sneaking in to feign what truth ought be light." Puck's voice lilts softly by my side, and I don't have to look to see him standing there in Paul's place.

A shiver passes through me. Oh. Oh shit. No.

Hearts made true. Green was the true-love potion, not true seeming.

I have completely and utterly screwed this up, and I have no idea how to fix it.

I feel something touch my waist and I jump back, turning to face Britney. She has my phone in her hand and she's typing something into it. Her lips press together in a pretty pout as she hands it back to me. "Call me later, okay? I want to know what's going on," she whispers. Her voice isn't any less high-pitched or wispy than usual, but there's a depth to it that isn't normally there.

I give her a sharp look. So *this* is the intelligent girl my brother was falling all over. "You're a better actress than you seem to be."

Her smile doesn't reach her eyes. "You learn to fit in early if you don't want to get bullied," she responds softly. "I'm serious. Call me. I want to know why that girl is all over my boyfriend."

"She's supposed to be my girlfriend," I whisper, confessing because it seems like a good moment to do so.

Britney's eyes widen, and then she smiles. "Good, then we're on the same side here very definitely. Call me when dinner's over."

"It'll be a little later; I have a friend stopping by and I need to wait for her to be gone, too." But yeah, once Maria's gone out, maybe talking to Britney will help make some sense out of the situation. Except I'm not sure there's any sense to be made.

Paul clears his throat. Except for Puck's weird comment, I'd forgotten that he was even there. "This isn't like Pepper," he says, glancing from me to Britney, relaxing when I nodded that yeah, he'd heard right, I'd spilled the secret. "She's into you, Jordan. I don't know what's going on."

I have a sick feeling in my stomach that I know exactly what's happened. I watch as James bends his head and kisses her one more time, lingering until Pepper's name is called from the stage. Dower sounds pissed off, and I realize that if he can only see James from the back, he probably thinks he's me.

I groan. "I'll figure it out," I promise them. Which really means what I have to figure it out is how to undo the mess I've made.

CHAPTER 15: Crowded House

THIS FAMILY dinner is unbelievable. Not in the same way that three magical potions are impossible to believe, but in that ridiculous my-life-has-turned-into-a-farce sort of way.

Mom has me put both leaves into the table to pull it out as far as it goes, which we normally only do for Thanksgiving and Christmas. She puts me and Maria to work (Maria was there waiting for me when I got home) setting the table, while Sam and Leigh finish putting together a salad in the kitchen. Karen sails in with her new boyfriend, David, just as Mom finishes putting the Chinese takeout into serving bowls.

And that whole time, I'm trying not to think about what Pepper and James might be doing in the living room.

At least they're in the living room, not downstairs in the basement. Mom's confused by why Pepper's here, and James hasn't exactly given a satisfactory answer except to say that he invited her. They've both got a dreamy sort of drugged quality about them, almost as if they're drunk on each other. Yeah, seriously. You've heard about people gazing into each other's eyes? They're doing that. And Pepper giggles sometimes.

They've kissed, too, I know that. But nothing more, since they're in a fairly public place, with my dad in the recliner nearby, switching channels on the television while waiting for dinner to be done.

We eventually settle in at the table, all ten of us, and it's just a bit tight. We knock elbows as we pass the dishes around, and Mom looks like she hopes we'll fill up on salad since she'd originally planned on there being only eight of us. Still, Mom usually cooks for an army, so I think we'll be fine.

Karen's boyfriend starts up a lively conversation about basketball, and I jump into that along with James. Turns out David's from New York, so he's a major Knicks fan, but we forgive him as soon as he shows he knows something about our guys in green. We end up talking about the classic Celtics team of the '80s, back when Bird was playing (who can forget him?) and the Dream Team of the Olympics. It might be stuff from before we were born, but hey, that's what classic sports TV is for, right?

Maria starts nudging me under the table, and I throw her an apologetic look. When she pokes my thigh, I catch her hand under the table.

David laughs. "I think I'm boring your girlfriend. Looks like you two've been together long enough to get past that starry-eyed phase." He nods at Pepper then, who's just watching James talk. James flushes, and my jaw tightens. Maria nudges me under the table again.

"Maria's not my girlfriend," I say. "She's my best friend, which is different. There's someone else I like."

Those words drop like a small bomb onto the table, but the one person I want to notice them doesn't even look my way. It's like I don't even exist anymore for Pepper. Weren't we just making out in a closet a couple hours ago? This can't be happening.

"Jordan," Mom says, tone soft and dark. I hear the unspoken reminder that I can't date yet.

I smile weakly. "It's okay, Mom. I don't think she even knows I exist." Not anymore, not since she drank a magical potion of falling in love with my brother.

"Either way," David says, apparently determined to keep things from getting awkward. "You're not much into basketball, are you?"

"Oh, I like basketball *players* sometimes, but I'm not that into the game." Maria says with a cheerful lilt, "I'd rather watch swimming and gymnastics. Or dance. I like dance shows a lot."

Mom glances at me, and I shrug and push my chair back. "Mom, Dad, can we be excused? Maria's got to be somewhere in a bit, and we've got some things to do first."

For a moment it looks like Mom might object. I can almost see what she's thinking: wondering what my best friend is getting me into, or wondering exactly who it is I like and how to keep me under wraps and safe. But Dad just waves and tells us to go on upstairs and keep the music down, and I decide not to wait for Mom to object.

"Nice meeting you, David." I nod to him, and then Maria and I tear upstairs.

We push the door closed and she collapses on my bed. "Ai dios, Jordan, what's going on with your girlfriend? I can't believe James'd do that to you."

"Neither could I, but there it is," I say dryly. I look in my backpack and pull out the empty vial, making a face at it before I toss it back in the underwear drawer. "One minute we're getting caught kissing in the closet, the next she's making googly eyes at my brother. It's like I slipped into bizarro world and can't figure out how to get back."

"I thought you were dating." Maria's got her own backpack on the bed, pulling out a skirt that looks way too short and a top and some heels. "Girls don't just up and do that to a guy."

"They do if magic's involved."

She gives me a look. "Chico, this is the real world. If we had magic, I wouldn't have to wear these." She pulls a balloon out of her bra and tosses it onto the bed, leaving her half-chested. "If we had magic, then poof, I'd just snap my fingers and I'd be Felipe at home for Mama, and the second I stepped out that doorway I'd be Maria again, all done up properly. I wouldn't have to spend my allowance on condoms and worry about whether my little sister found the pudding I'd made and ate it before I could use it."

Wait. "Pudding?"

She looks at me, eyes wide and innocent. "New trick I just picked up from the Internet. Pudding in the balloons feels more natural."

Oh. Crap. I sink down onto the bed next to her. "Maria, no, you're not letting him—"

"Just in case," she assures me, but she doesn't look me in the eyes, either. "He's a senior. He's not going to be satisfied with necking forever." She looks over at me, her eyes wide. "And I really *like* him, Jordan. He's so sweet to me. He brought me roses the other day, and yeah, I couldn't bring them in the house because Mama would've been all *mijo, no* about it all, but wasn't that thoughtful? He buys me dinner and takes me out to movies and ice cream. And he kisses like… like…." Her voice trails off, and she gives me a helpless look. "I don't know what to compare it to. He's the first boy I've ever kissed, and I feel like I'm going to go up in flames every time we do."

"I know the feeling." And I do. The way every time I got close enough I almost couldn't resist getting closer still, because I wanted to catch the scent of Pepper's hair or her skin. And when our lips met, my body tingled and warmed and I found myself wishing for all kinds of impossible things.

Maria's right: if magic were real, we'd be able to be everything we are on the inside on the outside as well. It'd be simple, just a flick of a wand or a gulp of a potion, and poof, everything fits.

Her hand settles on the back of my neck, rubbing lightly. "I'm sorry things aren't working out with Pepper," Maria says quietly. "Do you think it'll change again? What about that blonde bimbo James was into?"

"Britney's not a bimbo." And for the second time in as many weeks, I'm defending something I was against only hours before. Man, life has gotten weird. "She's completely different when she's not doing hair flips to attract an alpha male." I pick up the pudding-filled balloon and toss it back to Maria. "Aren't you supposed to be getting ready? Put your boobs on, girl."

Maria laughs, and I look away as she strips down. "I know you think I'm being dangerous, but Marco's a nice guy, Jordan, I promise. This is our fourth date in a week and a half and he hasn't been anything but a gentleman. He likes touching my butt but hasn't tried for anything else."

"That's a good thing, Maria, since certain other things that could get you killed are awfully close to your butt," I remind her, talking to the floor. I can hear her rustling about, moving as she pulls nylons on. "Don't you remember all those stories from when we went to Boston last year?" We'd gone in to the ceremony in Allston for the Transgender Day of Remembrance, and reading and hearing the names of those who had died had reduced both of us to tears. "They probably thought the people who killed them were nice, too."

The rustling stops, but I don't look up, not trusting that she's actually dressed yet. After a moment, the bed moves as she wiggles into her skirt, and I know it's safe enough then. I glance up as she's meticulously tucking one balloon into her bra. I could swear she's gone up a cup size since she first showed me how it all worked. I pick up the other balloon, letting it roll a little in my hand, feeling the difference between that texture and my packer, and wondering just how close to reality it is. Not that I'll ever get a live one in my hand to check out at the rate I'm going. I hold it up and she takes it from me.

"I promise, if Marco ever says or does anything to scare me, you'll be the first person I text," she promises. "And I'll go home immediately. Do you want me to start carrying mace?"

I'm tempted to say yes. She looks so contrite that I just sigh. "No, you don't need to carry mace. But I'm sure you can remember to kick him in the junk if you need to get away." I look over at my bureau, frowning slightly.

She sits back down, still just in her bra and skirt, her nylon-covered foot nudging my toe. "What is it?"

"You're going to think I'm nuts." I get up and go over to the bureau, pulling the drawer out so I can take out the three vials, one of them empty but the other two still full. I show them to her on the palm of my hand, smiling faintly at her confused look. "I had a dream where this guy gave me three magic potions. When I woke up, they were on my bureau."

She wrinkles her nose. "Right, Jordan. What are they really?"

"No, really." My laugh is dry, because haven't I been having the same thoughts about my sanity since the dream? "He said they were for true love, true sight, and true seeming. And I tried one out today."

Maria tugs her shirt on, pulling it down so it clings to her chest and covers her ribs, but leaves her belly bare. "Sure, right."

"I figured true seeming might help me out, right? Make people see me like who I am inside, since things have been weird as all hell at school," I tell her. I shake the empty vial. "I put it in my water bottle, but I didn't get to drink it. James stole it for him and Pepper. So then I put it in my other water bottle, but I stepped out of the auditorium when you texted, and when I came back, that bottle was gone too."

She's just staring at me, waiting for the shoe to drop. She doesn't see it.

"James and Pepper drank it," I say again.

"So suddenly they looked different?" she asks.

I shake my head. "No, I think I screwed up. I think I mixed up the vials and that was the true love one. I think what happened to them might really be a magic spell, and I don't know how to put it back right."

Maria blinks slowly once, then twice. "You do realize how insane that sounds, right, Jordan?" she finally says slowly. "This is the real world. There's no such thing as magic."

I was going to offer her the true sight potion, so her boyfriend would see her exactly like she is for who she is. Or true seeming for herself. If they share the drink, it can't hurt anything, even if I mix up the potions, because they'll either see each other for who they are, or be seen for who they are. It's a win-win situation. But at her disbelief, I change my mind.

"Yeah, of course I realize what it sounds like." I close my hand around the vials and turn away. "There's gotta be another reason for what happened."

"What are the other two supposed to be?"

Oh, so now she's humoring me. "True sight, and true seeming, since true love is gone." I shrug, my back to her as the vials go once more into the drawer to be hidden beneath the underwear.

"What're you going to do with them?"

"Stop humoring me." I give her a dark look when I sit down next to her again. "If you're not going to believe me, we're not going to talk about it, even though I could use some help fixing things."

She touches my cheek. "I'm sorry, Jordan." She leans in, wrapping her arms around my shoulders, and I pull her in for a hug. "But it is pretty weird, you know."

"My whole life is weird lately," I mutter against her shoulder.

Maria pushes me back to look at me seriously. "Did you talk to Dr. Hewitt about the dreams?"

"Yes." Okay, so that's sort of a lie. I did tell her about the dreams. I just didn't tell her about the part where the vials were real.

"So it's not some kind of testosterone-induced hallucination?"

I snort with laughter. "Maria. Testosterone does not induce hallucinations. You should know that."

She shrugs, all innocent. "Rage for no reason, hallucinations, they're kind of similar, right?"

Time to just let the conversation go before I get too mired into a discussion of me being nuts, or worse yet, Maria convinces herself it'd be the right thing to do to tell Dr. Hewitt that hormones have addled my brain. "I'm fine, Maria, don't worry about it. I promise, no more conversations about magic, okay?"

She pushes herself up, plumping her chest and smoothing her shirt and skirt. "Think Marco'll like it?"

A soft laugh, because oh yeah, given the chance to go back to talking about her date, and she's there. She still gives me a worried look, and I smile to show her I'm just fine. "Yeah, Marco'll flip for it, I'm sure. You look awesome."

My phone buzzes, and I flip it open to look. Britney. Who apparently types her number into people's phones as *<3 Britney <3.* "Hang on a sec, Maria, I'll be right back." I step out into the hallway, saying quietly, "Hello? Everyone's still here, it's not really a good time to talk."

My door opens and Maria follows me out before Britney can respond. "Don't worry," Maria whispers, "I need to go meet Marco anyway. You talk to Britney and get things figured out. I'll text you later when I get home, I promise."

"I guess it's a good time after all," I say quietly into the phone. Britney starts talking as I watch Maria walk down the stairs. I hear her saying her usual good-bye and blown kiss to James, and I hear his and Pepper's responses. It's like a kick in the gut to hear them speaking together.

With a soft groan, I apologize to Britney. "I'm sorry, I missed whatever you just said." How am I supposed to listen when the world is spinning out of control around me? I go back in my room and lean against the door, hoping that it will hold the world still, just for a little while.

INTERLUDE: Britney

BRITNEY TILTED her phone to one side, letting the virtual keyboard enlarge so it'd be easier to type. *Where are you?* she tapped out and hit send to her strangely acting boyfriend. She tossed the phone on the bed and tried to work on her science lab, hoping to be interrupted by the characteristic chirp of a text coming in. She managed to finish a graph in careful colored pencil before she picked up the phone again. Fifteen minutes had passed, and nothing had come back. *James?* she typed, well-aware that she was starting to sound desperate. Or possibly shrewish. She sent the one word, then a moment later sent another message with the words *We need to talk.*

She couldn't forget the way he had been that afternoon. Kissing Pepper Sullivan right there in front of everyone. His brother's girlfriend. Britney's lips pressed together, narrowing her expression into a sour visage that she knew her mother would tell her would wrinkle that way if she weren't careful. She looked at the phone, poking it as if that might make it sound.

Nothing.

With a grumbled sigh, she picked it up one more time and used it to sift through her e-mail, finding the electronic cast contact list that had everyone's cell number on it. Since Jordan hadn't called her yet, either, she might as well try to call him. She pressed the on-screen button to dial and set it to speaker, leaving the phone on the bed in front of her crossed legs.

"Hello? Everyone's still here, it's not really a good time to talk." Jordan launched right into the conversation without waiting for a response. There was a moment's pause, and then he added quietly, "I guess it's a good time after all."

Britney sighed. "Nice to talk to you, too, Jordan. Look, I know you don't like me very much, but I've been trying to get hold of James and he's ignoring my texts. I saw Pepper walking out with you two, and I know she's been hanging out with you guys a lot, but she left her brother behind today. And she and James weren't letting go of each other. Did he really bring her home? And is she still there?"

She heard a soft murmur like someone talking to someone else. "Jordan?" she nudged him verbally.

"I'm sorry, I missed whatever you just said," he responded. She heard a door thud, and a groan. "What's going on, Britney?"

"That's what I'm calling to ask you," she said, her tone sharp with frustration. "Your brother walked off hand in hand with another girl today, and I get the feeling I've been dumped without him even having the decency to tell me so. Did he say anything to you?"

Silence from the other side except for the sound of ragged breathing. When he responded, the words were slow and measured, "No, he didn't say anything to me. But he did bring Pepper over for dinner. I think they're still downstairs, and I can tell him to call you when she's gone."

Britney let her head fall forward toward her crossed feet and the phone. Her arms created a circle, so her quiet words echoed toward the phone in the hollow created by her bent body. "Jordan, I thought we established earlier that I'm not the enemy. My boyfriend and your girlfriend hooked up today. We need to work together, and you didn't call me."

She could almost hear him thinking, sorting through his words, and she wondered if he knew more than he was saying. "I'm not sure there's anything we can do," he finally said. "Everything's kind of out of control over here, Britney, and I don't know what to do about it."

"Then we figure it out." Everything could be figured out, she knew. All she had to do was address it like a science problem. Define the problem, create a hypothesis, then work toward the proof and solution. Even relationships fell prey to the same theories, or they had until this afternoon. She pursued James with her usual quiet logic, letting him believe he was the one in charge of the relationship. Maybe that was her failing, that she'd let him believe he could walk away just as easily.

"Do you really think it's that simple?"

She placed her hands on the comforter, pressing herself up enough to stretch out, lying down with her feet by her pillow, and her elbows propping her up by the phone. Her toe tapped lightly against the wall. "In the end, everything's that simple, Jordan. We have a problem, we find a solution, and it's done. The hard part is figuring out the solution."

He laughed then, a surprisingly bitter sound, although she guessed he was due a little of that, considering. "Right, then, you just get on that, Britney. I'll help you implement once you figure out what it is we're doing. In the meantime, I've got homework that hasn't gotten done because I was busy getting bullied at rehearsal and having a terrible afternoon and an extremely awkward dinner."

The line clicked dead before she could respond, and she stared at the phone as if she could bring it back to life by sheer will alone. She tapped out a quiet message and sent it to Jordan, not expecting a response: *For what it's worth, I'm sorry.*

Not your fault was the reply.

She knew, but that didn't matter. Britney felt miserable for herself, and bad for him as well. She was pretty sure she couldn't come up with a relationship scenario that sucked more than this one.

A quiet tap on her door alerted her before it pushed open and her mother stepped inside. Britney's pretty pale-blonde looks came entirely from her mother, and Mrs. Jenkins had frozen them in time. When they went out, people asked if they were sisters, surprised when she demurred, saying that she was Britney's mother. Impossible, they would say. Britney had spent years learning how to be perfect, but not so perfect that she was better than her mother.

And even now, late at night, her mother was still the picture of quiet perfection, not a hair out of place despite having changed into sweats and a tank top for lounging around the house. Only her smile wasn't perfect, quiet and cold, the one that Britney had learned to copy so she could blend in with all the other pretty people.

Britney let her lips form that same chill smile in return. "Hi, Mom."

"I've just had the most interesting conversation with Cathy Graves," she said. "About the play you're involved in."

Britney could hear the disapproval imbuing those tones. "I thought you said it would be good for my college transcripts. I'll have cheerleading, the AP classes, and now the play. I'm well rounded."

"Well." Mrs. Jenkins's lips pursed. "I'm not entirely certain I approve."

"My homework hasn't suffered," Britney pointed out. She wouldn't add that some nights she'd been up until midnight so she could manage rehearsals until six, then time with James afterward, and not get started on her work until after eight.

"It's not that." Her mother came in and sat on the bed, the image of a concerned parent if Britney only believed the act. "I don't approve of a school choosing to promote illicit behavior."

"What's illicit about a play?" Britney pulled away from her mother's light pat on her knee. "Mom, it's a good show. You should hear the way it's coming together, even after just a couple of weeks. I love working with Tyler and Zach and Lianne. And wait'll you hear the kid who plays Puck sing. Or Jordan. James's brother? He's got the most amazing voice. We were working on the finale today and he was knocking it out of the park."

Her mother's lips thinned into a twist of disapproval. "Jordan. That's the one playing a woman."

Cathy Graves—wait, was this about that girl Emily? "Mom, you can't listen to what she's saying about the play. Her daughter's just pissed off that she didn't get a part in it, and she's only a freshman. She can be in the play next year. She's been making trouble since we started rehearsing."

Mrs. Jenkins silenced her with a look. "Britney, facts only. Does the play promote homosexuality and cross-dressing?"

Britney shook her head, brow furrowed. "It's a play. It doesn't promote anything, any more than Bugs Bunny promoted cross-dressing. Yes, there's a gender change in the plot. And yes, there are some gay relationships in it, when Puck's magic tries to put Lysander and Demetrius together. But it's not telling anyone what to do. It's just part of the plot, and it's Shakespearean, which has always been about gender and relationships."

She didn't like the way her mom looked at her, that sour expression only deepening. "Mom," she said slowly. "It's a play. It isn't going to suddenly change anyone's mind about how they look or who they love. You know that."

Except her mom didn't believe it. She could see that, and Britney knew that no matter how smart her mom was, and no matter how many PhDs she had, that sometimes emotions ruled over the mind. She needed to come up with something quickly.

"You've always told me that it's important to live up to my commitments," she said, choosing her words carefully. "And that my transcript needs variation. I made a promise to the directors that I would perform in the play, and I can't back out on that now. How would it look to schools to see me dropping something simply because of politics?"

Mrs. Jenkins's smile was tight. "I'm not suggesting you drop the play, Britney. After the twenty-eighth, there won't be a play. I'll be helping Cathy with her presentation for the school board. We don't want this influence for our children, and we will not allow it to continue. Rebel as you want, but the play will be finished soon."

"You can't!" Britney protested. "That's ridiculous, Mom. It's just a play! Words!" She knew, though, that words were dangerous things. Words were how the world changed: words first, then actions.

But her mom only smiled and left, and Britney sank down at her desk, opening her laptop. She quickly composed an e-mail but chose not to send it, not yet. She couldn't make herself send something to Pepper, not after everything that had happened today. She'd wait until morning and talk to Jordan and Paul, who at least still seemed to be sane, and see if the three of them could come up with a plan. And in the meantime, she circled October twenty-eighth on the calendar in her agenda and wrote "school board meeting," because she knew that was one thing she couldn't afford to miss, not if they were going to save their play.

PART FOUR
Dress & Tech

JOURNAL: Thursday, October 22

I DREAMED again last night.

This time it was Titania and Oberon, and just a little bit of Puck. I don't remember it nearly as clearly, and we weren't in my room. We were in Titania's bower. Puck didn't say a word; it was Titania who looked at me, and walked over and touched my head.

"Wishes are a tricky thing when granted by a trickster spirit, are they not?" she murmured.

I nodded at her. I guess I expected Puck to look embarrassed, but he just watched me quietly.

Titania crouched down before me, both hands on my face. When I looked into her eyes, they were soft like grass, with all the shadings from pale straw to the deepest green blues. It was a weird sort of thing to notice in a dream, but I couldn't stop staring at them. "I grant thee wisdom," she whispered, and pressed her lips to my forehead. Then her fingers pressed against my chest. "I grant thee bravery for thy heart, and the ability to see the truth of thy heart with thine eyes." Her lips moved to brush against one eyelid, then the other.

In the background, Puck pursed his lips and rolled his eyes. As Oberon pushed at him, Puck leapt to his feet and yelled, "Fine! I go, I go, look how I go," his tone more sarcastic than playful as he leapt out of the bower and out of sight.

I just stared at Titania. True sight of my heart? What does that even mean?

Then James started pounding on my door and I woke up.

Everything about yesterday seems dreamlike this morning. From Ms. Jackson catching me and Pepper making out in the closet, to the whole nightmare with the school board, to Pepper and James making out at rehearsal, to my conversation with Britney (who still sounds like Minnie Mouse, but when she's not trying to be a bimbo you can hear that she does actually have kind of impressive brain cells). It was just a weird day overall, and I can't even explain most of it.

I keep hoping yesterday might've been a dream, too.

Because yeah, by the end of the day my almost girlfriend was kissing my brother. He dumped Britney and Pepper dumped me, and now James and Pepper are together. I don't get it. And no, I didn't tell Pepper the truth, so it's not one of those things where she ran screaming. I mean, we were making out in a closet earlier that afternoon and everything was pretty much awesome. If I'd had all the bits I'm meant to, it would've been a lot more embarrassing when Ms. Jackson interrupted us.

We should talk about the whole school board thing. I guess there are some concerned parents who are going to bring a motion before the school board to get the play canceled. Ms. Jackson and Mr. Dower say they'll support us, of course. Ms. Jackson's pretty emphatic about it all, like it's some kind of personal crusade. She kept looking at me, like she was expecting me to say something because I guess in a way it's personal for me, just like it's personal for Ryan and Zach. By saying that the play's immoral for portraying a character who changes gender, and for portraying gay love, that's saying we're immoral too.

But to fight it that way, I'd have to go public and then I'd lose the peace I have for the rest of my senior year. It would make everything harder. It might make some things impossible. I'd be opening myself up to all kinds of risk that I've avoided so carefully.

I'm not sure I'm strong enough to do that. The idea of opening up my mouth to tell perfect strangers that I was born biologically different than what I actually am terrifies me. I can't even imagine telling the people I care about.

I keep running through scenarios in my head, where I tell Pepper and she doesn't say a thing, just walks away. What I really need is for Titania to kiss her eyes with true sight, not mine.

I know what you're going to say. You're going to tell me that I've always had true sight, and that I should trust my instincts. But I can't go with that, since I trusted my instincts and I started a sort of maybe relationship with Pepper and look what happened.

I think I'm better off where I am. Hiding. Maybe I'll just stand by Ryan's side and let him lead the charge. I'll be an ally; that's a help, too.

I don't want to become the poster boy for transgender acceptance. It feels like a one-way trip to martyrdom. I like my life, and I like my skin.

I just want to live in peace. Is that really too much to ask for?

CHAPTER 16: Musical Relationships

WHEN I leave the house, I have the remaining vial in my backpack. Yeah, singular. I can't tell Dr. Hewitt when I write my journal for her, but I remember more of the dream about Titania than I'm saying. Because Puck came back, whispering in my ear just as I woke up. He told me that Maria had taken one of the vials.

I didn't believe him, of course, because for one, when could she have taken it last night? And for two, why? She didn't believe a thing I said about them. But when I went and looked in my underwear drawer, under all the tighty-whiteys, there was only one vial there, full of a pale-blue liquid. The purple was gone.

I can't believe she took it. I wonder if she was just that desperate that she palmed one before going out because she thought maybe I was right and she didn't want to admit it. I'm angry at her for taking it, especially since I don't even know which one it is, but I'm also not sure I can blame her since I don't know what to believe about them myself. I can't even prove that any of it was real to start with. Either way, I decide maybe I should just carry the last one with me and avoid it wandering off, since I swear these things are starting to have minds of their own.

I can't tell Dr. Hewitt that objects from my dream are appearing physically in the real world. I know I'm already diagnosed with a psychiatric disorder, but that's not the same thing as being insane. I'm not *nuts*; I'm just not built to the correct biological specifications. But dreaming about things appearing and believing in magical spells? I'm pretty sure that *is* nuts, even though I've got evidence that it's all *true*.

When we reach the school, Pepper and Paul are there waiting for us. I start to walk toward her, because magic isn't real and it had to have been some crazy hallucination. Besides, shouldn't it have worn off? But she goes right around me and slips her arm into the crook of James's elbow. He kisses the tip of her nose, and they walk on past me and Paul, heading into the school.

"It really happened," I say quietly.

"Apparently, yeah. She couldn't stop talking about James after he finally dropped her off last night," Paul speaks quietly back to me. "But that's not the only thing that happened yesterday. I talked to Zach on the phone last night."

Uh-oh, I have a really bad feeling about what he might be about to say.

"Ryan broke up with him last night, right after rehearsal," Paul said. "And I saw Ryan walking in with Caitlyn this morning, and they looked pretty close." He pauses then, and shakes his head. We can see James and Pepper through the long windows at the front of the building. They're leaning against the opposite wall, curled into each other; she looks more comfortable in his arms than I was ever able to let her be. My gaze drops away. I can't look.

"It's like we've turned into Hollywood," Paul muses. "People getting together with their partners on stage and breaking up with the people they've been dating for ages. How long were Ryan and Zach together?"

"Two years. It was a big deal back in the beginning of our sophomore year because Ryan had been out for a while but no one knew Zach was gay." I can remember it, and I start walking up the stairs again, not wanting to stand here talking, especially about this, in front of the thugs. "No one ever bugged Ryan because he was so Zen about it. But I guess he and Zach got together over the summer at an Arts camp, and when they came back, Zach was nervous about it. People started teasing him and pushing him around. Bashing him, really. And Ryan stood up for him, along with a lot of their friends. It wasn't easy, but they made it through, and most people don't even think about it anymore. They're just them, y'know?"

Which made it all sound so easy. And doesn't mention when Zach's arm was broken in a fight, or that Ryan's nose got broken in that same fight, which is why it has that little crook in it now. I remember the fights, and that's why the idea of people knowing the truth terrifies me. Some people get even more violent about transgender people than they do about gay people. Scary stuff, yeah, but I remember that list of names from last year's Remembrance ceremony. Those people didn't just get their arm or noses broken.

I pull open the door and hold it for Paul, and he just looks at me and shakes his head. "There's something in the water. But we'll figure it out and put it back right. We'll talk later, at rehearsal, if Pepper can keep her hands off your brother long enough to run it."

"Thanks for that lovely image," I say dryly. He gives me one of those teasing Puckish grins, then he's gone, disappearing into the crowd of moving students like he was never there.

It's easy to drift through the day. James isn't in any of my classes, and Pepper's a year younger. Zach's in a couple of my classes, but we don't talk. He looks so upset, and he's pulled in on himself to the point where everyone's leaving him alone.

By the time I walk into rehearsal, I've had a day away from it all, but that's not enough to prepare myself for the reality of the situation. Ryan sits on the edge of the stage, Caitlyn standing between his knees, arms looped over his shoulders. They aren't kissing, but she's nudged up pretty close to him, and Zach's studiously avoiding them by running lines with Tyler on the other side of the stage.

I don't even see Pepper and James, and I try not to think about where they could be. Like, oh, the supply closet off the music room. That's our place. She has to remember that we were together just *yesterday*, doesn't she? The magic wouldn't wipe away those memories, would it? I feel like all of a sudden, I never actually meant anything to her.

"Hi."

I don't even turn to look at Britney, just saying, "Haven't seen him yet." I don't try to hide the bitter tone from her.

"I did. They're out in the hallway, by the side door." She sighs. "It's so wrong. I just don't get what happened."

I open my mouth, and close it again. I can't tell her. "It doesn't make any sense."

"It's like the play is cursed." She goes up on her toes and waves to Paul, waiting for him to join us before she goes on. "I had this totally not good conversation with my mom last night," Britney says. "And I think you guys'd want to hear it. I think everyone actually needs to hear it."

"Like what?" Paul prompts. Britney motions to the row of seats and she and I sit, while Paul climbs to sit on the back of the chair between us, toes pressed against the seat bottom to keep himself balanced.

"There are people who want to make the school board cancel the play," she says quietly.

Oh. Right. I probably should've said something to someone. "How do you know about that?" I ask. Paul gives me a sharp look, and I shrug. "It came up yesterday, and I happened to be in the right place to hear about it. Ms. Jackson said not to tell people about it, and that she and Mr. Dower were supporting the play one hundred percent and not to worry about it."

"It's all Emily's fault," Britney whispers, "and her mom is calling other moms about it. Like mine, who was all over the part about it promoting immoral behavior."

"It's not immoral." So maybe I'm getting a little sick of hearing how Ryan and Zach and I are *wrong*, because the words just slip out before I think twice about it.

"I didn't say it was," Britney says quickly. I don't think she noticed how cranky I sound, so I just bite my tongue before anything else slips out as she continues, "My mom's the one who put it that way. Thing is, she really seems to believe it. I never knew how bigoted she was. And I think they're starting a big campaign to all be there for the meeting."

"Next Wednesday, on the twenty-eighth," I supply the date.

"Well, then, we all need to be there, too," Paul says firmly. "All of us who can. You guys, me, Pepper, your brother. Whatever else is going on, if we want to put our play on, we need to be there to fight this kind of stupidity. Doesn't it go against the anti-bullying policy somehow?"

"That depends on how the school policy against discrimination is written," Britney points out. "Some schools don't include sexuality. Plus, the school board is probably a bunch of older folks and pretty conservative." When I give her a look, she shrugs, "I spent some time online looking things up after mom talked to me last night." I have to smile, and she smiles back.

It's funny, but I like her better now. James is right, she's not unintelligent. She seems to have a good solid head on her shoulders. Logical. She's a good ally.

"But if the rest of the school isn't upset about Ryan and Zach being gay, why're they upset about the play?" Paul glances from Ryan and Caitlyn over to where Zach is trying not to look at them. "It doesn't make any sense."

"Emily," I say quietly. "And me. It's all my fault because Emily's pissed off that I got the part of Viola instead of her."

"So she's trying to ruin the play for everyone?" Paul rolls his eyes. "How mature, trying to get rid of the toy for everyone because she can't have it."

I laugh, but there's nothing humorous in it. "I never said she was being mature."

"She's playing on their fears," Britney says quietly. "Our parents want to protect us, and they want us all to grow up normal. Which means they want the boys to like the girls, and everyone to just be exactly what they're supposed to be, according to society's norms. Viola changing sex is totally Shakespearian, but it's not what most people think of as *normal*. And when Lysander and Demetrius get caught by the potion, they're being *made* to be gay, which can be terrifying to a parent. They think that somehow the play will teach their children to do things that aren't normal."

"That because of the play someone's going to suddenly want to change their gender, or kiss someone who's the same sex as themself?" I snort again and shake my head. "Shouldn't Emily's mother be more afraid that if her precious daughter had actually gotten the part, she might start wanting to be a boy?"

The thing is, in reality, it doesn't work that way, and I could tell her that. I know some people don't figure it out until later, but still, it's not as simple as doing it because a play told you to. It's something on the inside, and it's not easy to figure out. I was lucky to have really good people around me to help me get past all the confusion when I was a kid.

"Fear isn't logical," Paul said. "And I have to admit Emily's kind of brilliant in a scarily Machiavellian sort of way. If she weren't so evil, she might even be hot again."

"You could always take one for the team and learn her campaign from the inside," I suggest, trying to tease and lighten the moment. "Kiss up to her and see what she's got planned."

Paul's head cocks as he looks at me. The roll of his eyes, when it comes, is very deliberate. "I don't even want to try to fake it anymore. Not that she'd ever give me the time of day. She seems to like the big brawny kinds."

"Pfft. When true love hits her over the head, she might be surprised. I never thought I went for the petite girls." I shut my mouth quickly, a flush staining my skin with heat. Didn't mean to say that. Paul's look is sympathetic and amused, which is the oddest combination and makes his features more fey than ever.

"I like them taller than me," Paul admits. I'm thankful to him for covering my embarrassment.

Britney just looks at both of us, a faint frown marring her perfect features. "So what are we going to do about the school board meeting?"

The door at the side of the stage opens. I don't want to, but it's the right thing, so I stand up and wave to James. He catches sight of me and he and Pepper shift direction to join us like there's no reason why they shouldn't. And I guess in their minds, there isn't.

"People are finding out about the school board meeting," I say, hoping Pepper at least remembers that part about yesterday. She frowns in response, and I don't know if that means she's forgotten or if she's trying to reconcile exactly where she was when she found out about the meeting with where she is now. I ignore the look and just catch her up on what Britney's told us about her mom and Emily's mom. "We need to do something."

"Like what?" James asks. His hand is sliding against Pepper's shoulder as she leans into him, and I can't stop watching it.

"Like forming our own protest against the protest," Britney says. Her tone is short and clipped, and she won't look at them just as much as I can't seem to stop. "We get Ryan and Zach and Caitlyn and everyone involved and we show up at the school board meeting on Wednesday and we defend our play."

I want to ask what if Ryan isn't gay anymore but that'd get us back into a discussion of what happened yesterday, because that particular part of it really doesn't make any sense. Instead, I try to man up and lead the crusade. "Well, then, let's get everyone over here and start explaining. We've got less than a week to get our plan solid." I force myself to meet Pepper's gaze. "Don't worry. We'll save your play."

"Thanks." She smiles softly at me and it cuts deep into my heart. Fixing the play is easy. Fixing this relationship mess is what's going to make me bleed.

CHAPTER 17: Cornered

PEPPER'S WATCHING me as rehearsal winds down. Dower's talking, giving us direction on what he plans to work on tomorrow, with Pepper sitting silently beside him. I figure she must be looking for James, and I spot him down in the chairs, getting his things together. I point toward where he is, and her gaze shifts there, then returns to me, quiet and watchful.

I wonder if we're giving them a ride home.

And the way she's watching me, I wonder if I still have a chance. I mean, how "true" can true love be if one minute she's kissing me in the closet, and the next she's glued to James? Did it bring out something that was already there inside of her, or did it put something in her mind so she thinks she's in love, even if she's not?

I jump down from the stage and go to get my things together. I see her walking out that side door, so I call quietly to James that I'll meet him at the car and I follow her out.

She's just standing there, like she's waiting for me, and leaning against the lockers. Something in her expression, the wide green-gray of her eyes as I get closer, breaks my heart. I stop before I'm in her personal space, waiting for her to say something, but she doesn't.

"You were watching me," I say quietly.

"I know," she says, and her gaze finally drops away. "And before you ask, no, I don't know why. I'm dating your brother."

Which didn't stop her yesterday, when she started kissing him while she was still dating me. And I wonder if she even remembers. "But we—"

"We *what*?" she asks quickly. "What did we do? What were we? Were we *something*, Jordan? Because it doesn't make sense in my head."

There's a good answer for that, I'm sure of it. Just as sure as I am that this isn't it, as I step forward and frame her face with my hands and lightly brush my lips against hers. We were this. We kissed so many times and nowhere near enough, and then I lost her and none of it makes sense until this moment when I'm tasting her again. It feels so right.

She pushes me away, a soft hiccup breaking in her throat. "Stop it, Jordan. You know I'm—"

"You're what?" I interrupt quietly. I shove my hands into the pockets of my hoodie so I don't reach out to her again.

"I'm with James," she says. "Your brother."

"But you still like me," I tell her. "You kissed me just now."

Her small chin lifts, quivering slightly. "No, you kissed me. I just—" A soft hiccup of hesitation. "Okay, so maybe I kissed you back, but that's not the same thing as kissing you first."

"No, it's not," I admit. "But we—you don't remember, do you?"

She blinks, bewildered. "Remember what?"

"Why was I with you when Ms. Jackson told you and Dower about the school board?" I try to nudge the memories free. "Tell me that. Tell me what we were doing together, then."

And for a long moment, I don't think she's going to answer me. The silence stretches out and I take another step closer, but she moves back, right up against the lockers. I stop, not wanting to chase her away.

"We were getting some things out of the supply closet," she finally says slowly. "But Ms. Jackson said it was okay if you stayed while she talked to me and Dower."

Close, but that's not everything. Something in her mind has blocked it out, that something probably being a nice little vial of colored liquid that I never meant for her to drink. Paul's right: there's something in the water, and I'm the one who put it there. I take a slow breath. "If I kissed you again, would you slap me?"

She hesitates, which I take as a good sign, but in the end she reaches out and presses against my shoulders to push me back. "Don't," she says simply. "I'm not interested in you that way."

I turn when she steps past me. "You're lying."

"Maybe." She doesn't look back. "But I'm with your brother and it's pretty horrible of you to be trying this, Jordan. Don't you care about James?"

I don't answer, because everything that comes to mind isn't exactly nice considering what he's done to me. Except, it isn't their fault, is it? She goes back into the auditorium, and I let myself fall against the lockers, head back as I groan. I push at my eyes, as if I could rub the confusion away.

Footsteps come down the hall, light and almost dancelike in the pattern that they make on the floor. I open my eyes and let my head crane in that direction to see Paul coming from the restrooms. "That went well," he says, and I can hear the sarcasm.

"Don't rub it in. I can't take it right now."

"I can try again tonight," he offers. "It's like she doesn't even remember she was dating you, does she?"

"We weren't dating." Which is true. We'd decided we couldn't, not until the play was over. We were just enjoying each other's company and doing an awful lot of kissing. "But yeah, I don't think she remembers any of it."

He leans against the locker next to me, hands hooked in his pockets as he mimics my stance. "Which doesn't make any sense. There isn't something that can just erase a person's mind like that. And last I knew, you two were pretty tight."

"Ms. Jackson caught us in the supply closet," I admit. "That's why I was there to hear about the school board. Then not long after she was kissing up to James."

"It doesn't make sense."

"Magic wouldn't, I guess."

I realize what I've said when he goes silent. I glance over and he's looking at me, body stiff, waiting like I'm supposed to say something else. Instead I push away from the locker. I can just walk away before it gets any worse.

He reaches out, fingers wrapping with surprising strength around my upper arm, digging in. "Magic? You smoking something?"

I laugh. "You're not going to believe me anyway, so sure, why not tell you the whole story? You think there's something in the water? Yeah, there was. I put it there. I thought it was a potion of true seeming, and I was going to drink it so everyone would see me like I actually am because I'm sick of taking shit since we started rehearsals. Except I got them mixed up, and I think it was true love instead, and James took my water bottle and drank it and gave it to Pepper. Then I lost my second water bottle because I went to talk to Maria when she texted me with a 911, and I figure Ryan and Caitlyn somehow ended up with it. See, it's all really very simple, and we can put it all back to normal if we can just figure out how to counteract a love potion. Right?" The laugh I end with is brittle and sharp, like I'm on the edge of hysteria.

Paul blinks and it surprises me that he looks entirely real and not a bit like Puck. "Magic. Jordan… why would you even need a potion of true whatever?"

"True seeming. To look like what I'm supposed to look like," I say flatly. "Because this damned play is making people look at me sideways, and they're going to start seeing things."

"Just because they're calling you girly?" Paul shakes his head. "Jordan, take it from someone who's been hearing that since he was seven: it doesn't matter what they say. All that matters is what you know. And besides, with your build"—he motions at my shoulders, at the muscles visible in my arms—"they're obviously wrong."

"But they're not."

Oh God.

That was out loud.

He's looking at me, and I'm looking back, and I don't have any idea how to rescue the conversation now.

"You're a girl?" he asks quietly.

I shake my head quickly, hands clenching at my sides. I can feel the panic stealing in. "No. Not at all. Well. Biologically. But I'm not female. And if you tell a soul—"

"I won't," he says quickly, but at the same time, he takes a step backward, as if he can't stay too close to me. "Jordan. Did you tell my sister?"

"No way in hell. I don't plan on it."

Dead silence and his expression is mostly flat with an edge of angry. "Did it ever occur to you that she might've wanted to know that she's kissing a girl?" Paul asks quietly.

"She's not kissing a girl!" I press my lips together, the yell echoing off the lockers. Thank God we're alone out here. "Biology has nothing to do with who I am," I say as evenly as I can. "*This* is why I didn't want to play Viola. Everything's been *fine* until the play came along and messed everything up. Now people are looking at me funny."

"Which is why you had a magic potion." He still looks dubious, and I wonder what he'd think if I told him Puck had his face.

Hand over my face, I press fingers against my eyes, then slowly push my hand up, shoving my long bangs back from my face. "I'm going insane, I know it. But this—it can't be explained any other way, Paul. One minute everything's fine, the next it's turned upside down. It's like Puck skipped through and put his drops on their eyes and now they can't see anyone but each other, no matter what they'd prefer."

"You think she'd still prefer you?" he asks, and I can tell by the way his gaze skims over me that he's still stuck on the subject of my biology.

I try not to let it get to me. "Yeah. I do. I kissed her, and she kissed me back. If it weren't for the magic, we'd still be together."

"And you'd be lying to her," he says quietly.

No, I wouldn't, not in my eyes, but I guess I can see why he says it that way. "Telling her now isn't going to change anything. We need to figure out how to break the spell."

He walks up to me, coming in close, as strong as if he weren't smaller and skinnier than me. "I'll help you get her back, if you help save the play. And if you tell her the truth."

"If things go back to normal, I'll tell her." My jaw sets. "I'm already helping with the play." I refuse to promise anything more than that because I can guess where he's going with that thought.

"Fine." He nods slowly. "For what it's worth, I don't believe in magic."

"Yeah, well, neither did I." I nod at the door. "Go on out. Tell James I'll be there in a minute."

I wait until he's gone before I let myself collapse back against the lockers all over again. I close my eyes, the darkness closing in and enfolding me, the familiarity of the near panic attack almost comforting. It's a known sensation, and it doesn't scare me anymore. I let myself float in it for a little while before I take a deep breath. Nothing I can do about it now except trust Paul, and hope he's worth that trust.

CHAPTER 18: Panic Call

I SPEND most of Friday trying to guess where the next attack will come from. Paul knows the truth about me now, and no matter how much I tell myself to trust him, I keep expecting something to change. The guys in the locker room have a field day with how jumpy I am, slamming locker doors and laughing when I spin around and glare. There's nothing malicious about it, and it isn't even about me being Viola. It's just boys-will-be-boys kind of fun at my expense. I duck into the privacy space in the locker room to get dressed, and that's when it changes, when the catcalls start about whether the cut of my dress for the play will show off my scars.

I don't dignify it all with a response, and they go quiet before I'm done changing. When I come back out, Tyler is sitting on one of the benches, and he tosses my shoes to me. I put them on quietly and give him a nod, figuring he must have run them off for me. He nods back and goes out without saying anything else.

I guess the play is bringing us all together, one united front against the school. I wonder how long it'll last when Paul tells them the truth.

I twist and worry about it all day, my mind wrapped around the idea and unwilling to let go. But when I walk into rehearsal, Dower yells for me to get my tailbone down to the choir room for musical practice as if nothing's any different than it is at any other time. Paul looks up when I get there and holds my gaze for a moment.

I don't look away. High school's like the animal kingdom; don't show fear, especially to the weaker ones.

After a moment, his mouth twists into a sort of half smile, and he shifts his path to walk near me before he leaves. "We're thinking about getting together at my house this weekend to talk about the school board meeting," he says. "You'll be there, right?"

"Who's we?"

"Just about everyone in the cast." Paul ticks them off on long fingertips. "You, me, Britney, James, Pepper, Ryan, Caitlyn, Zachary, Tyler... I've left Lianne out of the mix, because she's still tight with Emily, and we don't need any spies passing secrets."

I laugh, and the sound is more forced than normal. "You're having fun with the whole secret ops thing, aren't you?" I try to tease.

He grins, and suddenly Puck is there again as he goes up on one toe and spins around, touching my forehead with a lazy fingertip as he comes down to the ground once more. "If must we deal in things we wish were not, then must we not deal in things as we wish they were?" A soft smell of earth and roses scents the air, and then the image is gone and Paul's standing a step away, grinning as if he had never been that close to me.

"Always wanted to get into spying, and I've got the organization to run this like an op." He shrugs, mischief in his expression. "Why not have fun with it while life's busy trying to suck?"

"With love's loss, find what can be found whilst seeking lost love." I don't know where the words come from, but there they are on the tip of my tongue and spoken aloud.

Paul gives me a quizzical look. "Something like that, I guess, yeah." The door to the choir room opens again, and James comes in, stopping when he sees Paul and me talking. Paul shrugs again. "I'll text you and let you know when."

Rehearsal goes on after that, and it's a few solid hours of singing, blocking, and more singing. By the end of it, my throat feels dry and ragged, and I'm just done with being in James's presence at all. When we get home, I plead headache and grab a bottle of soda and a bag of chips (unhealthy, I know) and close myself in my room. It's not just that I'm done with James, but I'm done with people overall.

Mom and Dad go out to a movie, and James goes out with Pepper (just what I wanted to hear him talking about, yeah). Sam's old enough to watch Leigh, so I make sure Sam has Karen's number in her phone (she already did) and tell them to pretend I'm not here so I can stay locked in my room.

No computer. No instant messenger. Nothing. I leave my phone on in case of emergency, then put my headphones on and crank the sound up for some headbanging loss of hearing.

I almost miss it when the phone goes off with a text. It's late, sometime after eleven, and I'm not even sure who's home at this point and who's not, although the girls ought to be in bed by now. I grab the phone and flip it open to find Maria's text.

Maria: *911 come get me?*

Me: *y? Whassup?*

The phone rings then, and I toss the headphones to one side, the music loud enough to still be audible while they're lying on my bed. Phone pressed to my ear, I lie down. "Yeah?"

"I'm on the corner of Wasserman and High Street, just down the way from Pond." Maria's voice hitches. "I need a ride. *Please*, Jordan."

"Are you hurt?" I start hunting for my shoes blindly, hand patting the floor to seek them out. Finding one, I shove my foot into it. "Do you need me to call your home?"

"No! Dios, no, Jordan." Her voice cracks, and she moans softly. "Don't call them. Please, don't call them. I'm not—I don't think it's bad. I just. I need you to come get me. Please." She hesitates before adding, "And I need a place to stay."

I shove my other foot into my second shoe, then grab my jacket. I can't quite shrug into it and keep the phone, so I have to pause. My heart's hammering, because I can hear her fear. "Are you *safe*?" And I wonder who found out, who saw her, who's hurt her. Because she can say she isn't hurt, but I hear it in her voice. Something happened. Something awful and terrifying.

Panic clutches at my chest as I imagine standing on the street corner in Allston, a slip of paper in my hand, and saying *Maria Jimenez died on October twenty-third*. I imagine having to *remember* her, and that spurs me into action. I grab my keys and I'm halfway down the stairs before I realize two things: if James isn't here, I don't have a car, and Maria hasn't responded yet.

"Are you *safe*?" I ask again, pushing her with my voice as best I can.

"I nodded," she says quietly, sounding almost defeated. "I—you can't see it. I'm just tired, Jordan. I'm going to sit down here a bit. There's a pagoda thing here, like some kind of memorial, I don't know what. There're flowers. And—thank you." Her hoarse whisper is almost too quiet to hear.

"Don't move," I order. "Just stay put and I'll be there as soon as I can." Which will be as soon as I can get my hands on a car.

I check the garage and the driveway, but my folks and James are still out, which means all the cars are gone. Plus I can't walk out while the girls are sleeping, just in case they wake up. I may've told Sam to call Karen if she needed anything, but my folks still think I'm the one in charge tonight.

So I call Karen first, and she's at the library studying but she says she can drive over to be here in case the girls need her. Sometimes having a big sister is amazing, especially when she doesn't ask stupid questions about where I need to go and why.

Then I call James. He's breathless when he answers the phone, and I try not to think why, blurting out instead, "I need the car. Maria's in trouble."

He hesitates. I'm waiting for some snappy comeback, and I'm ready to protest. But instead I get murmurs and him saying, "I can be home in fifteen minutes. Okay?"

What can I say? Wherever he is, he probably has to drop off Pepper first, then get here. Fifteen minutes sounds like it'll probably be pretty quick. So I just nod, then say, "Okay," for his benefit since he can't see me any more than I could see Maria.

I close the phone and stuff it into my pocket, finally managing to shrug into my jacket. I can't sit still, so I pace back and forth in the living room. When Karen gets there, she comes in quickly and wraps her arms around me. "What's wrong, Jordan?" she asks.

Karen's easy to talk to, and I let it spill out, or at least, what I know, which isn't much. Her lips press together. "You want to take my car?" she offers. "If she needs someone to talk to, you can bring her home, so we can talk... girl to girl." She only stumbles a little over it. Karen doesn't know Maria like I do, but she met her first as a girl, which I think makes it easier. It's harder when you have to shift pronouns after the fact.

I shake my head. "James is coming, and I want him with me for backup." Just in case Maria isn't as safe as she thought. Just in case we need to protect her.

Karen's smile flickers. "So now it's a guy thing."

And I almost manage to smile in response. "Yeah, it's a guy thing."

When I see the lights of my own car coming into the driveway, I'm out the door. Karen'll tell my parents, my parents'll get pissed off, but it's worth it. I yank open the passenger door and slide into the seat, kind of thankful not to see Pepper in the car still.

I give him the directions and he pulls out of the driveway, but not before giving me a pointed look. "What's Maria doing over by Pond on a Friday night?" His fingers are tight on the steering wheel, and I can see that his mind went where my mind went when I heard the address.

See, there're only two reasons to go to Pond Street. For one, it's a cut through from the north side of town to the south. Sort of a back route that takes a little longer but doesn't have any lights or much traffic, but you might get to see chickens crossing the road from a farm or two. This is only useful during the day, really. Which brings us to the second reason to go to Pond Street. At night, people pull off into various spots and walk down to the shore of the lake. Some don't bother leaving their cars and just steam up the windows. But in the end, it's all about the hookup.

Where Maria is waiting is close enough to Pond that she could've walked there. And there is pretty much no other reason to be down in that area; it's all suburban housing.

Which means yeah, she's probably been parking.

"She has a boyfriend," I admit to James.

His expression twists, and I see the shudder roll through him. I look away.

"Jordan, you have to admit—"

"What?" I interrupt him. "She's a *girl*, James. She might've been born with boy bits, but she's still a girl and she fell in love and what do you *think* happens? Just because God fucked up doesn't mean we're not still teenagers, with hearts and hormones and all the fun that brings. She's a girl, who met a guy, and yeah, they were probably parking on Pond because that's what couples *do*. You can't tell me you weren't just making out with Pepper somewhere."

"That's beside the point. We're both—"

"What?" I interrupt again. "Normal? Is that it?"

He pulls up to a stop sign, jamming his foot down on the brake. "Yeah. Normal, Jordan. She was born a girl and I was born a guy and it's just the way things are supposed to be."

"And Maria's not." My throat feels too tight. "I'm not."

Silence. Fuck.

I'm cold and starting to shiver. My teeth chatter audibly, and James reaches to turn the heat up.

"There's nothing wrong with you, Jordan," he finally says.

"I know that." But I don't believe he does. He doesn't say anything else, and I just let it go as we drive through the darkness.

CHAPTER 19: Delivering Maria

WHEN WE get to the corner, I can see the pagoda, half in shadow from a streetlight. James pulls up to the curb and I jump out running, which it occurs to me after about six steps might be stupid. But there doesn't seem to be anyone else here except me, James, and Maria, huddled in a corner. I fall to my knees next to her, hands on her face, touching to make sure she's okay.

When I get to her shoulders, she winces and pulls her jacket over where I can see a bruise forming.

"What happened?" It's a stupid question, but I ask it anyway, because even though I know it had to be her boyfriend, I don't know the details. And some of them might turn out to be important.

Her gaze flicks toward James who is hovering somewhere near the car, watchful but staying back. I don't know if it's because we were arguing, or because he doesn't want to get close to Maria, or because he thinks he'll see trouble faster back there. Whatever it is, it's handy for me right now, because Maria speaks, voice low and hoarse.

"I took one of your things." She doesn't look in my eye as she says that, so I just tell her I know and stroke her hair, encouraging her to go on without me yelling at her. "I thought it'd make him see me like I am. I mean, either that or it'd just be some random-colored liquid and not do anything at all. It seemed like I might as well take the chance."

Funny, that's pretty much how I thought about it when I tried to do the same thing. Look where it got me.

"So I slipped it into his soda when he wasn't looking, and we were down by the pond, lying down on a blanket, and we were making out. And things were getting kind of heavy, so I figured he was really into it, and that meant the potion thing was working." She flinches as I touch her shoulder. "That's when it all went wrong, and I saw him for what he really was."

True seeming. She'd meant to take true sight, but she grabbed true seeming. At least I know what the one in my backpack is, now.

She sits up, and as her jacket falls open, I can see just how bad it is. Her shirt's ripped, and her bra's half off one shoulder, and one of her balloon boobs is missing. There're bruises across her shoulder, and a really bad one around her eye. "How bad did it get?" I ask.

"He didn't kill me," she replies.

And she has a point. It could've been worse. It could've been a lot worse.

"He started yelling about how I had a hard-on and how gross was that, that I've got a dick under my skirt. And I yelled back because what the fuck does it matter if I'm a girl with a dick? It happens! God fucks up and this is how we come out and I happen to like being me." Her voice raises, and I see James glance over at us. He has to be hearing us, but I can't see his expression.

I stroke her hair, because it's a part of her I'm pretty sure isn't bruised, and it seems to help settle her some to have that contact. This isn't what I thought would happen with true seeming. I mean, if he's an asshole, I thought she'd just see it. I didn't think it'd make him become his true self and act like even more of an ass. Fairy magic doesn't work the way we think it would, I guess. It's something I need to think about more, later. Maria's more important than my problems right now.

"We need to get you to a hospital. Or home. Or something," I tell her. We can't just sit here all night and I'm not sure I can take her to my home. I don't know what my parents would do. Probably call her parents and then tell me that they have the right to behave however they want since she's only sixteen. No, that's not an option at all.

"I can't go home. I—" Her voice hitches. "I called Mama, and she said it was my own fault, going around dressed like a girl and making out with boys. She said if this is who I am, then maybe she doesn't want me to come home at all. Ever."

Oh crap. That's worse than I thought.

"What about your psychiatrist?" James's voice comes from nearby, and I realize he's crept up quietly while I was focused on Maria. I look at him, then put my arm under Maria's shoulder and help her stand. He hesitates for a moment before he comes in to support her from the other side. And he has a point; if anyone can at least tell us what to do, it's Dr. Hewitt. Especially since it sounds like the Jimenezes have essentially tossed Maria out.

Dr. Hewitt gave me her number at a time when I still had bandages on my wrists and stitches that hadn't yet turned into scars. I remember she both gave me the number on a card, and she wrote it in Sharpie on my bandages. She told me to call her any time I needed her, day or night, even if it meant waking her up. She never wanted me to feel so alone that I did that again.

I've called her three times since then. Once that night, just to test out that I really could. And it helped, knowing she was there. Once was right before I started hormone suppression therapy, when I was terrified that my boobs were going to become huge overnight like some of the other girls' had, and she talked me out of the panic attack I was having. And the last time was after my first day of school in eighth grade, when I'd been through an entire day as a boy and no one had said a word that meant they thought otherwise. I'd wanted to tell her some good news for once, and I didn't want to wait until our appointment.

I make sure that James has Maria securely first. They walk slowly, Maria limping and James's jaw set and angry. I let myself fall a few steps behind while I dial the number.

It's midnight now. She's not going to be happy about this.

The phone rings four times, and an answering machine picks up. I listen to her voice talking, and I panic, because it's her cell phone and I don't have her home number, and what if she can't hear it ringing? So I hang up and try again, just in case I need to wake her up. It's rude, but I need to do something other than standing around here shivering in the cold, while Maria shivers out of fear.

This time she picks up on the second ring with a sleepy-sounding hello. For a moment I forget how to speak, then I force out, "Dr. Hewitt? It's Jordan. And it's kind of an emergency."

"Are you okay?" She sounds tired, but the words come quickly.

"I'm fine," I reassure her, "but Maria's not. She's been beaten up, and her mom told her not to come home."

Silence on the other end of the phone.

"Dr. Hewitt?" I prod gently, worried that she's gone back to sleep.

There's a rustling noise, and a moment later she finally speaks. "She should go to the hospital."

I shake my head, stopping to stand still for a moment, the phone cradled by my ear. "She won't go. Her mom kicked her out, and she doesn't have any way to pay for it, and she's scared."

Silence again, for a long time, then a murmur of voices in the background. When she comes back, she asks, "Can you get her here?"

I feel the breath rush out of me. She's going to help, thank God. "Yeah, James is driving. I'm going to sit in the back with Maria."

"How bad off is she?" There's more murmuring in the background, the deep rumbling voice of her husband close by.

I glance over at where Maria is leaning against the car. She has the jacket pulled in tight around her while James sits inside the car already. "She says nothing's broken, but she's pretty bruised. Her boyfriend ripped her shirt, and um, given how it went, I'd bet he kneed her in the nuts, too. She didn't say that specifically, but he was pretty offended by her anatomy."

Murmurs, while she relays that information. "I'll take a look at her, but if she needs more care, we'll have to take her to the ER. She needs to think about whether she wants to file a police report, too. And we're going to have to contact child services."

Well, the police report would be awfully practical, but I have a feeling it isn't going to happen. I don't even want to think about the child services part. "Yeah. We'll be there soon. And thanks, Dr. Hewitt."

"You're my kids," she says, voice softening. "What else can I do?"

The phone clicks and she's gone. I hurry over to the car and open up the door to the back, nudging Maria in before I climb in with her. "Dr. Hewitt said to bring her over." James has dropped me off many times, so I know he knows where to go. It's not all that far from where we live.

Dr. Hewitt's a great psychologist. She's probably not supposed to get so personally involved with us, but she's always been good to those of us that she calls her kids. When she started the group for transgender teens, she tried to get to know us, get us talking about our lives in the real world. And she lets us know a little more about her, too. Maybe it's not perfectly professional, but it makes her real somehow. And I like that about her.

And it means we can trust her when we need her. Like now.

When we pull up, there's a light on the porch, and I can see a few lights inside the house. The door opens and Dr. Hewitt's husband comes out, coming down to pull open the back door to the car as soon as James pops the locks. I slide out and reach back in, gripping Maria's hand; she clings to me in return.

"It's okay," I whisper. "I'm not going anywhere until I know you're safe, okay?"

She hesitates, looking at Mr. Hewitt, and I'm not sure if she's ever met him before. "That's just Dr. Hewitt's husband. He's cool," I tell her, tugging a little. "She's going to take care of you, and we'll figure out where to go from here."

Maria finally emerges from the car by inches. She clings to her jacket with one hand, the zipper twisted in her fingers, and clings to me with her other. I try to switch my grip to help her out, and she only holds on tighter, so I let her. I can only imagine what she's going through, and reality looks so much worse than what I can come up with. Although I can think of some pretty awful things and I'm hoping none of those happened.

Mr. Hewitt takes a step toward Maria and she fades back, hiding behind my shoulder. He's a big guy, dark-skinned and hair close-cropped in a kind of buzz cut. He's ex-military, I think, but in business now. I don't really remember the specifics. But he backs up when Maria shrinks from him, and his voice is low and mellow as he says, "Come inside, and Ann'll take a look at you, Maria. I'm not going to hurt you."

Her mascara is smudged, making her eyes look like a raccoon's even as she blinks at him. She nods, and moves slowly up the walk, limping like something aches. James moves in close to her other side and she lets him slip an arm under her shoulder so she can lean on him to get up the three steps.

Mr. Hewitt kisses Dr. Hewitt when we get inside, and she shoos him up the stairs to check on BethAnn. Then she looks at the three of us. It takes a long time, like she's not just looking at us, but through us, trying to divine exactly what to do. I glance sideways, and James isn't looking at any of us. A point on the wall has caught his fascination, like he's there for that, and he isn't holding on to Maria anymore. And she's still clinging to me so hard it's a wonder I've got any blood left in my fingers.

"Maria, let's go down to the guest room and take a look at just how bad it is," Dr. Hewitt suggests, her voice softer and more gentle than it is in our counseling sessions.

Maria's hand tightens on her jacket, and she swallows, leaning into me. She takes me with her when she walks, but James stays behind. Dr. Hewitt glances at him, but doesn't tell him to stay or go, just lets him stand there in the entryway.

The guest room is down the end of the hall. I've never been in here before, but it looks a little like an interior decorator threw up. Pink and lace, with a few country cow figures on corner shelves as decorations. It's just not my style, and I hadn't figured it for Dr. Hewitt's either. But the place is clean and neat and it smells like roses. Maria relaxes, slowly, when the door shuts and it's just the three of us.

She lets go of me finally, her head dropping so that her hair hides her face in a wave of darkness. Both hands come up to pull the jacket from her shoulders and let it fall. When she hands it to me, I see that the zipper is broken, half torn out, which explains why she was holding it closed so carefully.

The shirt beneath used to be a soft blue baby-doll tee. I remember when she bought it at the mall, with the swirled heart printed on it. It's not anything fancy, which means she'd been getting comfortable with her boyfriend. She was still dressing for him—the shirt only comes to her belly button, and she wears low-rise jeans—but it's a T-shirt. The bra on the other hand... that looks like it used to be a lacy thing, but it's shreds now. A half-flat balloon falls from it, and she stares at it on the floor.

Her narrow chest has red imprints on it, like a fist, and as she crosses her arms, she bares one side of her ribs and I can see what looks like a boot cast in red there. Shivering, she finally lifts her chin and I get my first good look at her face in the light.

It's pretty awful, the bruising to her chin and cheek already starting to turn purple and swell, and there's a dark slash of red over her lip and chin where something was cut and bled.

"Is that all of it?" Dr. Hewitt asks. She checks with gentle touch to make sure nothing's broken, asking Maria to breathe in deeply, hold, and let it out.

"Nothing else is hurt," Maria says. "He kicked me, but I got away."

Dr. Hewitt looks crushed, as if seeing Maria in this condition has somehow ripped her heart out. We three all sit on the bed, and I keep thinking I should leave them alone, but then Maria's hand grips mine again and I couldn't go if I wanted to. When Dr. Hewitt asks what happened, it all spills out again, everything but the potion Maria took from me.

"This is assault," Dr. Hewitt says.

Maria stares at her knees. I nudge her shoulder lightly, and she says, "I know. But I'm not going to charge him."

"Why not?" I try to keep the outrage in check, but honestly? I want to go find him and hurt him as badly as he hurt her.

"Because he's right," she says flatly. "I lied. I didn't tell him there was a dick under my skirt. I didn't tell him that I wasn't born a girl. And because when he said I sounded like I was proud to be a girl with a dick, well, he was right. I am. I don't need to have it cut off to prove I'm a girl."

"That doesn't give him the right to beat you up, Maria." Dr. Hewitt is using her counselor's voice, soft and urging, trying to bring Maria around gently.

"I know. But I don't think I want to go through a trial or anything, either." Maria looks at us, first me, then Dr. Hewitt. "Can you imagine what it'd be like, standing there on some witness stand, in front of some jury of people who don't get it, trying to explain who I am and why I am? It's like trying to swim uphill. Even when you think you can trust someone, you can't."

"Not everyone's like this guy. Some of them are like James," I remind her.

She just looks at me, smile sad. "James hardly wanted to touch me. And he's afraid of me."

I want to protest, but I remember how he looked when we left him out there in the entryway. I wonder if he'll still be there when I get back.

Maria shrugs, shoulder brushing against mine. "He wouldn't have done it if I hadn't gotten hard while we were kissing. I don't think he'll hit a normal girl." And it makes me ache to hear her say that, like she's *not* as normal as the rest of them.

"We'll sleep on it," Dr. Hewitt says firmly, and I know it's not settled yet. "And we're going to get you checked at the hospital." Maria gives her a wary look, and Dr. Hewitt smiles gently. "I had to call child services. I'd be risking my license if I didn't. They want you taken in to the hospital, and we'll work out how to pay after. Someone will want to talk to you there as well, and you may change your mind after that."

Maria shakes her head, but I hope she does. I don't want Marco to get away with attacking her.

Dr. Hewitt looks at me then. "Jordan, you and James should go home." Maria grips my hand again, and I make a small noise of protest as Dr. Hewitt continues, "Let him go, Maria. You'll be safe here, and you can text Jordan first thing in the morning. It's better that he go home before he and James get in trouble with their parents."

Maria looks so lost. I wrap my arms around her, pulling her in close and hold on tight, pressing my lips against the side of her hair. "You're going to be okay," I whisper to her. "I won't let it be any other way. And if you have to go to trial to get this bastard, I'll go with you, and even if I can't be next to you on the stand, I'll be there for everything else. You know that, right?"

She laughs, her smile weak as she pulls back and kisses my check. "Best. Friend. Ever. Thank you for rescuing me, Jordan."

I touch her hair, then cup her cheek. "I'm just glad you called. I'll be your white knight any time you need one." I kiss her forehead then, and when her breath hitches, I pull her in for one more hug. It's a little while before I can convince her to let me go.

CHAPTER 20: Arguments

JAMES IS still standing in the entryway where I left him. His jacket's buttoned up, and his arms are crossed as he stares at the family pictures hanging on one wall. There's no one else around. I'm figuring Mr. Hewitt went back to bed, and hopefully we never woke BethAnn up.

He looks at me when I walk in.

"Maria's going to be okay, thanks for asking," I say.

"We need to get home," he replies.

Okay, so we're just supposed to ignore everything? We're supposed to pretend like tonight never happened, like my best friend wasn't beaten up just because she's a girl? I don't think so. I catch up with him as he pulls the door open, but he goes through and lets it start to close behind him, like I'm not even there.

"What the hell is going on?" I ask as soon as we're outside. I run down the steps, catching up to him again at the car. "What's got you in such a snit? Are you pissed off that I dragged you away from a date with *my* girlfriend to go rescue my best friend?"

He looks at me. Just stands there, hands by his side, balled into fists, and stares at me, using those few inches of height he has on me to really get a good glare down going. "That could've been you."

So, looks like we're ignoring the entire subject of Pepper. Fine. I'll come back to it. "But it wasn't. No one knows, James." A lie, and I remember how awkward things were between Paul and me as soon as I'd spilled the beans. But I just keep lying. "And no one's going to find out. Y'know, Maria doesn't even want to press charges because it means standing up in front of people and talking about it. And I can't blame her for that part of it, because it's not like I want to strip myself emotionally in public either!"

"Just because you don't want it to happen doesn't mean it won't, Jordan." He pushes at the short spiky strands of his hair, threading his fingers through in frustration. When he's done, it's all standing up on end. "This is your life, Jordan. You're always pretending. You're always going to be worried about getting caught. It's probably not the last time I'll be out here in the middle of the night picking up after you or Maria, is it? Because you'll never be happy just trying to be yourself. You'll want more."

Is he saying this? Is he really, truly, going off on me about this? "You're the one who told me you weren't surprised I had a crush on Pepper," I say quietly. "You're the one who told me Mom'd kill me, but go for it anyway. And now you're telling me that I *should* live a loveless life just in case some nutcase gets offended by my genitals? Or are you just saying it because it'll make you feel better about stealing my first *girlfriend* away from me?"

He gives me a bewildered look. "She wasn't your girlfriend, Jordan. You can't date. You can't risk it. Just like you can't piss in a urinal or strip in the middle of the locker room. You're not actually a *boy*."

I can't believe he just said that.

I stand there with my mouth hanging open, waiting for the punch line. Waiting for him to tell me he's joking, that it isn't real. That this is some weird fever dream because we've been driving around for half the night. I'm half tempted to pinch myself, because we've slipped over into a bizarro world where my best friend and supportive brother is telling me he doesn't believe in me anymore.

There is honest bewilderment in his expression, like he's waiting for me to agree. I feel my breath starting to shake in my chest; I can't quite get enough oxygen. "That's not true," I force the words out.

"You were born a girl," he says. "You're on your way to being a guy as best you can, but underneath it all, your biology is female. And until that's different, that—" He waves a hand angrily at the house. "—could be you. Some girl could realize you've got breasts and go completely insane and beat you, or get some guy to beat you up for her. And it could be even worse if a guy figures it out. *Think* about it, Jordan, just *think* what could happen to you. I'm supposed to be protecting you from that, which means that yeah, sometimes I've got to be the realistic one. I've got to be the one who remembers who you actually are."

"I thought you knew who I was." My voice sounds hollow, and I take a step back. Maybe this is the real James. Maybe he's saying what he always thought, and he's never really been the supportive brother I thought I had. It sounds like he thinks it's some phase I'll grow out of. "I'm taking T, James. I'm not a girl. I've never really been a girl, not where it counts."

"When you get a girlfriend, try telling her that. *Before* you get physical. She'll probably want to know."

The pain in my chest feels like he sucker punched me. All the breath escapes in a soft whoosh and I'm left gasping, hungry for air, desperate to breathe normally again. "I had a girlfriend," I whisper.

He shakes his head. "Pepper? No, Jordan, you never had her."

I'm walking before I think about it, stalking off down the street. It's about five blocks to our house, which isn't far, but they're suburban blocks, which means it isn't close, either. It'll give me time to think. And cool off, before I put my fist in my brother's face.

I don't even really know what I want to punch him for first. He called me a girl. He stole my girlfriend. He—he infuriates me right now. I feel betrayed by everything he said tonight, like after seventeen years I'm realizing that he doesn't know me at all.

My footsteps slow. Is it the potion making him act this way? True love. I don't see what's so true about it. Did he have a thing for Pepper before? Or did it *make* them fall in love, the way it made Marco act like an ass? That's it, I think. Just like Puck's flower eyedrops. Fairy magic makes love where it didn't exist before, with the first person they laid eyes on, which was each other for James and Pepper.

The problem is, it's obvious that true love from a vial lasts longer than a few hours. It's been a day already, and he doesn't seem to think there's anything wrong. I want to ask him about Britney, but it's too late. The car's starting, half a block behind me, and a moment later he drives by without even slowing down.

The worst part is that his words sting more than any taunts I've heard from anyone else, just because it's James that's said them. He's always been right there by me. When I was little, we played in the same soccer league. I always played with the boys anyway, because I played harder than the girls did, and I didn't want anything to do with them. I wanted to play on James's team. We were inseparable.

When things happened, when my whole life turned upside down, James was right there with me. It was confusing for a few years there. I didn't know what was going on, and he didn't know what to think. But when I needed someone to back me up, he did, without hesitation. He wasn't going to let anyone tease his sister, and when I informed him sharply that I was his brother, he just said *that too* and went on with life.

He's always been the most amazing person I know. The *best* person, and my best friend.

Now this.

And I can try to rationalize it away all I want, that it's some side effect of the potion somehow, but I don't think that's right. Why would magically falling in love with Pepper suddenly make him hate me for who I am? Why would it make him stop being my rock?

It wouldn't.

Which means he's always resented me, somewhere underneath it all. And tonight just made it come out.

I trudge home slowly, not really wanting to get there. My phone tells me I have a text so I flip it open to see a *g'night my knight* from Maria that makes me smile. I also see that's it one thirty in the morning, and my parents' car is next to mine and James's car in the driveway. It looks like Karen is already gone.

Time to face the music, I guess.

I go in through the garage, and they're waiting there, in the kitchen. There's no sign of James. I'm surprised when they don't just start yelling, and I don't exactly know what to say to them, either. So we stand there, me with my hands in the pockets of my hoodie, them sitting at the table, and we stare at each other. I finally shrug and offer a quiet, "Hi."

"James told us about Maria," Mom says. The whistle on the teapot sounds, and she gets up, pouring hot water into three mugs. She drops a spoon into one, giving it a quick stir before she hands it to me and sits down again, nudging one cup to Dad and keeping one for herself.

I take a long sniff: hot chocolate. It may be from a packet, but it's still comfort food, and one way for Mom to say *I love you* with a mug. I give her a wary look, not sure if I'm being comforted or chastised. When she answers by pointing at the chair, I sit.

"James told us what happened to Maria," Dad repeats. He has that serious look, the one that makes him look exhausted by life, as if we kids have worn him out. "We understand why you left."

"I made sure Karen came over, in case the girls woke up." Which doesn't entirely defend me walking out after curfew when I'm technically sort of maybe but not exactly babysitting for my sisters. "I didn't want them to get scared."

Mom's hand covers mine where it rests on the table. "You're grounded for going out after curfew, and for not calling us to let us know what was going on before you left. You could have both been walking into a very dangerous situation, and no one knew where you'd gone," she says. "Two weeks, and we'll talk then about it being lifted. James is grounded as well. That means you've got school, your play practice, and your doctors' appointments, and that's it. No going out on the weekends, no having friends in."

I just clench my teeth and nod. It could be good, right? I mean, if James can't go out, or have anyone over, he can't date Pepper. So that's a nice little side benefit.

I could protest, but I don't want to get into another argument. Besides, I walked out, and it's way past when I should be home and in bed. I can't argue getting caught, even if it was for a good reason.

"About Maria," Dad says, and he pauses there. Mom's hand tightens over mine.

I don't have a good feeling about the way they're looking at me. I weasel my hand loose so I can drink some of the hot chocolate. I think I'm going to need it. "She's still my friend, Dad. She's staying with Dr. Hewitt, and child services will be figuring out what else to do tomorrow."

Mom's lips purse together. "James tells me she was dating a boy."

"That's what sixteen-year-old girls usually do, Mom." Flippant, I know, and I brace myself for the added grounding time for my sarcasm.

"But she's not a usual girl," Dad says. "And you're not a usual boy."

"James also tells us you want to start dating," Mom continues before I can get a word out.

Me? I'm going to kill James before he can tell them anything else.

My jaw clenches. "I've already had this argument with James tonight. Can we skip it so I can get some sleep? I promise, you can spend all breakfast tomorrow reminding me that I'm not a real boy, and that I'm still dangling from the feminine puppet-strings. But right now, it's almost two in the morning, and I'd kind of like to get some sleep."

Mom sighs. "It's for your own safety, Jordan."

"You can't wrap me in a bubble!" So much for shutting down the argument. Good going, self, maybe we should stop talking?

"Jordan." Dad's voice has that end of discussion tone, and I bite my tongue to keep from saying anything else. "Fine, we'll talk in the morning, when you're ready to be reasonable. But I think you can at least agree that you are in no way ready to date."

"When?" I ask. "In this perfect little world you've got going in your head, when are you going to admit that your *son* is ready to have his first *girlfriend*?" Because it's not fair. I remember Karen going on dates when she was fifteen. James asked a girl out for the first time when we were in seventh grade. I never even kissed a girl until recently. I'm ready to *live*, damn it.

"When my son is my *son*," Dad growls. "I won't let you risk yourself until I can be sure you'll be safe."

I don't want to deal with it right now. I don't want to feel like my life is being put on hold because God fucked up when I was born. "Yeah, whatever." I push my chair back, shoving myself to my feet. "I need to get some sleep."

My dad makes a noise, but I hear the murmur of my mom's voice, and neither of them comes after me as I walk out.

James is waiting in my room when I get there, sitting in my desk chair, idly twisting it back and forth.

"Are you going to apologize or yell at me more?" I walk by him and drop my jacket on the foot of the bed. I can't get ready for bed while he's in here, but I can at least pull out my pajama pants and a T-shirt. When he doesn't say anything, I walk out of the room, heading for the bathroom and a chance at some privacy.

"Jordan, wait." He catches up with me in the hallway, grabbing my wrist so I have to stop. "Is Maria going to be okay?"

"Do you care?" He winces when I say it, and I feel guilty after. "Yeah, she'll be fine. He didn't—" I don't want to say the words, and I look down at the floor. "He kicked her in the nuts and beat her up, but nothing worse." I figure that'll get the point across, and James nods.

"It could be you."

"You said that earlier." I pull my arm free and head for the bathroom. "I'm not planning on making out with any psycho guys since I'm *straight* and I don't think most girls could beat me up. Plus, I'm going to make sure I can trust a girl before I tell her." Maybe. Unless Paul tells Pepper first. The thought makes me start to shake. I groan softly. "Look, James, bad timing. Whatever your guilt is, it'll keep until morning. Just—leave me alone. I want to sleep. I want to talk to Maria tomorrow. That's it."

And I want everything to go back to the way it was just a few days ago, but I don't know if I can manage that miracle. I always thought having magic at my fingertips would improve life, not make it more miserably complicated the way it has. I've read enough Shakespeare, you'd think I'd know better. "All's well that ends well," I murmur, and God, I hope that's true in the end. But how do I get to the ending well part of it?

"I'm just trying to protect you," he says, and I'm starting to feel like it's a broken record. Him. My parents. Him again.

"I get it," I say sharply. "But someday the baby bird gets to fly on its own. So deal with it already."

I slam the door to the bathroom behind me, giving myself some brief moment of privacy. For a moment I catch a glance of the angry boy in the mirror glaring out at me, then I refuse to look at him. It's late enough at night, and it's been one of those days, that I'm half-afraid that if I look hard enough, I'll see *her* staring back at me instead.

INTERLUDE: Paul

JUST YESTERDAY Paul had listened to Jordan blurt out that he was a biological girl, and that he believed he'd used a magic potion to confuse everyone's relationships. A day later, Paul watched those relationships just keep splintering even more as rehearsal wore on. Jordan wasn't speaking to James but watched Pepper all the time. Britney was late, arriving red-eyed and angry. Ryan and Zach had fought at the start of rehearsal until Caitlyn dragged Ryan away, whispering soothing things to him. She took him outside the auditorium to neck in the hallway by the bathrooms.

It was madness, and it wasn't lifting. Which meant Jordan was wrong, it wasn't some Shakespearean fluke. It was something deeper.

And the worst was, Paul felt like it was somehow his job to sew the show back together, and yet, he couldn't manage to even thread the needle. He'd tried talking to people at the start of rehearsal about having a meeting over the weekend about the school board problem, but with James and Jordan both grounded for reasons neither of them was willing to explain, it had fallen through.

The school board meeting was less than a week away, and no one knew what to do.

Paul climbed the metal stairs at the back of the stage, walking out with quiet steps onto the catwalk until he could sit with his legs dangling over the edge. He leaned out, trusting his balance to keep him safe, fingers wrapping around the metal edging, as he peered down to the scene below. Jordan, as Viola, spoke to Ryan, as Orsino. Jordan's body language as a woman was stiff and awkward, everything seeming held in and closed down. "Relax," Paul whispered, even knowing Jordan couldn't hear him. He reached out, wiggling his fingers as if to sprinkle pixie dust, and Jordan spoke again, the words flowing more easily.

Paul grinned to himself. Sometimes all it took was the power of positive thinking. Better than any magic.

Below him, Pepper walked up to the couple, and Jordan stiffened at her approach. When she reached out to show him the blocking, trying to demonstrate by moving his hand, he jerked away and walked out, calling that he needed a bathroom break.

It was his third already this rehearsal. He was averaging about ten most days, in the several hours between when school ended and the rehearsal was done.

They were all at the breaking point. They needed something to forge them back together better than they had been before.

He heard cautious footsteps and glanced over. Britney hovered at the top of the stairs, one foot at the edge of the catwalk, looking at the narrow waffle-weave metal. She gulped and whispered, "It's an awful long way down."

"Afraid of heights?" Paul pushed easily to his feet. He didn't exactly skip back to her, but he moved on his toes, gait light and flowing, the same as he used for Puck. Heights had never bothered him, not even as a child. Being up here, in his hidey-hole, felt like home to him. He could see everything, but they could see nothing. He felt omnipotent.

Britney stared down through the holes in the weave, her fingers curled tight around the railing. "Academically, I know the tensile strength of the materials and that it can hold a lot more than my weight. In my gut, though, it sways every time I take a step, and I'm afraid we're going to go plummeting down." Her smile wavered. "So yes, I guess I'm afraid of heights. Or at the least, I'm afraid of falling from a height."

Paul pointed to the step and was surprised when Britney sat without hesitation. He crouched on the edge of the catwalk, close to her. "I like a girl who can look at things analytically," he commented.

"If that's a pickup line, you're going to have to do better." Britney glanced over at him.

Paul spread his hands, expression innocent while Puck's mirth danced in his gaze. "I'm attracted to your mind isn't enough of a compliment?"

She sighed and looked away. "If you asked to talk to me up here because you were hoping for a make-out session, then no, it isn't. I'm still trying to figure out how to break up your sister and James." Her smile was rueful when she looked back at Paul. "No offense. Pepper's a nice girl, but she's messing things up in a major way. It took me two years to get James to notice me."

Paul couldn't believe that. He was sure every boy in school noticed Britney, but most of them thought there was no way she'd even notice them. He mentally translated it to *two years of acting like enough of a ditz that James thought he had a chance* and decided that made a lot more sense. He had a feeling that he was going to be doing a lot of translation around Britney, as if her attempts to be intelligent and blonde at the same time had left her not speaking either language.

He cocked his head. "Well, that's part of what we're here to discuss. I need to fix a few things, and I need an ally whose brain isn't completely confused by hormones to help me out. And you, well, you're invested in the problem, but you're also smart, right? I think we can work together to fix our situation."

The group of actors below had shifted and reformed to work on a scene with Sebastian and Olivia. Pepper leaned in against James to direct him, nudging him into position. Paul let his gaze drift away; he didn't need to watch James groping his sister's backside.

"How?"

This was the difficult part. Paul had been watching everyone for the last day, but he had been watching Jordan in particular. "That's the complicated part. And I'm going to have to ask you to suspend your disbelief, because some of what I'm about to tell you seems... impossible."

"The whole situation is ridiculous," Britney commented drily. "My boyfriend changed his mind about me practically midsentence. What could be more impossible than that?"

"Magic." Paul whispered for effect, grinning at the dubious look Britney shot him. "At least according to Jordan, and after putting together all the variables, and some fairly intense observation, I'm thinking that maybe we should believe him." Him. Her. That part was still more complicated, and Paul frowned at the scene below as Jordan came back to the stage. The slender blond boy hesitated at the edge, expression troubled as he watched James and Pepper. When he walked forward, there was a careful *I don't care* swagger in his step. Whatever else Jordan was, Paul couldn't deny how the boy felt about his sister. Jordan wore his heart on his sleeve.

Britney stared down as well, leaning out for a moment until she caught herself and pulled back into the safety of the stairs with a small shudder. "Magic. Where's the joke, Paul?"

"No joke. But there's some history involved." Paul inched onto the step with Britney, shoulder to shoulder with her, looking out over the stage with the same perspective. "It begins with Jordan's birth. You see, he's a she."

Britney blinked. "Huh?"

"Jordan was born a girl," Paul said, voice low. "It all begins with that. Now imagine hiding a secret like that, and then having to deal with the whole school scrutinizing you for playing a female character. The stress got to him."

"It explains a few things."

Paul gave her a sharp look. "Like the fact that he only changes in the privacy room in the gym. He claims he has scars, and he's too embarrassed to have people staring at him. Or the fact that he always uses a stall in the men's room, even when he's pissing."

Britney's gaze narrowed as she looked at him. "I was just thinking that it made sense now why he's so sensitive about playing Viola, when he doesn't seem like the kind of guy who thinks girls are second-class citizens. But are you positive? Who told you?"

"Jordan did." Paul shrugged. "And I can't see any guy lying about it—no offense. It's not that it'd be bad to be a girl, but that most of us happen to like being guys. But if he was telling me the truth about that, then he was probably telling me the truth about the potions."

Below, Pepper had finally stepped back, holding the script with her arms crossed as James and Caitlyn worked their way through the scene. Jordan sat cross-legged nearby, watching Pepper, rolling something in his hand like a worry stone.

Paul grabbed Britney's arm and directed her attention. "There. Look."

Britney leaned into Paul, and he slipped one arm around her back to help steady her. "What am I seeing?" she asked.

"In his hand. He's been playing with that little glass bottle almost constantly," Paul said. "That thing in his hand is the proof that he wasn't lying. Jordan said he had some kind of magic potion, and that he meant to drink it himself, only something went wrong and it made James and Pepper fall in love. Caitlyn and Ryan, too, I think. If Zach could kill Caitlyn, he would. I talked to Zach for a long time last night, and he said Ryan's so gay he couldn't even think about kissing a girl before, but now he's making out with Cait in every corner of the school. It doesn't make sense when you look at it scientifically. Or socially. But it makes perfect sense when you look at it magically."

"This is bullshit." Britney pushed to her feet, wavering as the catwalk swung lazily under her weight. Paul watched her knuckles turn white, she gripped the side rails so tightly. He stood lightly next to her, balanced on the tips of his toes, swaying with the catwalk. "There's no such thing as magic," she said.

"Has anything else worked, or made sense?" Paul asked. He'd reasoned through it for five days, and he didn't like the conclusion either. But when everything else was eliminated, magic was the only thing left that even came close to fitting the facts. "He said something about getting them mixed up, which means that one in his hand is the other potion. And I think we'll need magic to fix magic."

"If the first part makes any sense, then that answer makes sense, but I'm still not sure on the first part." Britney wrinkled her nose. "It's not scientific at all. I want to make charts, look at things more closely."

"I have," Paul said. He glanced at her sideways. "Come over after rehearsal and I'll show you."

She stared at him warily. "Is *that* a pickup line?"

He laughed, spinning away, back up the walkway and a few feet away, where he stopped and bowed low. "My dear Hermia, as beautiful as you are, I know you are meant for Sebastian and not this poor Puck." He grinned, taking quick steps back toward her. "It's not a line, Britney. We'll work together, and figure it out. While we're at it, we need to figure out what to do about the school board."

Britney still stood where she'd been left, tightly gripping the rail of the stairway, leaning against that thin metal bar as she looked out over the rehearsal. Below them, Jordan walked slowly out to take the stage with his brother, the two standing stiffly as if it hurt to be on stage together. Paul couldn't remember them exchanging a single friendly word that day.

Pepper instructed the two to greet each other as if long lost; Jordan awkwardly put his arms around James but pushed back before James could clap him on the back or say a line.

"I need—"

Pepper's shout of "No!" cut off Jordan's quiet, anxious words. "No break," she ordered. "Nothing. Nada. Zip. Not until you two finish the scene and I say you can go while I work with Puck and the fairies. Got it? You are *mine* until I tell you otherwise."

Jordan looked at the floor, then out to the audience, nodding at no one. "Got it."

"She's being brutal," Britney said quietly.

"We're falling apart," Paul replied, just as softly. "Everyone down there is too clouded by fairy juice to see anything else. You and I can see clearly, so it's up to us to pick up the pieces and figure out how to put the mess back together."

PART FIVE
Performance

JOURNAL: Wednesday, October 28

IT'S FUNNY how I used to be afraid of mirrors. Okay, maybe not so funny in the laughing sense, and maybe not so unexpected, either. But it's hard to believe now.

I was looking in the bathroom mirror this morning after my shower. Everything was foggy and blurred, with little droplets left on the glass after I tried to rub the fog away. I was trying to see if I have any facial hair. I know, I've only had two shots. I won't grow a beard yet. Still, I can't help but wonder and look. I fixed my hair while I was there, then gave myself a good, hard look.

And I saw myself staring back.

That's where it gets funny.

Normally, I see me, right? But sometimes it's like I can see through myself to my bones, to the person I was born as, and that's what makes me worry that other people can see that as well. Like *she* peeks through my skin, waiting to be noticed.

This was the first time where I couldn't see any hint of her at all.

I twisted side to side, checking myself from all angles. I let the towel fall, looking critically at my body. I don't like my body because it's still wrong, and it's going to take a lot of time before I can fix what God messed up. My shoulders are good and broad, my pecs strong, my abs just as strong. It's the gentle curves that seem out of place, softness where I should be hard (not to mention parts that are tucked away instead of hanging out).

It didn't bother me this time. I saw all those incorrect bits, but I looked past them and I just saw me—Jordan—staring back. Exactly who I've always thought I am, and there he was in the mirror.

I smiled all the way through getting dressed, then through most of breakfast.

Then James came down, which pretty much ruined it all.

I know we talked about it. And I know you told me that I can't do anything about it. It's Pepper's choice to date James, and his choice to date Pepper. They aren't doing it to get back at me, or to ruin me, or even because I like Pepper.

But knowing all of that doesn't change the fact that it just hurts to think about.

I started taking the bus yesterday. It stops down the end of my street, and it's mostly freshman and sophomores who take it. I know in city schools, like Maria's, most kids take the bus all the time. But around here, kids get cars when they're sixteen, and after that they drive. It's a mark of status. So people look at me a little funny when I climb on the bus, but it's easier than going with James when he picks up Pepper to drive her to school. I get that I can't argue about them dating, but I don't have to watch it, either.

Because it really does still hurt.

What's worst is during rehearsals, because James and I have to work together all the time. The cast is divided up into the three basic groups, without a lot of overlap. So if I'm on stage, he's either on stage with me, or waiting in the wings and running lines. And then she's there.

I caught her watching me yesterday. I was just finishing the scene with Olivia, and I'd done my monologue at the end. I finished, and everything went silent. I looked over at Pepper, waiting for some kind of reaction, and she was just sitting there, with her elbow on her knee, chin on her hand, watching me.

I cleared my throat, and she jerked back, flushed. God, I love how her freckles look when she blushes. She told us it was fine and to take five, and gave me a look as she suggested a bathroom break before we started up again. It was my turn to flush, because okay, so maybe I've been taking a lot of those lately. I just can't stand there and watch her touching him in front of me. So I take a break to cool off. I figure it's better than punching my own brother, right?

We're getting along again, mostly. He's asked after Maria, and he seems worried about her, which is good, I think. And he's stopped being ridiculously overprotective for now. Being grounded has been sort of good for us. We spend most of the evenings in the basement, finishing up homework and watching TV or movies. Dad put in a projector over the weekend, so our TV is now a huge screen against one wall, which is pretty much amazing. It's almost like he was trying to apologize for something, but we're still grounded, and I'm still not allowed to date. I just have a big screen to watch movies on, by myself or with my sisters, once James starts going out with Pepper again.

I guess the only good part of all this is that no one's saying I got the part because I'm dating Pepper. Hard to spread rumors with so much evidence in the other direction. The hazing hasn't gotten worse, not really. There's always someone from the cast in my classes, and except for Lianne, they all pretty much seem to be rallying around me.

I hate that I'm the weak one, that they're all trying to protect me. It shouldn't be that way, should it? There's nothing funnier than Paul and Zach flanking me, walking down the hall and glaring at guys who look like they're going to say something. In some ways, it's better for all of us, and in some ways it's worse. They don't come after us physically, but it's all mental.

I came out of History the other day and FAG had been spray-painted on my locker, on Paul's, and on Zach's. On Ryan's they'd painted "used to be a FAG" and on Cait's they'd put "FAG HAG." No one caught who did it, and no one was punished. Someone said it's just kids being kids, and I asked about the zero-tolerance policy.

He said maybe it doesn't cover fags.

I was going to point out I'm not gay, but Zach pulled me away before we could start a fight there in the hallway. It's like they're trying to get us to make the first move. It's getting harder not to.

I looked things up later, and guess what? The zero tolerance policy very specifically states that the school will not tolerate bullying about race, religion, or sexuality. They give examples that are pretty much what happened to us. Except I read online that transgender issues aren't always covered. It's slippery. It's not exactly sexuality, after all; it's gender, and I guess they don't talk about hate crimes for gender. I also read online about how people can get around these policies by saying that they aren't bullying about sexuality because I said I'm straight. So maybe I should just shut up and take the joke.

Things are poisonous at school, and no one's doing anything about it. I think they don't see it because they don't want to see it, because if they do see it, they have to take sides. And the only people I actually trust in the whole damned school are Dower and Ms. Jackson. And people are very careful to avoid getting caught by those two.

Ms. Jackson did save us from having to clean off our own lockers. She made the janitorial staff repaint them overnight. Zach asked if he could do his in rainbow colors; I don't think he was serious at first, but when she said he could paint his own graffiti on it the next day, he told the janitors to leave it alone.

The next day he brought in paints and he outlined the word FAG in rainbows, and wrote "and proud!" next to it.

Way to own the word, Zach. I'm kind of proud of him. And kind of envious that he can do that, and not let it all get to him. I'm nowhere near as good about it.

I keep wanting to go back to where I was a month ago, when I was just one of the guys. I knew some kids from classes, I knew some kids from sports a while back, and I was in chorus. I wasn't on stage, and no one was looking all that hard at me.

Maybe I should've stayed invisible.

CHAPTER 21: Truth and Lies

WHEN I get off the bus in the morning, I see Paul sitting on the edge of the steps of the school, as far from the ever-present thugs as he can get. As I walk over he stands, hunched in his jacket that looks too big for him, his hands shoved deep into the pockets. It's cold, even for October, like winter's coming early.

Even after almost a week, it's still on the tip of my tongue to ask *where's Pepper* but I manage to bite the words back before they slip out. Paul glances at me with a small rueful smile that seems out of place on his Puckish features. "She's already gone in with James. I was just waiting for you and Britney."

Right. So I stand there next to him, trying not to lean closer (he's about the only pocket of warmth out here) and trying not to lean away. Stand casual, Jordan, that's the way to do it. Don't attract attention. Ignore the sudden loud wolf whistles as Britney joins us.

"It's so tempting to shove my tongue down your throat just to shut them up," Britney grumbles, but the look she shoots me is wary as she says it.

I just shrug. "If I were even the littlest bit interested, I'd say go for it, but you're still my brother's girlfriend. Even if you're not right this second." Paul told me in e-mail last night that he's told Britney about the magic, and that she doesn't believe it. She's still staring at me, and I start to wonder what else he's told her. "What?" I ask.

"Inside." Paul grabs my wrist and Britney's as well. "This isn't a conversation we want to have on the front steps."

"Music room?" Britney suggests. Paul nods, and as soon as we get inside the front door, we all turn to walk toward the music wing. I pull my hand back from Paul; that's just what I need people to see and comment on, adding more fuel to the fire.

"The school board meeting's tonight," Paul starts talking as soon as we make it into the music wing. No one'll be in the practice room right now, so we take it for ourselves. I try not to think about the storage closet, or Pepper, but it isn't easy.

They seem to be waiting for me to say something. "I know," I tell him. "James and I are going. The grounding's being lifted for that."

"What do your parents think about the whole thing?" Britney sits on one of the desks, one leg neatly crossed over the other. Paul leans back against a desk, his phone out, fingers flying as he sends a text.

That's kind of a loaded question. We sat down to talk about it as a family over the weekend. I want to go to the meeting, and James wants to go because it's Pepper's play and all (which might be the same as my reason, but I can't say that to him). My folks are afraid things'll be dangerous for me since it's my role everyone's arguing over. I let out a sigh in a soft huff of breath. "It's complicated," I try to push it off. "What about yours?"

"Is that because of what you are?" Britney's question comes out half-interested, all calm, and too bald for me to ignore.

I clench my hands in my pockets, feeling blunt tips of my fingernails pressing against my palm. When I glance at Paul, he nods faintly, and I have to take several more breaths to get myself on an even keel again. I glare at him, but he doesn't look at all apologetic. "Yes," I say as calmly as I can manage. "They… they don't have anything against Shakespeare, or the gender switching, or the potential gay romance. But they think that all the publicity means I might not be safe. Especially with what's been going on lately around school."

There. She's asked, I've confirmed. Now what? Other than me wanting to strangle Paul, but I can save that for later.

"I wouldn't have guessed," Britney admits. "I mean, I've known you for what, more than four years now? And you've always just seemed all guy to me."

"I *am* all guy," I mutter. "Biology aside, there's no question about that. I'm a boy. Is there a point to dragging this onto the table?"

"Yes." Paul sets his phone on the desk and walks between us. "Betwixt and between, thou art neither one nor t'other."

Oh no, not again. It's been days of sanity (aside from the mess made of my life by the potions) and now the world's spinning again with Puck's words. He touches my forehead and things slide sideways. When I blink, there are leaves in his hair, and his eyes are bright and mischievous. "Fear lies within that which thou knowst not," he says with a laugh, "but that which is known cannot be feared. Show that they have but gone unseeing. Make them see, and they will know no fear."

I stumble back, grabbing on to the edge of the desk behind me to hold me up. His words are weird, but I know what Puck's saying. Be myself. Tell the truth. Make them see that we're not changing anything, that the world is just as it always has been and it wasn't scary before. That I can't hurt anyone.

I start to shiver, cold taking my bones. *No.* I try to speak, but I don't know if it's audible, because I can't hear anything. The world is black light with bright spots, swallowing me whole behind the shutter of my eyelids. There's a vibration through my whole body as I moan, and the shivering starts all over again.

I'm losing myself. They want me to tell.

I can't tell.

I'll never be safe again.

"Jordan?" A soft touch against my shoulder, then warm fingers on my chill cheek. "He's freezing, Paul, this can't be good."

He. Britney called me he. That's good—we haven't taken six steps backward there, at least.

The creak of a door far in the distance and a rumble of voices. "Is Jordan okay? He looks kind of gray."

"He got some difficult news," Paul says, then he's there as well, on my other side. "Jordan, if you don't want to talk to the board, that's okay. We just thought that if you and Ryan and Zach spoke, it'd be the best way to get our point across. Zach's already said he's in for it, so we needed to talk to you and Ryan this morning."

"Why Jordan?"

Okay, so that's Ryan's voice. Another person to tell, another person to hear, another person to look at me strangely from now on and not see me the way I am anymore. Because once they hear, there's no going back. I can't make them unsee the underpinnings of who I am. I start to laugh, the sound too bright in the darkness of nervous hysteria. "You're gay, Ryan. Zach's gay. Me, I'm... I'm...." The laugh tangles in my lungs, and I cough.

Britney pounds me on the back, then ends up rubbing it as I drop my head between my legs. Oh God, now I'm here and I know I'm here. The darkness recedes, but the problem hasn't gone anywhere. When I peek up, Ryan's still looking at me.

"You're gay too? I thought you said—"

"No," I cut him off, trying not to start laughing again, although I can still feel hysteria nibbling around the edges of my mind. "I'm Viola. Except, I'm not, I'm Cesario in truth."

He blinks at me, not getting it, and my laugh is weaker now, hovering like a groan in the air. "I was born a girl, Ryan. I haven't truly been one since I've been old enough to know the difference, but biologically, I'm female," I finally manage to get out.

Silence.

Ryan shrugs. "So. What does that have to do with anything?"

For that, I could kiss him. Relief at this one reasonable response slams into me, taking my breath away all over again, but when I close my eyes, the darkness holds only peace. I let my lungs fill and empty, relaxing.

"The school board." Paul hitches himself up onto the desk next to where I'm leaning. "Everyone's up in arms about how the show is going to lure unsuspecting kids in and somehow convert them. I want to tell them that for one, this is Shakespeare, which has always been gender-bending goodness, and two, knowing that they aren't alone gives kids strength, and helps them."

"And three," Britney added, "that there isn't anything terrifying or scary about discovering gay or transgender people in your community. They're just normal people, like everyone else."

"And you really think that'll work?" I ask, just as Ryan asks what this has to do with him.

Wait, what?

"You're gay," I point out. "You were dating Zach up until a couple of weeks ago."

"Yeah, well." Ryan shrugs with one shoulder. "I thought you were just too shy to change in front of the guys until a few minutes ago. Not everything's what we assume, right?"

Britney looks at Paul, then moves to his side and leans in to whisper something. I could see part of their arguments crumbling in their hands. I haven't said yes yet, and without Ryan, things get awkward, because a guy who used to be gay really only helps the whole "gays can choose" argument, which is not the one we want to put forward.

"So you don't like Zach anymore?" I ask. And it occurs to me that it might be a good time to find out what the limits of the potion are, since I've got someone here right in front of me, and this time I'm not emotionally invested in his relationship. "Do you still think about him at all?"

Ryan glances away from me, toward the door. One shoulder rises and falls in a shrug.

I try pushing a little harder. "So let's say you're locked in a closet, and next thing you know, you're locking lips with someone. The lights come on. It's Zach. Do you freak?"

The look he gives me is so sharp that I feel the bite, but I just smile. "Do you freak?" I repeat.

"No."

Britney and Paul have gone silent, watching us as we talk. I just nod, because I was kind of hoping for that response. "Do you still love him?" They were dating forever; they had to have said the words at some point, I figure.

"I love Caitlyn." His tone starts definite, but there's a confused lilt at the end of it, like he's not altogether sure.

"So, what's it like, making out with her? And how'd you fall in love so fast, anyway?" I'm looking for the chinks that I know are there, digging away to try to make the wall fall down.

"I don't know." His finger traces over the graffiti on the desktop. "I just felt drawn to her, like there wasn't anyone else in the world for me. But…." Ryan's voice trails off.

"But—?" I nudge verbally. Ryan flushes, and I cock my head, waving with my hands. I want to know whatever it is that's embarrassing him.

"Sometimes I think about Zach when I'm kissing Cait," he admits quietly. "I want her. I love her. I *need* her. But in here—" His hand rests against his chest. "—I'm still gay."

"Magic can't hide the truth, nor can it create truth where it is not," Paul says quietly. It takes two looks and I still can't decide if that was Paul or Puck speaking.

"Magic?" Ryan asks.

"Long story," I say quickly before we can go down that road. "Just—have faith, okay? It'll get unconfused eventually." Maybe it'll wear off, or we'll figure out how to put things back to right. Magic can't change anything permanently, can it? In Shakespeare, everything always goes back to normal eventually.

Of course, this isn't Shakespeare. This is my life.

"So you're on board?" Britney asks, nudging my shoulder.

"Yeah." I clench my hand so tightly I can feel my fingernails making little half-moons on my palm. But it keeps the cold away and lets me nod as I answer. "I'll talk to the board. As long as Ryan and Zach talk, too."

The bell rings then, like an exclamation point on my statement. There isn't time for anything else; I have to gather up my things and run to my locker so I'm not late to homeroom.

CHAPTER 22: Emergency Meeting

I DON'T call first before going over to see Dr. Hewitt. Dower canceled rehearsal for today, since all we could talk about was the meeting anyway. James takes the car (and Pepper), and I walk over to Dr. Hewitt's house, hoping she won't mind seeing me unexpectedly. I don't even know if she's working in the office today or if it's her day off with BethAnn.

But I need to talk to someone, and if Dr. Hewitt is busy, maybe Maria will be there.

I waste time on my way over. It's not a quick walk to start, and I need some time to clear my head. I can't believe I agreed to do this tonight. I can't tell James or my mom and dad. They'll freak. I'm going to freak. My life will never be the same. So it's maybe an hour after school lets out when I'm knocking on the door and Maria pulls it open.

She throws her arms around me, kissing my cheek noisily as she drags me into the house. "Jordan! I thought you were grounded."

Crap. "I am. Mom and Dad think I'm at rehearsal, but it was canceled, and James is out with Pepper so they don't know." My expression sours because I don't want to think about that, either. "I figured I'd come over and see Dr. Hewitt, if she's here."

"She's upstairs with BethAnn." Maria skips—yeah, skips—into the kitchen. "Want something to drink? And look," she stops and twirls, arms out, showing off her V-neck sweater over a cami, her denim mini skirt and the leggings under it. "New clothes. It's all my money, but Dr. Hewitt took me shopping."

I pull out a chair at the table and twist it around, sitting on it backward so I can rest my chin on the back. "Where'd you get the money?"

"She convinced Mama to give it to her. She said she talked to Mama and Papa for a long time last night, it was her third time going over, and they finally admitted that they ought to at least send some money to me to live on. She told them that I want emancipation." Maria's expression is serious as she sits down at the table and nudges a cola toward me. "Then I can get a job, move out on my own. I could live anywhere I want, maybe even here, if I can get that."

"Does Dr. Hewitt want that?" This kind of blurs the lines between job and well, parenthood. Or friendship. But it isn't at all what a doctor does for her patients. "What about child services?"

"Child services doesn't have any place for me, so they said Dr. Hewitt could foster me for now. And I could work for her," Maria says cheerily. "She hasn't said yes, yet, but BethAnn likes me. I could be here every day after school for BethAnn and pick her up from daycare and make dinner and do the laundry and the cleaning. Like an au pair girl, or a maid. I'd be that extra pair of hands she doesn't know she needs."

I don't want to burst Maria's bubble, but I wonder if she's making things out to be too easy. So I take a gulp of my soda instead, and change the subject. "Are you coming to the school board meeting tonight? Not to say anything, but just to be there."

She looks at me, her head cocked, and she reaches out to nudge my leg with her toe. "Chico, is something wrong? I thought you were looking forward to this fight, so you could save your play."

"It was better before it was really my fight."

I hear footsteps, and I glance up to see Dr. Hewitt coming in. She motions for us to keep talking, and well, I want her to hear it too, so I tell them everything about meeting with Paul and Britney and Ryan that morning. Dr. Hewitt brings a glass of water and joins us at the table. It's a little weird talking to her like this, here in her kitchen, more like a family friend than my doctor. I guess that's what she really is now, more than anything else, after everything with Maria. She doesn't feel like just a doctor anymore.

"Why did you come here to tell us this?" she asks. Okay, so maybe she still *sounds* like a doctor.

"I don't want you to talk me out of it," I say quickly. "Or into it. I'm going to do it. I feel like—there are words somewhere inside my head, and they're almost ready to come out. Like when I start talking I'll magically know what to say and how to say it." Magic again, and I wonder if that's true, if Titania touched my lips as well as my eyes so I can speak truth. I lick my lips, uncertain.

"But?" Dr. Hewitt prompts.

Maria's kicking her feet back and forth, toes sliding with a soft rasp against the linoleum floor. Every once in a while she touches my ankle, but she doesn't apologize, just smiling at me and I know she's making contact on purpose. She's letting me know she's there. I smile back and reach out with one foot, dragging her foot toward me and trapping it, leaving us intertwined, and her smile widens.

"I need moral support," I admit. "It isn't about being me. It's not about being transgender, or about being gay, or about being straight. It's about living in peace as yourself, and more importantly, being allowed to do it. It's about being able to be safe at school no matter who you are. And it's about respecting tradition, and not being afraid of differences."

"That's a lot of abouts." Dr. Hewitt smiles then. "Bob'll take BethAnn tonight, and I'll be there to cheer you on. But you understand that you don't have to do this. No matter what you told your friends, if you change your mind, they should respect that. The only person who can decide to out yourself is you. And the one who has to live with it afterward is you."

I don't want to think about what it'll be like once everyone knows; that scares me. But I'm stronger than people think. I'm sick of hiding, I'm sick of being afraid. I just want to be me. I want everyone to shut up and just *let* me be me. I nod slowly. "I know. It's my decision, and I've made it."

The doorbell rings, and Maria bounces up to run and get it. Both Dr. Hewitt and I look that direction, even though we can't see the hallway; her head is cocked, listening.

The door squeaks when it opens, then silence for a long moment.

"Mama?"

I'm up and moving before I think about it, coming down the hallway in time to see Serena wrapping her arms around Maria's thin waist, hugging her hard. Her Mama stands back in the still open door, and she looks at me, nodding like she's not surprised at all to see me here. I can't read what's in her eyes, but she doesn't look pissed off to see me, which is new.

"Gracias." She speaks to me first, not to her own daughter. It takes me a minute to realize that, since she doesn't normally talk to me at all. "You saved my—" She hesitates, and the word comes so slowly that I can almost see her sifting through her options before she says, "—daughter."

I hear Maria's soft inhalation, then a choked sob.

"De nada." I might not know much Spanish, but I've picked up a little from Maria, and it makes her Mama smile. "She's my best friend. If she needs me, I'm going to be there."

Maria almost knocks me over, throwing her arms around me, kissing me on the cheek. "That goes both ways," she says emphatically. She buries her face against my shoulder, using me a little like a shield. I manage to get my arm around her waist, pulling her next to me, and we all just stand there while her Mama looks her over.

In the end, her Mama just nods, and there are tears in her eyes. "You are a beautiful girl."

She's talking to Maria this time, thankfully. Maria makes a soft little snort, but her eyes are wet too. "I've been telling you that all along, Mama. It just took you some time to see it." There's a small hesitation before Maria asks, "Papa?"

Mama shakes her head. "He's not ready. You're—you were his *son*. He grieves for you."

"I'm not dead." Maria sighs.

"Sí. But you are not Felipe anymore, either."

There's really nothing any of us can say to that, because she's really not. She's just Maria. I'm not sure Felipe ever did exist the way her Papa thinks he did.

"I should go." Not because I'm interrupting, even though I feel a little like an extra in this scene right now, but because I want to shower and get changed for the meeting tonight. If I sniff hard enough, I think I can smell the lunchroom's french fries, and that's never a good impression to make.

Maria hugs me hard before she steps away. "I'll be there tonight. I promise. I might be in the back of the room, but I'll be there."

And that really means a lot to me. "Thanks. It'll help, knowing that. Wish me luck?"

She shakes her head. "No luck. Break a leg, Jordan."

In a way, I guess she's right. I'm planning on telling the truth, but it's still a performance. I just need to not get stage fright.

CHAPTER 23: Treading the Boards

THE ROOM is packed. I didn't expect there to be this many people here but somehow, all the seats are taken and we're standing off to one side because our legs are young. I can see Dr. Hewitt and Maria sitting in the back, and when I glance over, Maria wiggles her fingers at me. Next to me, Britney reaches out and squeezes my fingers. I glance at her, then past her to the rest of the cast. Me, Paul, Britney, Ryan, and Zach, of course. Pepper and James. Tyler's here too, and Caitlyn. The fairies are sitting in the audience with their mothers, and I can see exactly what the fairies will look like when they grow up. I bet the moms have been friends since they were freshmen, too. The only person from the cast who is missing is Lianne, but when I look around again, I finally spot her, sitting with Emily Graves and her crowd on the other side of the room. Lianne won't look at me. Good. I'm angry at her for not sticking together with the rest of us.

Paul manages to slip in between me and Britney. "I haven't told anyone else," he says quietly.

"Well, gee, that's handy, but shouldn't you have thought to keep your mouth shut before you told Britney?" I have to ask. I glance at Pepper, wondering if he'd told her already, but Paul sees where I'm looking and shakes his head. Not that it matters now, considering.

"I thought it'd be better if everyone was surprised," he says. "You know we're all with you. We all have been, all along, even when it was just stupidity over the play. Nothing's going to change."

Paul has a lot of confidence, and I wish I did too. Because that's the point I want to make today, that things shouldn't change.

Pepper has a clipboard in her hands when she comes over, James close behind. "Okay, right after the opening remarks they'll go over old business," she says. "Then they'll introduce the new business, and they have to recognize us before we speak."

"I'm going to speak."

She looks over at me, startled. "Oh?"

I nod twice, then decide I probably look like a bobblehead doll and stop doing that. "I have a speech." Sort of. In my head. I hope. "I think it'll say a lot of what needs to be said. And since it's my part everyone's freaking out over, I think maybe I should be the one to talk about it."

"It's my play," Pepper says quietly.

She's standing right in front of me, the clipboard held like a shield between us. I look down at her and smile sadly. "I know. And it's important to you. It's important to *all* of us. But I'm the one who's been harassed about it, and just trust me when I say I have a speech that's really going to blow them away. I promise. And if you feel like you need to tell me to stop talking at any time, just do it. But please, try to trust me."

Her green eyes are wide, expression assessing for such a long time that I feel warmth in my cheeks because she's staring at me. A faint pink underlines her freckles as well when she finally looks away. "Okay. But if it starts to go off the rails at any point, I'm jumping in."

"That's cool."

I don't know what she means by going off the rails, so I guess we'll see if she lets me get through it all before she interrupts me. And I only half lied about having a speech. I didn't write it down, but I can feel it burning my tongue, the words wanting to come out. It tastes like magic.

The board members come in and sit at the table at the front of the room as solemnly as if it were a Supreme Court judges' bench. There are five of them: two guys, three women. All of them look at least old enough to be my parents. One of them looks like she's probably a grandmother.

I'm starting to shake with nerves. Out of the corner of my eye, I see James slip an arm around Pepper's shoulders. She shrugs it off, stepping into her own space, the clipboard still hugged to her chest. She's watching the board members speak, even though they aren't talking to us yet.

Puck's whisper reaches my ear in soft, sibilant tones. "Speak truth," he murmurs, "and they will hear only truth. From your heart to your lips to their ears to their hearts. Heart to heart, truer words ne'er spoken than this."

The room spins. I hope it's time, because I'm ready to go.

Everyone is looking at me. Waiting. They must've said something, someone must've responded. Pepper nudges me from behind and I walk up to stand at the end of the table. I can see everyone on the board, and I can see everyone in the room. There is no time to be nervous. There is only the magic, and the words, and the truth. Time to speak.

"Centuries ago, when Shakespeare wrote his plays, he wasn't trying to create something that would be taught in our English classes," I say. "He wrote to entertain people. He wrote so that patrons would come into his theater and give him money so he could keep writing, and he wrote so people would listen. Sometimes he wrote so they would laugh, sometimes so they would cry. But he always wrote so they would recognize themselves standing on that stage."

Aside from my voice, it's so quiet that I hear when someone shifts in their seat, the metal chair leg scraping across the floor, the noise aching in my ears. I try to smile. "Shakespeare wrote about people. *All* people. Short and tall, thin and fat, male and female. He wrote about the heart and mind. He wrote about everything he saw around him, bringing it up on stage for viewing, because that was what people wanted to see. If he were writing today, he'd have a play about gay marriage. He'd have a history about the war in the Mideast. He'd tell stories about the conflict between church and state—wait, I think he did that already, in one of the histories, didn't he?"

There's a soft titter of nervous laughter. Not much, but I'll take it, absorbing it like courage to go on. These thoughts are mine, but the words aren't. They're better than I could ever create, spilling like drops of potion between me and the audience.

"Shakespeare found humor in the most basic parts of the human condition. He showed us love and mistakes, he showed us when we are right, and when we are wrong. But most importantly, he showed the people who came to see his plays that underneath their skin, no matter what comes and goes, we are all the same."

I have them now, my voice stronger than when I began, and I step forward. I feel confidence like a role I play, and I use that. "In *Twelfth Night*—the original version—Viola takes on the guise of Cesario for safety. Women couldn't travel then, so she plays a man. When it first played on stage, imagine the humor in it. All players were men then, so a young man played a woman playing a man. It was a difficult role, and one fought for and earned by the best. Shakespeare used this role to show so many things, though. He showed the differences in how men and women were treated by outsiders. He showed the difference in the freedoms they had. And he showed the difference in how it felt to be Viola or Cesario. But in the end, when it all came undone, who was she?"

Here, this is the crux of what I'm about to say. I pause, waiting until I hear a whisper start, and then I say it again, my voice louder than before. "In the end, *who was she?*" I wait two beats, then lower my voice to say, "She was Viola. And when the makeup came off, the player was just a boy who played a role. The point is, we all wear masks at times, but underneath, we are still the same person. Sometimes we put on a mask because society tells us to. Because we are told we cannot be accepted as we are. And that is what Viola did. She was told she could not be a woman, so instead she tried to be a man. But she never changed in her heart."

Heart. God. Mine is beating so fast I'm shaking, so loud I have to wonder why they all can't hear it.

My breath shudders in my chest, then slips out in a soft whoosh through my lips as I try to keep composure. "Our version of the play threatens beliefs even more than Shakespeare does, because it crosses the gender boundaries and because it crosses the boundaries of sexuality. It's scary to some people, because they look around and to them the play is talking about something so far removed from what we see as *normal* that it might as well be alien. There are gay people out there, but they're somewhere else. They're not in our school. And there are people who change genders out there." My breath hiccups, throat tightening as I repeat, "Somewhere else. They're not in *our* school. But the thing is…."

I have to gulp in a breath, holding it to loosen tight lungs, before I can blurt out, "The thing is, they are. Here. Being gay is a fact of life, and our school managed to get over the fact that Ryan and Zach dated for two years. They were the same people after they came out as they were before, and it wasn't easy for them, but they got through it. And gender—"

I stop. I don't know what to say, how to put it into words. And I remember Puck's whisper, from my heart to theirs, so I touch my fingertips to my heart. "Gender isn't always how we look, sometimes it's how we are inside. Viola is a woman, and she never changes that, even though magic makes her male. In the end, she's happy to go back. And I get that, probably more than anyone else could. Because I'm the opposite. I've always been a boy, always known that was what I was, even though I was born into a female body."

The silence doesn't feel good anymore. It isn't awe—it's shock. I have to go on.

"That doesn't change who I am," I say firmly. "I'm still Jordan and I'm still the same boy you've all known since eighth grade. And the play doesn't change who we are either, and it won't change how we think about the world, except maybe for the better. The play opens eyes. It looks at people honestly, and it doesn't judge. It just shows what some of us have known all along: *we are who we are*. You can't change what's in your heart, whether people are able to see it clearly or not. Sometimes, you just have to help people open up their eyes."

James is at my elbow, and he tugs me off to one side. Pepper doesn't look at me as she takes my place. I can't hear what she says because the darkness is rushing in around me, narrowing the world down to a tiny dot of focus. James gets me into a seat on the floor, my back against the wall. I don't know if I did good or if I did damage, but I know I said what needed to be said. The question is whether any of them will listen.

CHAPTER 24: Aftermath

THE MEETING isn't over yet, even though I'm done talking. But it might as well be, since everything seems to have turned to chaos.

I'm where James left me, sitting with my back against the wall. Maria is pressed against my right side, and Paul is pressed against my left, making a shield of human bodies out of themselves. My eyes are closed, as if it'll help me center myself, but with all the noise, that seems impossible. I hear James's voice as if from a distance, mixed with Pepper's voice and others, arguing with the school board. I'm not sure if they're arguing about the play, about morality, or about whether I should even exist.

"She's been lying about who she is!"

Emily's voice, strident and sharp, cuts through the chatter. I feel Paul's wince, and he mutters, "Can't believe I thought I liked her."

Maria snorts softly. "We all have bad judgment sometimes."

"Part of being a teenager." My throat hurts, the words scraping as I finally speak. I open my eyes and offer a weak smile. "Have they decided to burn me at the stake yet?"

When I look out at the audience, Emily is standing on a chair to get her head over the sea of adults around her. "She's a girl, pretending to be a boy," she insists, her voice pitched high enough to hurt my ears.

"Jordan's a boy." James cuts her off. "Jordan's always been a boy. It's not his fault he was born with fucked-up anatomy."

"Language."

James shrugs at the admonition from Dower. I grin, because that's my brother. That's the guy who's always been there for me, and even though we fought, here he is, standing up for me. Again. The grin fades as Pepper steps next to him, and his arm goes around her shoulders.

Emily's smile twists, sharp and vicious. "Is that why you broke up with him, Pepper? You figured out you'd screwed up and he had girl bits in his pants? So you went after his brother instead? I don't know who to pity more, the one you dumped or the consolation prize."

James goes to move forward, but Pepper holds him back. "You're jealous, Emily," he says, trying to keep his tone quiet. "Jealous as fuck because you can't sleep your way to the top, and you can't win the part on your own. You were pissed off when you thought you were beat out by a boy, now you're pissed off because you know that he's stronger than you'll ever be. Face up to it: he's better than you at the role. It's not about morality. It's not about anything but your feelings being hurt."

Her outraged shriek hurts my ears. "It's about him being a fucking tranny and using it to get the best part in the play!" she shouted.

I could probably hear a pin drop in the silence that follows her outburst.

"At least she got the pronoun right?" I whisper, and Maria laughs nervously.

"Emily Graves, no matter what decisions are made today, this school has a no tolerance policy towards bullying, and that language will not be tolerated." It's the grandmotherly one who speaks from the school board. She reminds me of Ms. Jackson, all small and tough, her voice like nails. "Sit. If you continue to spout hateful obscenity, you will be removed from the room."

I wonder if that policy extends to the school. I wonder if she'll get suspended when she incites guys into beating me up, or if she'll just get detention. I'm cynical, I know, but I'm scared. The funny part is, I'm here. There's no blackness, no panic, just me and the feeling of people pressed against me, keeping me anchored in the here and now. I wish I could still retreat, but I'm not, and I don't know why. Something to ask Dr. Hewitt, I guess. I still feel… weird. Floating. Like I'm watching it all from the outside, and if it weren't for Maria and Paul, I might float off entirely.

The grandmotherly one continues speaking. "We will step out to discuss the issues on the table. Please enjoy the provided coffee and cookies."

My stomach turns at the thought of food. Still, when Maria and Paul stand, and offer me hands to help me up, I stand as well. Maria hugs me first, wrapping her arms around me, slight body curled against mine as she kisses my cheek. "How do you feel, Jordan?"

"Weird," I admit.

Then I'm surrounded. Ryan and Zach hug me, and Tyler claps me on the back, pounding his support roughly into me just like two guys in the locker room. Cait kisses my cheek. And they all talk, a steady stream of words that tumble over each other, telling me that it doesn't change anything, that I'm still Jordan. There's some disbelief, and some talk about my locker room habits of hiding when I change. They dissect my habits, picking apart the places where I have always been different and noting the reasons for it now. But none of them try to hurt me for it. I feel dampness prick the corners of my eyes, and when Maria's hand finds mine, I squeeze tightly for all I'm worth. This moment, at least, is good.

Then Pepper is there, and there are glances and whispers as the rest of our friends step away. I flinch when Maria pulls back—I need my anchor—but they all leave us alone.

"Why didn't you tell me?" Pepper asks.

I can't read her expression. Her green eyes are wide, her hair in little russet flyaways around her face and coming loose from her ponytail. Her freckles are sharp against her pale skin. I reach up, but remember she's not mine to touch, especially not now, so instead I push my bangs back from my face. "I couldn't. I couldn't tell anyone, because of what could happen. M—" I start to tell her about what happened to Maria, but I can't out her, not without asking first, so I shrug one shoulder. "People get beaten up for being transgender. I just wanted to live my life, Pepper. A guy's life."

"So you lied to me."

Ouch. I nod slowly. "Yeah. I guess I did."

She nods as well, breath coming out in a soft huff of a sigh. "It explains why your voice is so perfect."

"Would you have—" *kissed me* "—cast me if you knew?"

Her lips press together, a faint pink coloring the skin under her freckles. "Maybe. I don't know. It made your life more complicated. If you'd told me, maybe I would've let you out of the role instead of talking you into taking it."

A wry smile tilts my mouth. "If I'd liked you less, I wouldn't have let you talk me into it. I did it for you, Pepper."

Her arms cross tight across her chest, and she looks at the floor. "And this? Telling me by telling the whole world?"

"For your play," I say. But it's not enough, I can see her retreating. "Pepper—"

"Don't." She takes a step back. When she looks up at me, her lower lip is caught in her teeth, worrying at it. "I don't hate you because of what you are, Jordan. But I don't know what I think, either. And I'm angry that you didn't trust me enough to tell me before you got up in front of everyone and blurted things out because you think you were doing it for the play. They didn't need to know it. I could've saved the play. It was just Emily being a bitch, and we needed to point that out."

"We did."

She shakes her head. "No. Not exactly. I'm not sure what you did. But I hope it did whatever you wanted it to do, for you. You're a good actor, Jordan, and you play the role well. Maybe it's because you're used to it, I don't know. I guess... congratulations on coming out."

That wasn't what I meant. "Pepper—"

She steps back again. "I'm going to go get coffee."

And then she's gone, and I'm on my own. And I get the feeling I've fucked up but good, and I can't remember why this seemed like a good plan in the first place. I see Paul and Britney watching me, and Paul looks worried. Guilty, maybe. They start to come toward me, but I wave a hand, pushing them away. I don't want anyone around me right now. What I really want is to get away and think about tonight, pick apart my feelings. And I don't want anyone else's help with that.

I sink back down to sit on the floor again, my head back against the wall, eyes closed, and I float there, waiting. When the board comes back, the decision is made: we get our play, I get my part, and they make all the proper noises about bullying not being tolerated. Noise erupts, both protests and elation, and I try to ignore it all. I'm still stewing on what Pepper said about how I didn't need to say what I said. Didn't I? Didn't it make a point about how the play isn't changing us because we already are who we are?

INTERLUDE: James

JAMES HAD to wait for Jordan, once everything was said and done. He'd promised to make sure Jordan got home safely, even promised to go straight home except for dropping off anyone who needed a ride. James knew that his parents thought that having Jordan in the car would make sure James didn't linger when he took Pepper home.

They were probably right.

But that didn't mean he had to rush. He could let Jordan talk to Maria and Paul, while James waited off to the side, his arm around Pepper's shoulders. And it meant no one was looking when he turned just enough to lean down and brush his lips against Pepper's. He tugged her with him, moving into the hallway and out of sight, wrapping his arms around her so he could pull her in closer for a kiss.

He felt a connection to Pepper that drew him in. Whenever he wasn't with her, he thought about her. When she was in the room, he watched her. When they were close enough to touch, he couldn't resist doing so. He was obsessed by her, and the best part was, she was obsessed by him in return. He had never felt like this before about any girl; she was the first girl he could honestly say he loved. This was it, it was perfect, and it was going to last forever.

Pepper's small hands pressed against his shoulders as she pulled back, putting space between them. Her lips were red, a faint blush under her freckles as she looked at him. He'd never realized just how much he liked freckles. Small curvy redheaded girls with freckles. Why had he ever thought that leggy blondes were his thing?

"We need to break up."

James blinked. "What?"

Pepper sighed, her fingers ghosting over the spiked hair on his head, expression soft and sad. "I'm breaking up with you, James."

"Why?" He refused to let her go, as if by holding her there she would change her mind and remember how perfectly they fit together.

"You're my heart, Pepper. My restriction will be up soon, and I'll take you out, and everything'll be back to normal."

Her brow furrowed and for a moment she looked uncertain. Her gaze shifted to look at the doorway, then back to meet his. "Something's wrong, James. I can't say exactly what it is, but it doesn't feel right."

"It feels perfect," he insisted.

A small smile on her part. "Yes. It does. That's part of what feels wrong. I feel like I can't live without you, and that's too much for me. Tonight I should be in there." Pepper pointed at the doorway where people gathered, still talking over the decisions that had been made, and the direction of the play. "I should be thinking about the play and what we still have to do to make the production right. And instead I'm here because I can't keep my hands off of you. That *scares* me."

"It scares me too, Pepper, but that doesn't mean we should stop being together," James insisted. There was a slow ache building in his chest, thudding painfully with every beat of his heart. "We can slow down. I'll stay on the opposite side of the room when you're directing. Unless you're directing me," he added with a grin.

"Maybe I should have Dower direct your scenes."

James's smile faded. She looked serious when she said that, her words soft and matter-of-fact. "No, you shouldn't. We can behave. I'll make sure Jordan even behaves."

At that, Pepper's gaze skittered toward the doorway again. She was still looking that way when she spoke. "We need to break up, James." She pushed at his chest until he released her, and she took several steps backward. "I could still use a lift home, though. If you don't mind. Mom wasn't coming to get me and Paul since she figured you'd be bringing us."

"You're my heart." It was a last ditch effort, said uncertainly because the words felt unfamiliar but absolutely true and necessary to say. "Pepper—"

Eyelids lowered as she looked at the floor. "You're mine too. This hurts. But it's right. Because there's something really wrong with us."

He couldn't move as she walked away, feet rooted to the ground like a nightmare. Breath hissed out in a rush as he leaned back against the wall, letting it support him as his legs folded and he slid down to the floor. The ache thundered now, each breath shuddering through him. Something wrong? No, *this* was wrong. Being separate from her was wrong. He was desperate to get up, run after her, sweep her into his arms, and declare his heart all over again. He needed her. *Needed* her.

James leaned forward, elbows on his bent knees, head cradled in his hands. He wouldn't cry over a girl, not even if it felt as if his heart had been torn in two. And he wouldn't go after her. He wouldn't give her that satisfaction.

"Hey." Jordan crouched next to him, his hand touching James's shoulder. "You all right?"

Paul was there too, standing just beyond Jordan, thumbs hooked in his pockets as he stood, loose-limbed and angular. James looked from one to the other, fighting for something to say.

"We need to fix things," Jordan said quietly.

"Friday," Paul replied. "We've got the perfect excuse now, and I think our idea will work. It ought to set everything back to rights."

"Set what back to rights?" Questioning gave James something to focus on that wasn't Pepper, and wasn't the pain of her absence. He could feel the hole by his side where she ought to be and wanted to go find her. But he held on to that question and waited for an answer.

Jordan gave him a rueful smile. "Everything, James. Everything that's messed up. I'd say more, but you wouldn't believe me."

James blinked. "Try me."

"You and several other members of the cast are caught under a magical spell that needs to be reversed in order to make you sane again," Paul said easily. "You, Pepper, Ryan, Cait... we can fix it. You're hosting a party Friday night."

There's something really wrong with this, she'd said. James didn't believe that. Not when it felt so right, and not when Paul was spewing such complete nonsense. He ignored it in favor of the part that made sense: the party. "Have you asked Mom?"

"I did, before we left to come here," Jordan confirmed. "She said if we won tonight we could have a party in the basement Friday after rehearsal, with the whole cast, to celebrate. Which means our grounding's done, then, I guess. If you give me the car, I'll go buy all the food myself and I'll get everything set up. Paul and Britney said they'd help. You don't have to do a thing."

Britney's name gave James a moment's pause, a faint sense of guilt and something left undone. But it was good that she was hanging around with Jordan. It might make him feel better about things, James thought, and stop seeing relationships where they weren't. "Okay," he agreed, not sure they actually needed his agreement right now.

Jordan budged up closer to him, nudging him shoulder to shoulder. "What's wrong, James? You seem really out of it. You going to be safe to drive home?"

Yes. No. He wasn't sure, because his mind had followed his heart into the other room, and as he looked down the hallway, he saw Pepper coming back. She hesitated in the doorway, watching him, and for a moment he thought she would disappear again. He pushed Jordan away, stepping toward Pepper, and she took two steps toward him. A hesitation, then she was in his arms, lifted for a kiss, her face buried against his neck afterward.

"I was wrong," she said quickly. "I was wrong. I love you."

And just like that, everything was right with the world again. The ache eased, and James smiled, fingers tangled in her hair, coming through the red curls. "I love you, too."

Someone cleared their throat, but James ignored it.

"I'll be in the car." Jordan's flat, angry tone sent a twist of guilt into James's center, but he ignored it.

"Friday," Paul said, and both boys walked off.

James didn't care. He'd meet them in the car soon enough. Right now he had Pepper, and everything was exactly the way it was supposed to be.

PART SIX
Curtain Call

JOURNAL: Thursday, October 30

I KNOW we'll be talking about this next week, so I might as well get it all on paper now to make it easier to remember the details. Things weren't all that bad yesterday, but they weren't all that good, either.

Ms. Jackson met the buses, making sure everyone went straight inside the school in the morning, rather than lingering on the steps. All the teachers were right there, directing students to go to their lockers, then straight to the auditorium for a special assembly. We sat by homerooms, so they could take attendance, and there was a lot of noise and laughter as people settled in. I found a seat at the end of the row, and no one sat next to me. I wasn't all that surprised, given how many of them were looking at me.

It wasn't a long assembly. Ms. Jackson told everyone about the school board meeting. She didn't go into specifics, and she didn't talk about me at all, but people kept looking at me so I know it went around the social networks between the meeting ending and school starting. I'd bet there's a video of my speech out on YouTube, too, if I go looking. She explained that bullying will not be tolerated, and that she expects everyone to respect those who are brave enough to act on stage. She said that the guys who painted the lockers have been given a two-day in-house suspension, which sucks for them, I'll admit. I'm glad, though. It's the only way people will listen, if they're forced to take responsibility for their actions.

Then she said that the remainder of the rehearsals will be closed, which those of us in the cast cheered about, and I'm pretty sure it was Emily booing along with more people than I'd care to think about.

I don't know what to think about her last announcement.

Ms. Jackson has decided that there will be a mandatory assembly in December for us to perform the show for the whole school. Anyone missing it without a valid parental excuse will be given detention, but parental excuses will be accepted of course, because she can't force anyone into seeing something they don't morally agree with. But overall, it'll be considered a part of our health and society classes, with sign-in and everything. She also said something about some changes in our English classes to include literature to encourage us to be open-minded. Can't wait to see what the school board thinks is appropriate for that.

I heard rumors later going all around the school about Ms. Jackson. Some people are saying she's going to be fired because of how she handled the situation. Other people were complimentary about how she'd handled things. It's a pretty mixed bag right now.

I was asked if I wanted to skip gym yesterday. I said no, because I haven't changed. What everyone else knows about me has changed, but I'm still the same guy who was in there two days before, and if they can't deal with that, then they need to get over it. So I walked in, grabbed my stuff from my locker, and went into the privacy stall. When I came out, Coach was there waiting for me, and all the rest of the guys were gone. He told me he'd be doing locker room duty every time I'm in there, for the rest of the year.

I tried to tell him he didn't need to do that, that I can take care of myself, but he insisted. Said Ms. Jackson said he had to.

I don't think Coach really approves of me. He's known all along, because Ms. Jackson made sure he did since I insisted on being in normal gym and locker rooms are a vulnerable place. But I didn't want to be different. And Coach never treated me any differently. If anything, he's always pushed me harder, I think. Maybe he thought it'd make me quit, but it didn't. I can bench more than most of the guys in my gym class can even think about.

The thing is, even though Coach doesn't get it, and even though I'm pretty sure he doesn't like what I am, he still protected me. When the guys started getting on my case in the middle of class (something about bouncing boobs, and let me tell you, there was no bouncing going on) he shut them down. Coach is good people.

It wasn't all good, though. One of the guys stole my regular clothes, and I got stuck for a while until another guy—Brian—brought them back. Don't think that meant he was being nice; he called me a fag and tried to get me to change in front of him, like him seeing me is going to make me suddenly want to acknowledge my second X chromosome. I asked if he got off on watching other guys get naked, and that finally got rid of him.

So I get the feeling life's going to be an absolute bitch until the play is done. Maybe even longer, because they can't forget that I'm different underneath. Which is exactly what I didn't want, all these people staring at me. Talking about me. Dissecting everything I do and trying to second-guess me. Saying it's a phase or something I'm going through.

What's funny, though, is that it's getting easier in a way. Now that they all know, there's nothing to hide. I can just be me, and say fuck 'em if they don't get it. And I do. It's on them to deal with their own inner hater thoughts. I'm still the same guy who was in their class before the meeting, and I'm not changing any time in the near future. Except for the better, when my voice starts changing and I have to shave.

God, I can't wait to shave. Months? Seriously? Time needs to pass faster already.

I talked to Maria last night after I got home from rehearsal. I'm glad she's going to keep staying with you, but I'm also really glad that she's trying to spend some time with her Mama and Serena. Are they being good to her? I know her Papa still doesn't get it, but maybe he'll come around eventually. I have my arguments with my folks, but it's hard to imagine them giving up on me entirely just because my brain doesn't match my bits. I know I'm lucky in my family, I really am. Blessed, I guess. But it sounds like maybe Maria's finding her blessing too.

I supposed you're going to ask about Emily Graves, aren't you? The thing is, I don't have anything much to say yet. I saw her once yesterday, and that was right after the assembly. She walked past me in the hall, and she didn't say a word. The look she gave me might have meant "this isn't over yet" or it might've been "you are invisible to me." Either one, really. I'm watching out for her.

It's a pity, because she's spending so much time on anger that she could channel into something better. Like voice lessons so she'll be ready for next year's musical. I heard a rumor that someone's pushing for something traditional, like the Sound of Music. I bet she'd make a great Liesl. Maybe I'll tell her that. Course, maybe she'll bite my head off if I do.

I don't hate her. I did, for a while, I guess. But it's hard to hate her now. We won. She's been proven to be a bigoted idiot. Everything's good. Hate would only make things bad again. I'd rather do what any good senior in the theater program should do and try to make sure that the kids who are left when I'm gone are ready to carry the torch properly. And she's got a ways to go before she gets there. Maybe there's some way to get her to take my help. Hah. I'm delusional, right?

Anyway. School, then rehearsal, then I have to get home and get things set up in the basement because tonight we celebrate. Cast unity.

I think things'll be even better after tonight. I can't explain it, but trust me. Sometimes the heart just needs to see true.

CHAPTER 25: Heart on My Sleeve

MS. JACKSON isn't outside today when the bus pulls up. I guess she figures they got the point yesterday, but I'm not so sure. Brandon and his thugs are there, waiting, when I get off the bus and head up the stairs with the crowd. There's a shout: *hey little girl!*

It's funny how quickly I'm on my own, the others from my bus going left or right, leaving me alone in the middle. I ignore Brandon and keep going, step by step. Don't look, don't even think about making eye contact, and God, don't try to say a word. Chin up, eyes straight ahead, keep walking.

There's tap on my shoulder, and I make the mistake of turning because it's an automatic reaction to the touch. Brandon's taller than me, and heavier, although I'm betting he's not as strong; it looks more like weight than muscle. He's using that height to lean in and try to intimidate me. "Looks like we were trying to take apart the wrong girly boy." He grins, all sharp teeth and feral attitude. "Or maybe we weren't wrong. Maybe you both are. Maybe that's why you stick together, to make sure no one finds out about your girl bits."

He's in front of me, Toby's behind me, and another thug stands to either side of me… there's no place to run. Can't just ignore it anymore, and my backpack feels far too heavy, weighing me down. "We beat you last time," I remind him, my voice pitched low. "You want something worse this time?"

Okay, so maybe threatening him isn't the right thing to do.

I'm grabbed from behind; Toby uses my backpack and jacket to pull both down my arms, trapping me so I can't move when Brandon takes a swing. He hits right over my left eye. The impact snaps my head back, the world spinning and out of focus for a moment. I see stars. I've never seen stars before, but there they are, casting him in a sparkly halo, except he's sure as hell no angel.

I step back, ducking my head and stomping down hard on Toby's foot behind me. I'm wearing boots, he's wearing boots, but my heel pushes a lot harder than his toes can handle. He yells and his hands tighten on my sleeves as I yank forward, managing to get one arm out of my jacket. I swing wildly, trying to hit someone. Anyone. My goal here is to stay alive, not any kind of finesse.

My fist connects with flesh and bone, and it hurts like hell. One of them grunts and pulls back; then he twists away to deal with a threat on another side.

Fuck yeah, I've got help. Good. I'm going to need it.

It's a blur after that. I pull a punch when I realize that Caitlyn's there, in my way. It sends me off-balance and Pepper grabs me to help me get back upright. I'm about to turn away from her when I see a hand closing over her ponytail, and I punch. This time it's more satisfying, knocking him back, and he trips over the steps, sitting down hard.

I see Paul struggling with one of them, and James taking a hit, then giving one back.

Then there's something coming at my face. It hits me just above the eye, same place as Brandon got me earlier. My head snaps back and I lose my balance completely. There's someone behind me when I fall, but I lose track of everything for just a minute in the spinning bright sparkly stars.

"Stop!"

Ms. Jackson's voice is the next thing that makes sense. Ms. Jackson, Dower, and two other teachers as well. They separate us out until somehow it's the thugs in one group, Paul, Caitlyn, and Ryan in another small knot, then me, with James and Pepper holding me up after Ryan hands me off to them.

Ms. Jackson's not saying anything, just inspecting us. She sends Brandon and the rest of the thugs to her office, telling them that their bruises will wait until she's done with them. She frowns when she gets close to me, and I blink because there's blood on my lashes. Great. Mom's going to kill me. "Nurse," she says quietly.

I try to take a step, and Pepper's right there, insinuating her shoulder under my arm. "Just in case you're dizzy," she says, as James takes my other side.

Here I am between them. Coming between them. Separating them. Isn't that what I want to do?

Maybe. After I feel better.

"Guess they didn't get the point yesterday," James mutters.

"I think they got the point," Pepper replies, just as softly. "I don't think they liked it. I hope they don't suspend all of us for helping out Jordan."

"M'right here," I remind her, in case she's somehow forgotten, since she's talking about me like I'm not here. "Can't suspend me for self-defense."

"They could suspend the rest of us for coming to your rescue," Pepper counters.

I shake my head. Oh, crap, that's a really bad idea. I have to stop walking for a moment, staring at the wall just long enough to get my equilibrium. "They won't." My head hurts, but I'm getting less dizzy. "You did the right thing, because if you hadn't, I might be a puddled mess against the stone steps. No one on my bus even thought about stopping."

But my brother stepped right up. Even when we're arguing, he's there for me. No matter what.

"I can't blame them for being scared." James nudges me and we turn right, heading down another hallway toward the nurse's office.

"I can blame them for not saying anything." Pepper sounds indignant. "What if it were their best friend? Would they just let those bullies beat him up? Why should they let them beat up Jordan just because he's—"

"*Different?*" I can't help but interrupt.

Pepper hisses in a soft breath. "Yes. Different."

Getting that statement out into the open doesn't feel as good as I thought it would. Having her arm around me doesn't feel great either. It's just reminding me that she was angry with me on Wednesday. "We should talk," I say.

Silence.

"Maybe later," she finally replies.

I open my mouth, intending to protest, but she shakes her head. "Don't," she says. "Not yet. You're bleeding. We're going to deal with that before anything else."

Then when? When is later going to be? Because I have a feeling that if I don't push at it, I'm going to lose her completely, potion or no potion. God, what'll happen tonight at the party? What will true sight do? Will it make things better or worse? Suddenly I'm not so sure I want to know the answer to that, but it's too late not to do it. We have to fix what I broke.

The nurse, Miss Habernathy, points to one of the cots, and I sit down, Pepper still on one side, James on the other. She is on the phone, and she takes it into her office so we can't hear, leaving the three of us alone.

It's awkward. And weirdly comforting at the same time.

Fingers lightly touch mine, and I glance over. Pepper's not looking at me, but her hand closes over mine, curling around my fingers. I can barely breathe as I turn my hand in hers so our fingers can tangle properly. I'm afraid to take meaning from her gesture, but she leans her head against my shoulder. On my other side, James is silent.

He loves her, I remind myself. And she loves him. And if that's still true after tonight, then I have to step back and let them be. But right this second, with Pepper's hand in mine, I pray that maybe things will go back the way I think they belong. I hope.

CHAPTER 26: Man in the Mirror

IT'S AWKWARD, waiting there while Miss Habernathy is on the phone. When she finishes, she writes out two notes, handing one to Pepper and one to James so they can get back to class. James claps my shoulder, and I wince because something there hurts, and Pepper squeezes my hand. She slides off the cot, then pauses and comes back to lean in and kiss me on the cheek. I blush.

Miss Habernathy pulls a curtain around the cot, giving me some privacy in case someone else comes in. "Does it hurt anywhere other than over your eye?" She sits on the cot next to me, like she's trying to be a friend instead of an authority figure. I shrug, and when I wince, her lips press together. She reaches to touch my ribs, just under my left breast, and I wince again. She sighs and stands. "If you've got any damage to your ribs, you might want to go to the ER," she tells me.

I shake my head. "No way. I'm going to class." If I walk out of school right now, I feel like they've won. "What about my eye. Does it need stitches?" Because I know she can't do that.

Her fingers are light and cool as she touches my eyebrow. I have to work to hold still because I can feel every touch, feathered as some of them are. She goes to get a swab to clean it properly, and I wince as she carefully applies antibiotic cream. "No stitches, but we'll butterfly it." She shows me the clear bandage that I've seen used before instead of stitches sometimes. "This should stay on in the shower, at least for a few days, and give that a chance to close up properly. You're going to have a shiner. Let me get you some ice."

Putting the bandage on hurts more than I expected, as Miss Habernathy makes it pull on the skin, pressing the edges of the small wound together. I bite my lip, not wanting to make a sound about it. I can finally breathe when she tugs the curtain and steps past it, walking away and leaving me alone. My hands are shaking, and when I tighten them into fists, my whole body starts to shake. Oh fuck. I wrap my arms around my center and hold on, waiting for the slide into the darkness.

It doesn't come.

It's not panic, I realize. This is the aftereffects of adrenaline as it slips out of my system, and I can't stop shaking, but I'm still *here*. All the little aches and pains are coming to me now, and I feel a spot on my left side twisting as I breathe and I'm not so sure about it. I try to focus on the air in my lungs—in and out, in and out—and not think about whether someone broke my ribs or not. I wonder if I did any damage to Brandon or Toby or any of the others. I wonder where they are, and how soon they'll be coming down here to get checked out after Ms. Jackson's done with them. I remember the feel of skin and bone under my hand and I look at my knuckles, seeing how red they are. When I stretch and curl my fingers, it hurts. Fuck. I hope I did good damage, since I hurt myself well enough, it looks like.

Maybe I *should* go to the hospital and get checked out. Maybe Ms. Jackson's already called my folks and they'll be dragging me out of here any second. Maybe I should just do the right thing.

But I'm not weak. I don't want them to think they can just push me around and force me out. This is my school. My home. My place to be.

It takes some time, but I wriggle out of my hoodie and drop it onto the cot beside me. Then I take off my T-shirt, and undo the bindings below it. I can see the shadow of a bruise forming on my ribs, angry red and just starting to darken around the edges. An elbow, I think, not a fist. Or a knee. I can't remember the specifics when I look back on the fight; it's all just a blur of impact and pain.

There's a sound and I quickly drag my T-shirt back on, whimpering at the feel of my shoulder pulling. Fuck, that too? Not fair. When Miss Habernathy pulls the curtain back just a bit and looks in at me, she blinks a moment. She's seeing the binding there beside me, I know. I raise my gaze to meet hers. "Just make sure I'm not broken," I say. "I'll go to the hospital if you say I have to, but I don't want to. So tell me."

"You don't have to—"

I laugh, soft and sharp. "Yes, I do. It covered up part of the bruises, and you wouldn't have been able to really check my ribs. It's just clothes. It doesn't change anything, Miss Habernathy."

She hands me the ice and I lean back against the pillows, closing my eyes as I put the pack of ice against my brow. So cold and sharp, it bites into my skin, and I sigh and let go and focus on that. Her fingers press on top of my shirt, deft and careful, checking over my ribs. I wince at some points, but nothing makes me scream. And the funny part is? For the first time since I can remember, I don't care that she's touching my chest.

I've always hated doctors. I hated them when I was little, and they told me what a pretty little girl I was. I hated the way they forced me to look at myself, and I hate when Dr. Patil acts like he doesn't approve of the hormone suppression therapy, or now my T. I hate nurses who make me pay attention to my girl bits by checking them like they're suddenly diseased.

But this isn't bad. Miss Habernathy's nice, which helps, but mostly, it's like I just don't care that she's touching my body. I don't care that the binding's off. I don't care that I know she can see the shape of what little breasts I have. I'm not ready to walk through the halls unbound or anything like that, but I'm not embarrassed. It's just my body, and it's just the way it is, and someday it'll match what I see in my mind's eye. Right now it doesn't. But that doesn't make it any less me.

"Do you have a mirror?" I ask.

"Do you want to see the bruises?" She looks almost amused. "I don't think anything's broken, but your parents may want to get you checked out later anyway. Ms. Jackson might insist on it."

I smile wanly. As long as they don't take me out of school, or make me miss the party, it's all good as far as I'm concerned. I can have that conversation later. "What about the other guys? Where are they?"

"In the principal's office. They'll stay there until you're done here, then I've heard they need to come see me as well."

I can't help but grin at that. "Good."

Probably not what I should say, but hey, Miss Habernathy doesn't say anything about it, either. She just grabs a mirror out of a drawer and hands it to me. Not quite what I was looking for, but it'll do.

I look into it resolutely, keeping my gaze fixed on my image. And I see a boy staring back at me. His pale hair is long on top, bangs falling across his face, shorter on the sides. There's a thick purple stain starting around his left eye, and two butterfly Band-Aids holding together a strip of red to keep it from bleeding. His shoulders are broad, his neck more slender than it would be if he worked out more. Maybe T will change that, maybe not. His shirt's faded, his knuckles are bruised. When I lift the edge of the shirt, his ribs are red and starting to darken as well.

His.

It's as if I look into the mirror and for the first time, *she* doesn't lurk anywhere in the image. I'm all boy. I'm all me, seeing true for the first time. I touch the reflection with careful fingers, murmuring, "Thank you, Titania."

"What was that?"

No way am I explaining that, so I just hand over the mirror instead. "I need to get dressed and get back to class."

Miss Habernathy tucks the mirror back into a drawer. "Get dressed, but you're going to the office before class. Ms. Jackson wants to have a talk with you."

My fingers still as I reach for my bindings, my stomach cold and twisting. "Is she going to suspend me for fighting?"

"I don't know. I doubt it." She looks at me, and her expression holds sympathy. "But I'm sure she's called your parents by now, and you did get into a fight on school grounds. Get dressed, and I'll give you a note for the hall."

Right. That's reassuring. Except not.

I wait until the curtain falls closed again, then skin the shirt off. I dive for the drawer, pulling the mirror back out and look at myself, daring my eyes to see a girl, but even with the evidence right there I only see myself. Grinning, I put the bindings back in place, feeling, for the first time, right to be me.

CHAPTER 27: Performance

EMILY GRAVES is sitting outside the principal's office when I get there.

She's the last thing I want to deal with as I ache from head to toe. I wondered if she was the one behind getting the guys to attack me, or if it was all their own idea. She's here, so I'm guessing they pointed something at her. Ms. Jackson's door is still closed, so I settle into the chair next to Emily. It takes a moment to find a comfortable way to sit, leaning back, my legs stretched out and sprawled.

Her arms are crossed, her head tilted back, blonde hair pressed against the wall as she stares at the ceiling. Her legs cross at the ankles, and when I sit, she reaches to tug her skirt down to cover more of her thigh. I snort.

"I don't care how short your skirt is," I tell her. "You could be the hottest girl in the school and right now I wouldn't be interested."

"Freak." She glares at me. "Lesbian freak."

"I'd have to be a girl to be a lesbian," I remind her. "And biology aside, I'm not. Whatever you think, I'm a boy." And her opinion doesn't really matter. As long as she keeps her fists to herself (and doesn't goad anyone else into attacking me either), I can just ignore her words. I grin, because she can't win if she can't get to me. And I remember what I wrote in my journal; suddenly I'm in the mood to give a little something back.

"Y'know, you'd have a much better time around here next year, or even in the spring, if you stopped acting like a jealous hateful bitch," I tell her. Okay, so maybe I'm not giving *nicely*. But it's good, honest advice.

She twists so that she's leaning back again, staring at the ceiling. Her arms are crossed tightly, fingers gripping her own skin. She glares so hard I swear she could burn holes in the tiles over her head. "You're ruining this school," she hisses. "You're ruining my life."

God, *seriously*? "How am I ruining your life by living mine, Emily? So you missed being in one fucking play in high school. You don't even *like* the play. Why would you want the part?" That's what I really don't get. She wanted to be Viola and she's pissed off at me for getting the part instead of her. But she's angry about the whole play. So why would she want to be Viola in the first place?

She twists back again, sitting upright to turn that glare on me. "You don't even care, do you? That you're out here twisting reality and someone's going to end up hurt. You don't *care*."

Whoa. I hold my hands up, inching back because she's coming at me, leaning into my space. "What're you talking about?"

"You." She jabs my chest with her finger. "Unnatural. Freak. Just like Jessica. Can't be happy being the pretty one. Can't be happy being the *good* one or the *smart* one or the one with the perfect pitch. Can't be *happy* unless you try to pretend you don't have tits. Jealous of a fucking *cock*. You're a *girl*. Be happy with it. Be happy or else someone's going to come along and—"

She stops, shock twisting her face.

I have a sick feeling in my stomach. "Who's Jessica?" I'm trying to think if I've ever heard the name. If there'd been someone else transgender who was outed in our town, I would've known, right?

"Nobody." She turns away, shoulders hunched.

"She's dead, isn't she?" I ask quietly. "Or was it 'he' when he died?"

"*She*," Emily snaps. "Her name was *Jessica*."

I'd bet my life on what I'm guessing now, that whoever Jessica was, she's dead now, because she wasn't happy with who she was and tried to make a change. And Jessica was important to Emily. "Look—"

"Don't."

"If anyone has any concept what you're going through, it's me." I want to call her an idiot, but I restrain myself. Barely. I'm trying to be nice here. "First thing, whatever happened to Jessica, it wasn't Jessica's fault. Any more than me getting beat up this morning was my fault. I'm a guy. That's the way things are. Brandon and his crowd are stupid idiots who can't help but feel threatened by my lack of a dick, apparently, but that's their problem, not mine. Second, there's a thing in Boston in November—Remembrance Day. You should go. It might help."

She doesn't answer. Fine. I can't force rationality on her. But I can't be as pissed off as I was with her, either. I sigh, thinking about Jessica Graves. Jess Graves. *Jesse*. Oh.

I remember now. He was a freshman at BU two years ago when he was attacked at a frat party one night. They tried to rape him, and he fought back and one of the frat boys ended up blind. Jesse was the one who went to jail and the frat boys went free. He hung himself after two months. I thought I remembered reading that he'd grown up in Newton; maybe the Graves family had moved here after that.

I think I need to change the subject. I don't like her, but in a strange way, I might *get* her. And it makes me want to help, even if I can't replace the big brother she lost, and I sure as hell can't replace her older sister that she never had. Still, I have to say something. "Look, have you ever thought about getting vocal lessons?"

"My voice is fine," she snaps.

"It's an honest suggestion," I say. "I did, when I was younger, but I stopped a couple of years ago. I learned to breathe in the right spots, and how to get rid of some of the roughness I had with the phrasing. If you learn how to shape your mouth, you can get a better sound, earn some of those lower notes and more depth in your tone. Make sure your pitch is dead on. I could give you the name of a good vocal coach, if you want."

"I know a vocal coach," she mutters.

Right. I bet Jesse had voice lessons, if he was all about the perfect pitch. I nod slowly. "Good. Because you're sitting here telling me not to be something I'm not, right? But you're doing the same thing. Try again next show for a part that's better for your voice. Something where you'll knock their socks off. I'll come back and see it if you do."

She snorts. "Like I'd care if you did."

"You wouldn't. But I'd do it anyway." I shrug. "You're not as evil as you try to be. And I don't get anything out of seeing you as evil. I'd rather put my energy elsewhere."

Ms. Jackson's door opens, and Brandon, Toby, and four other guys walk out, heading down the hall with an office assistant escort. Emily is called and she goes without even looking at me. I don't know if I made an impression—probably not—but hey, I said something. And our conversation was almost civil. Mostly.

I cross my arms and lean back, head against the cool wall. I have a bit of a headache starting; I probably should've asked Miss Habernathy for painkiller while I was there, but I wasn't thinking about it then. I hear footfalls moving around, and the bell ring for the end of first period, then a soft scrape of the chair next to me.

"Jordan."

My eyes open quickly. Shit. "Mom."

She smiles and reaches out to nudge my bangs out of my face. "I talked to Miss Habernathy."

I can't tell how much trouble I'm in. She doesn't have that worried look that says she's panicking, or that hard line between her eyes that says she's pissed off. She looks more—sad. "I'm okay," I tell her. "Didn't need stitches. Don't need the ER for anything. Nothing's broken, just a little cut and bruised." I have to add, "It wasn't my fault." Maybe not the best to start out on the defensive, but it *wasn't* my fault. I shouldn't be getting in trouble for fighting.

"I know." Her lips purse with displeasure. "But Ms. Jackson asked me to come in for your meeting with her."

Right on cue, there's the door. Emily walks by, a pink note clutched in her hand as she keeps her head down, refusing to look at me on her way past to get out of the office. I stand and offer my mom a hand up. Always polite, that's me. That just lets her get close enough to hug me, right there, in front of everyone.

"Mom," I protest.

"Am I hurting you?" She lets go and checks my expression.

Well, yes, but I'm not going to tell her that so I shake my head. "Embarrassing me. I'm not six, Mom."

She rolls her eyes and nudges me toward the office. Oh right. Ms. Jackson's waiting.

I take one of the two visitor chairs in the office, slumping down and letting my legs stretch out, my hands folded against my waist. "Am I getting suspended?" I figure I should get the question out of the way first off, just in case.

"Not for defending yourself, no, nor are your friends being suspended for helping you," Ms. Jackson said firmly. "However, if there is anything done in retaliation, you will be facing the same punishment that those four are: three days in-house suspension. If they do it again, they will be expelled. We have a no tolerance policy, not a three strikes rule."

"Why didn't you do something about it before?" I have to ask the question, because this wasn't the first fight on the steps. It might've been the first time they jumped me in particular, but there've been a few fights over the years I've been in high school, like when they took Paul's phone weeks ago.

Ms. Jackson sighed. "It's complicated. They've walked a thin line to avoid being caught before now. But they were blatant today. They didn't care who saw what they intended, and they made it very clear that they intended damage to you. My concern is that due to your unusual status, it may not be an isolated event."

Mom pushes into the conversation. "Do you believe we should be concerned for Jordan's health and safety?"

Oh, I can feel the disapproval. It's all about her worrying for me, but still, Mom's not happy about the decision I made the other night. This was why she didn't want me out in the open. This was why she fought for me so hard with the school, to make sure I'd be safe. And this is why I have to speak up. "I'll be okay. I have to be, if I want to prove I have every right to exist and be exactly who I am. I'm just a guy, and if you guys start making a big deal about how I'm a different kind of guy, they won't be able to forget the difference. If I want things to go back to normal, I have to just act normal."

Ms. Jackson's nodding, and I wonder if she thought I might say something like that. "And if they try again?"

"You'll expel them." I sound a lot calmer than I feel. I've heard enough about how people die, in the hallway with a knife between their ribs, or in the parking lot by a single gunshot that somehow no one hears. But I can't act afraid. "Or I'll fight back. Either way, I get to keep my dignity a lot better than if I run away, scared."

I look over at Mom; she's dubious so I have to try to convince her. "I already got my fresh start when we moved here, Mom," I tell her. "I can't do that every time things get hard. I have friends here, and the play, and I'm a senior. Everything changes next June anyway."

"You have a point," she says quietly, and I smile, because of course I do. And she's listening to it. She's letting me grow up.

Ms. Jackson scribbles out a pink note and hands it to me. "Go on back to class, Jordan. I'd like to spend a little more time talking to your mother about how we can best ensure your safety here at the school, without being overbearingly obvious about it."

"Sounds good." I fold the note and put it in my backpack, then kiss Mom's forehead because she looks like she's waiting for it. "I'll see you after rehearsal, Mom. James is bringing me home, along with Paul, Pepper, and Britney. I'll make sure pizza starts getting delivered around seven or so."

Mom reaches up to ruffle my hair like I'm a kid, then touches the butterfly bandages over my eye. I'm sure I still look like a complete mess, but I don't care, because I'm still here. They can't get me down, and they can't get rid of me.

CHAPTER 28: Party On

I'M GLAD when the day is over. I make it through classes, then our closed rehearsal, and finally James drives us home, with me crammed into the backseat of the car with Paul and Britney. We split up when we get to the house; James and Pepper start getting food together in the kitchen to bring downstairs, and the rest of us go downstairs with the ingredients for the punch.

Maybe punch is a bit hokey to have at a party when we're over the age of ten, but we have an ulterior motive. Britney mixes it up: some blend of ginger ale, fruit juices, and fruit slices. Then I take out the last vial.

"True sight." It's the only one left, and the only thing it could be. "Do you really think true sight will fix true love?"

"It's not true love," Britney says practically. "It's a magically induced infatuation. If any of those couples are meant to be together, they'll survive being able to see things truly. And if they're not, it will open their eyes."

Guess I can't really argue with that. I hold up the little vial, then twist the top off and quickly upend it, letting it empty into the punch bowl. Hopefully it's not too diluted, because this is our last option. I hand the spoon to Paul. "Work your magic, Puck."

He grins at me and gives the punch three quick stirs and pronounces it done. Just in time, as the first of our castmates comes down the stairs.

It's showtime.

I ladle punch into cups, setting it out for easy access. James and Pepper bring down plates of cheese and crackers, vegetables, little eggrolls, and mozzarella sticks. I bought enough for an army when I was shopping yesterday; we deserve the celebration.

"Here you go, Cait." Britney hands Caitlyn one of the prepoured cups. "Family recipe for punch. No calories," she teases.

Caitlyn smiles back, taking a sip while her gaze sweeps the room, lighting where Ryan and Zach are talking in a corner. She blinks and takes another sip, then another, her expression slowly shifting from fond smiles to dawning concern. "I—" She goes silent for several seconds before asking, "Was I—what was I doing?"

I step back; I don't want to be involved. I'm not even sure what to say. But Britney's elected herself spokesperson and she puts an arm around Caitlyn's shoulders. "Something wrong?"

Cait shakes her head, then stops and nods slowly. "I'm not sure. I feel—odd. Like I was doing something and I can't remember why."

Britney throws me a look, and I motion at the filled cups. She nods and holds one of them out to Caitlyn. "Why don't you bring Ryan a drink? I'm sure you'll figure it out."

The hard part is, I can't tell how much they remember. How does this all seem reasonable to them? Do they rationalize away the magic of it by finding reasons that make some crazy sense to them inside their own minds? While under the effects of the potion, James doesn't even seem to fully remember that I was dating Pepper, but she does seem to remember it. For Caitlyn, it doesn't look like drinking true sight erases it all, but then, how could it? I'm just hoping things go back to where they were without getting too messy.

I try to fade into the background—not like I need to drink the magic Kool-Aid after all—and drift closer to where Caitlyn's offering Ryan the punch. He takes a sip and smiles, his free arm around her waist. He doesn't seem to notice how stiffly she stands, how uncomfortable she is. Ryan talks with his other hand, gesturing with the cup of punch. When it almost spills, he takes another long gulp quickly before he sets it down.

Ryan's describing the movie he saw last weekend, down to the last detail of the stunt design and the car crashes. He lets Caitlyn go, both hands in motion now as she puts distance between them. His expression is animated as he leans toward Zach, intent on getting his point across. He only stops when Caitlyn touches his shoulder.

"I'm sorry," she murmurs. "I don't know what I was thinking."

And just like that, I see it click through in his mind. He looks from Zach to Caitlyn, then back again, naked pain in his expression. Shit. I don't want to be watching them.

I backpedal quickly, getting myself away. I need a break from people, especially these people. They're my friends, but right now I'm feeling intensely guilty about the trouble I caused. I don't want to see how much it hurts to untangle it. But where can I go? If everything's going as planned, somewhere around here James and Pepper are figuring out how wrong they are.

Or how right. But I can't really think about that. And I definitely don't want to see it.

"Pizza's here!"

And that would be my cue to escape. "I'll get it!" I run up the stairs, leaving the noise behind as I burst into the quiet of the kitchen. I go through to the living room and meet Mom at the front door and bring out the cash I collected earlier to pay the pizza guy. In return, he piles my arms high with boxes of pizza, wings, plates and napkins.

"You look flushed, Jordan. Everything okay down there?" Mom sounds concerned, but she looks more like she's assessing me for something. She reaches out to touch my cheek, rubbing at something with her thumb, and I duck away.

"Mom!" God, do they ever stop treating us like we're a little kid with mud from the playground on our faces, needing a quick spit bath to clean us up? I can see it now, the morning before graduating, and she'll be wiping smudges from our cheeks with her thumb and sending us out there to meet the world.

"Seems quiet down there." She takes the wings from the stack and brings them into the kitchen. Pulling down platters, she empties the wings out of their Styrofoam boxes.

"Mom, stop, we can live with the boxes," I tell her, but she shrugs and keeps going. I guess it's not good enough or something. "It's not quiet if you're down there. We've got music, and everyone's talking. Wait until long enough and I bet you'll hear us singing. I think Cait said she was bringing some disks over for karaoke. Oh and Maria might be coming by; just send her down when she gets here, okay?"

She's still looking at me like something's wrong.

"Am I bleeding again?" I touch my eye, but no, other than the bruise and the bandage, it seems fine.

She shakes her head. "No. But you're looking so grown up right now. I can't even see my baby anymore."

I hear the unsaid *baby girl* in her words. "Mom, you're getting maudlin."

"You're almost eighteen; I'm allowed," she retorts. "I've got one child out of the house already, and I'm about to lose both of my sons. It's a mother's prerogative to get weepy over these things."

I really wonder if she's been drinking the punch, the way she's looking at me like she's never seen me before. Maybe it's just the T, and she's seeing the changes. Or my male aura shining through. I hug her before I can think about how much it's going to hurt my ribs (and it does), and kiss her cheek. "I'm pretty sure neither James or I will go very far. We'll need someplace to do laundry, right?"

She laughs, but there's a sadness to it. "Go on back downstairs, Jordan. Your friends are waiting for you."

Mom helps me bring everything downstairs, and the whole cast descends on the food in a crowd of laughter and conversation. Relaxed. Easy. The undercurrents are calm, like the stress from the last few weeks has melted away. Maria arrives while we're eating, and we end up sprawled together on a beanbag chair while Ryan and Zach fiddle with the karaoke machine, trying to convince it to work.

I set my piece of pizza down and Maria steals it to take a bite, laughing when I try to grab it back.

"Want to dance?" Tyler joins us, giving Maria a friendly grin.

Maria looks up, uncertainty in her expression, and she glances at me, so I introduce them. "This is Tyler, and he's a good guy. Perfectly safe, knows how to keep his hands to himself."

He bows, grinning at her. "As long as that's what you want." He holds one hand out to Maria, and after a moment she takes it, and they join the impromptu dance floor where Ryan and Zach already are. A new song comes on, slow and sweet, and Britney and James join them on the floor as well. James looks at her like the whole world is held in his arms, and I'm relieved that everything seems right with them.

The world is starting to reset and I hope it's going smoothly. But I can't bring myself to go find Pepper.

I guess that's why she comes to find me.

"Hey." Her voice is soft, almost hard to hear over the music. She sits cross-legged next to the beanbag, and I think for a moment about budging over, offering her space on the chair, but I'm not sure what to do if she won't take it, so I don't.

"Hey." My bangs fall in my face as I turn to look over at her. Red hair is drawn up in pigtails on either side of her head, curling slightly, the tips brushing her shoulders. It makes her look younger, her heart-shaped face rounding slightly. "So—"

"I talked to Paul." Her voice is flat, and she's looking at the floor rather than at me. Great. So now she thinks I'm insane on top of everything else. "He told me about—about the things that happened. It sounds crazy, but—" She stops and looks at me now. "I guess I can't think of any other reason to explain what happened between me and James. I look back on the last week and it all seems like a dream. James doesn't seem like he even realizes there's something wrong. He's not hurt, he's not angry, he's just out there with Britney like it was nothing."

There's something cold in my chest. "You're hurt?" I ask slowly. "Do you love him for real, then?"

Because this needs to be messier than it already is. Because I need to have fucked up that badly. I can't breathe, my chest aches so bad.

"No." A quick shake of her head. "But something did happen, and I did feel it, and I can't just turn things on and off so easily without feeling *something*, Jordan. I thought I loved James, and we did—"

I raise one hand. "Pepper, I don't want to know what you two did all those times he was late getting home. It was bad enough watching it."

"I know. I didn't even realize what we were doing to you. It was like I remembered kissing you once, but I didn't remember anything more, or feel anything about it." She draws her knees up, wrapping her arms around them, chin resting there.

"And now you do?"

"Yeah. Now I do."

She looks so forlorn, and I feel like I should do something. I don't know what *to* do. When I think about it, I realize just what that potion meant, taking control of them like that. And maybe it's better to be like James, not really remembering it, or thinking about it, than it is to be Pepper, who's sitting here feeling all of it.

I touch her shoulder cautiously, and when she tips toward me I open up my arms, letting her lean against me, and I hold on gently.

"What now?" I ask, afraid to be any more specific than that.

"I don't know."

Oh, well, then. I try to think about how this feels, right now, that she trusts me enough to come to me for comfort. I try not to think about kissing her. I try really hard, because I'm failing, and I want to kiss her and damn it… I can't. Not when she's all miserable. There is no such thing as *kiss and make better*.

"You were born female?" she asks quietly, her head tilting to look up at me, so close I could steal that kiss before she knew it. So tempting, and I bite my lip against the temptation.

I nod. "Yeah. But I never really was a girl inside my head. I was James's shadow and did everything he did, including trying to pee while standing up, which was a huge mess. But—" I grin. "—now I can."

Pepper blinks at me, green eyes wide.

Maybe that was too much information. I try to figure out how to change the subject.

"How?" she asks. It doesn't sound like a polite question; it sounds more like she honestly wants to know. I start to relax again, and I explain it in clinical terms, describing the STP packer as my cheeks go warm. It's not a romantic topic, but she wants to understand and I want her to understand, so it seems to work for us right now.

She has more questions then, and my skin is hot and flushed both from how close she is and from the fact that I am spilling more personal details than anyone knows about me. She laughs at my story about the first time I tried to make the homemade packer and got hair gel all over my hands. She kisses my cheek to test for peach fuzz when we talk about T (still smooth, unfortunately). I assure her that everything I've read says my voice won't change until after the play is done, and she says she can lend an ear when it finally does, to help me settle into my new singing range.

"I know what I'm getting you for Christmas," she decides.

"Oh?"

Pepper shakes her head. "You have to wait until Christmas."

"I'll wait until New Year's Eve, if you'll go out with me. You owe me a date."

For a moment, I think I've gone too far. That I've scared her off. Then she kisses my cheek again. "Let's take it slow this time, Jordan. A date for the new year sounds about right."

It's not perfect, but it's going in the right direction, and I can take that. "This time we'll get to know each other properly first."

"Good." Her fingers tangle with mine, and her hand feels right where it is, smaller than mine and softer too. "I want to know everything about you. And I don't want you to leave anything out."

"I won't. I promise."

And eventually I will tell her every little thing. There's nothing I want to hide.

WHEN D.E. ATWOOD was in second grade, she finally grew tall enough to see the shelf above the mysteries in the bookmobile. She discovered a rich landscape of alternate worlds, magic, and space, and has never looked back from the genres of fantasy and science fiction.

When she was twelve, she declared that she was going to be a writer and share the stories that she saw happening all around her. She wanted to create characters that others would care about and that would touch their lives, like the books that she read had touched her own life.

Today she has combined her interests, creating genre stories about the people who live next door, bringing magic into the world around us.

When not writing, D.E. Atwood is a mother (to two children, a cat, and a dog), a wife, a reader, a knitter, a systems administrator, almost a black belt in tae kwon do, and a music aficionado. Sleep, she claims, is optional.

E-mail: deatwood.writes@gmail.com

Twitter: https://twitter.com/DEAtwoodWrites

Facebook: https://www.facebook.com/pages/The-Fiction-Worlds-of-DE-Atwood/102482069899266

Tumblr: http://deatwoodwrites.tumblr.com

Blog/Website: http://deatwood.wordpress.com

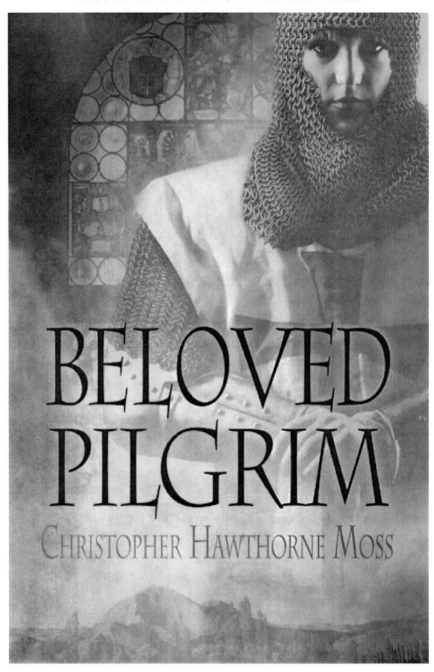

BELOVED PILGRIM

CHRISTOPHER HAWTHORNE MOSS

http://www.harmonyinkpress.com

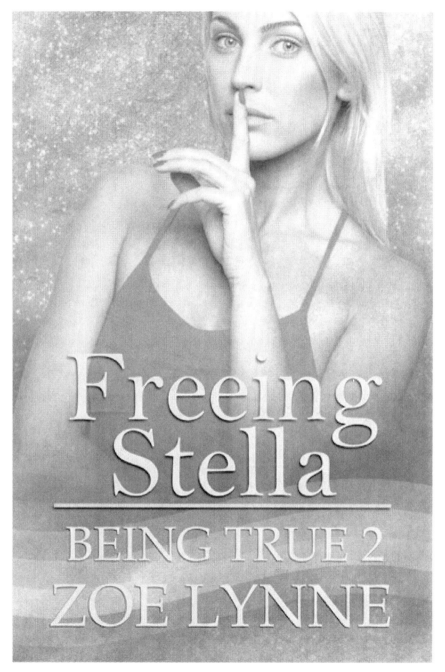

Freeing
Stella

BEING TRUE 2

ZOE LYNNE

Also from HARMONY INK PRESS

The Other Me

Suzanne van Rooyen

http://www.harmonyinkpress.com

Harmony Ink

CPSIA information can be obtained
at www.ICGtesting.com
Printed in the USA
LVOW10s0012210617

538826LV00008B/124/P

9 781627 988209